Worth Any Price

Boulder Beaumonts Book 1

Nika Rhone

P9P PARK NINE PUBLISHING

This is a work of fiction. All characters, organizations, places, and events portrayed in this novel are products of the author's imagination or are used fictitiously. Any resemblance to actual events, locales, organizations, or persons, living or dead, is entirely coincidental.

Book Cover Design by 100 Covers

Published by Park Nine Publishing

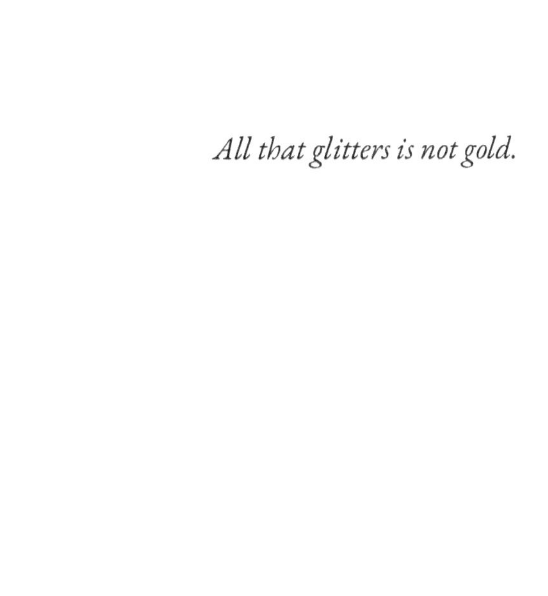

All that glitters is not gold.

Chapter 1

It was all kinds of wrong to lust after your son's martial arts instructor.

Even as she reminded herself of that fact for the third time, Amber Lovett shifted against the wall to get a better look at the man in question. Tall, trim, dressed in dark blue sweatpants and a baby blue t-shirt that made him appear entirely too edible for any woman's peace of mind, he stalked through the double line of kids checking form. He gave gentle correction when needed, praise where warranted, demonstrations when requested.

A happy little hum escaped her as a stretch of his arms doing just that pulled the tee tight across his back, emphasizing the flexing of lean muscles underneath.

Lordy, lordy.

It might be wrong, but he sure was making it hard to stop.

Besides, she'd come here to check the man out, hadn't she?

All right, not exactly like *this*.

When Derek first mentioned the man who'd stepped in to take over the class after Sensei Steve broke his leg, she hadn't paid too much attention. The only thing that mattered was knowing the community center's twice-a-week program her son adored wouldn't be cancelled. But after weeks of listening to Mister Rick this and Mister Rick that, she'd needed to come down and have a look for herself what all the fuss was about.

And boy, was she ever glad she did. The man was *fine*.

Dark brown hair with a slight wave in its thick depths framed a face that could only be classified as classically masculine, with chiseled cheekbones and a firm jaw emphasized by the hint of five o'clock shadow covering it. For such a tall man, his movements were graceful and precise, almost like a dancer moving across the stage.

Or a big cat prowling the savannah.

Obviously, none of that was why Derek seemed to worship the ground the man walked on. Since he didn't normally warm up to strangers easily, his sudden fixation had been a little worrisome. No one liked to think the worst, but she knew better than most that sometimes people weren't who or what they seemed to be. Better to be suspicious than caught by surprise.

Especially when it came to Derek.

Her gaze went instinctively to her son. In the second row, amidst the twenty or so other kids, he was noticeably smaller than almost all of them. Even though at ten he was squarely in the middle of the eight-to-twelve age range for the class. A sharp thorn of concern wormed its way into her brain like it always did.

Was he getting the right amount of protein? Enough exercise and fresh air?

Was she failing somehow as a mother?

"Just a slow grower," his pediatrician had assured her at his last check-up. "Nothing to do with his health or asthma and everything to do with genetics. He'll have a growth spurt before you know it. Nothing to worry about."

Yeah, easy for him to say.

She was *always* going to worry about her baby. They'd been all the other had for so long now, she didn't know any other way.

In her head, she knew the doctor was right. Just like she knew she couldn't keep holding a monopoly on her son's social life. Like it or not, he needed a chance to stretch his wings without his mommy helicoptering over him. Which was why after nervously observing the first class with Sensei Steve to make sure it wasn't too strenuous for him, she'd stayed away, much as it killed her to.

Of course, if Sensei had looked anything like Mister Rick and his very biteable ass, she might have found it a lot harder to stick to those good intentions.

Mind out of the gutter, Amber Lee.

Easier said than done when the ass in question was currently aimed in her direction as he demonstrated some kind of kick that both started and ended in a half-squat position.

Day-am.

Why couldn't he wear the baggy white uniform Sensei did instead of sweats that pulled taut against his delicious butt with every downward thrust? Maybe then she wouldn't have to mop up the mental drool currently running down her chin.

Okay, time to go. The last thing she needed was him to notice her skulking in the corner like a pervy stalker.

With the class's attention focused on their instructor, she slipped from the room. Not taking one last look at heaven was tough, but she managed. Barely. She grinned to herself. It had been such a long time since she'd done anything *but* look, she wasn't sure she'd know what to do if she ever got the chance to do more.

But oh, it was sure fun to think about.

She glanced at her watch as she climbed the stairs from the basement. Forty-five glorious minutes all to herself. Long enough to finally finish her current library book. She *really* wanted to find out who the killer was without having to go back on the wait list to check it out again. Maybe she'd even splurge for a latte and cinnamon bun at the coffee shop across the street while she read.

For the second time that night, her mouth watered.

A quick mental tally of her wallet's contents, however, squashed those plans. After tucking away this paycheck's allotment toward Derek's birthday present fund, that kind of needless indulgence wasn't an option. Which was a good thing, really. Her thighs would thank her for skipping the extra calories.

Her taste buds, however, were going to sulk for a week.

"Ms. Lovett, hello! It's so nice to see you."

Amber turned at the familiar voice, her smile for the older woman genuine despite the paperback practically burning a hole in her purse. "Hi, Mrs. Gandy."

A handsome African American woman with steely gray hair and an ample figure, Mrs. Gandy was the grandmother every child wanted as their own, right down to the peppermints she kept in her pocket. As the program director, she seemed to know everyone who walked through the community center's doors by name. And had an uncanny knack for matching them up with which program or activity suited them best, even if they didn't think so at first.

She'd been the one to suggest Amber enroll Derek in the karate class instead of chess club, which had been her original intent. To Amber's surprise, Derek jumped at the idea.

She'd taken a little longer to warm up to it.

But despite her initial reservations, her son had flourished over the past five months, making new friends and growing stronger by the week, despite his lagging size. Mrs. Gandy had been right, as usual. And for that, she owed her more than she could ever repay.

Although she did try, because life had taught her being in someone's debt was an uncomfortable place at the best of times.

At the worst, it could be downright precarious.

"I wanted to tell you how much my granddaughter absolutely *adores* the quilt you made for my great-grandbaby's crib. Thank you again. It was so sweet of you."

"I'm so glad she liked it." Her skill with a needle and thread came to her rescue more than a little over the past few years. It had been nice to do something besides remake old clothes for a change.

Mrs. Gandy's expression and tone turned cajoling. "Are you sure you wouldn't want to teach a class here sometime? There would be lots of people who'd love to learn how to make such beautiful quilts and blankets and things."

It wasn't the first time she'd asked. The same jolt of queasy panic hit her like it did every time she thought about being the sole focus of an entire roomful of people.

That would be a big hell no.

She summoned up an apologetic smile. "Sorry. I'm a much better doer than a teacher. I'd turn all thumbs if I even tried." Or toss her cookies. A lifetime of trying to fade into the woodwork and be ignored wasn't easily overcome.

"That's all right, dear. I had to ask." Mrs. Gandy looked disappointed despite her reassuring words, increasing Amber's guilt.

Which was why she found herself saying, "If there's anything else I can do to help out here, though, I'd be happy to volunteer. Just...not in a classroom. Behind the scenes is more my comfort zone."

She wanted to grab the words back as soon as they were out. Was she crazy? She didn't have time to volunteer for anything. Between her job at the hospital, her second job, and Derek, her dance card was already full. Past full, sometimes.

But a part of her still felt she owed something to the center for her son's free program. Taking something for nothing didn't sit right with her. Never had. So, if she somehow had to squeeze a few more hours out of her week to repay the debt, she would.

Sleep was highly overrated, anyway.

Mrs. Gandy's face lit up. "Oh, how sweet of you, dear. Thank you. We can never have enough volunteers." She tapped a crimson-tipped finger against her chin. "I'll have to see what events we have coming up that might suit you."

Well, that's that. You're stuck like a tick now.

"Sure. Just let me know when you do. I'm not picky. But Derek comes first for me. Whatever it is can't interfere with his schedule." That was non-negotiable.

"Oh, of course!" Mrs. Gandy smiled indulgently. "Derek is such a good boy. And so enthusiastic. I don't think he's missed a single class yet since he started. Except for when he had his breathing problems, of course. That's the kind of dedication I wish we would see in everyone who signs up for our programs. So many drop out after only a few weeks, or don't even show up at all."

The happy buzz from hearing her son praised instantly dimmed as the rest of what Mrs. Gandy said registered. "Wait. What breathing problems? Derek had an asthma attack? When?"

Mrs. Gandy's smile faltered. "Well, no, not an attack, exactly. But he was a little wheezy and needed to sit out most of the class. You didn't know?"

"No." Her lips pressed tight as she fought back the irrational urge to berate the woman. If Derek felt wheezy or short of breath, all he needed to do was use his inhaler and rest. The rational side of her brain knew that.

The rabid mom side wanted to pitch a howling fit.

Because her son had had a health crisis *and she hadn't known.*

Perhaps sensing the crazy hovering just below the surface, Mrs. Gandy said fretfully, "I did call you, but I got your voicemail."

"I never got any message." Something niggled at the back of her brain. "When was this?"

"A few weeks ago, during the Friday class. But I swear to you, I left a message."

She'd picked up a last-minute dinner shift a few Fridays ago, which explained why she didn't get the initial call. Rule number one was no phones on the dining room floor. That's why Derek had the number to the restaurant in case of an emergency.

Which he clearly hadn't shared with anyone.

The missing voicemail she blamed squarely on her crappy phone service. Cheap didn't always mean reliable. Something she'd have to fix first thing tomorrow.

"I sent a note home with Derek since I couldn't speak with you directly and you weren't here to pick him up in person that night. It said to call if you had any questions or concerns. When you didn't, and you didn't come in to talk to me when you dropped him off at class the following week, well, I assumed he'd given it to you and everything was fine."

And why wouldn't she? Derek wasn't the kind of boy who lied.

Until now, apparently.

Her teeth ground together as impotent frustration made her muscles tighten. He knew better than to hide any breathing issues from her. Mild attack or not, she wanted to know.

She *needed* to know.

Her son was the most precious thing in the world to her. And she knew just how easy it could be to lose the things you loved most.

It took a lot, but she managed to unclench her jaw. Balancing her need to ensure Derek's well-being against his budding adolescent independent streak was a tightrope she was still learning to navigate. She didn't want to start a fight over this with him. But she also didn't want him to think it was okay to keep things from her.

The one thing they'd always had between them was honesty. To find out he was keeping secrets didn't sit well.

At. All.

It was times like this she really wished her mother was still alive. Not only to ask for her advice. But so she could apologize for all the angst and grief she'd no doubt caused during her own rebellious youth.

Thinking about Derek being anything like her as he headed toward his teenage years was enough to make her break out in a cold sweat.

Tamping that thought down along with her annoyance, she managed a tight smile for the woman watching her with genuine concern in her eyes.

"It's fine, Mrs. Gandy. You handled everything right. I'll talk to Derek about this when we get home."

"Oh, dear. I didn't mean to get him into any trouble."

"Don't worry. He did that all by himself." A sickening thought occurred. "Did you say this happen *during* one of his classes?" Was this new instructor making the workout too difficult for him to handle? God, had she let herself get too distracted by his good looks to notice he was pushing the kids too hard?

"Yes. Missy—one of the older girls in the class—came to get me, but by the time I got down there, everything was already well under control. Mister B...Mister Rick had everyone sitting around them as he explained exactly what poor Derek was going through."

Her head snapped back. "He *what*?"

"Oh, yes, he explained all the symptoms, and what it feels like to have an asthma attack, and how the medicine in Derek's inhaler helps. And what to do if someone has an attack and doesn't have it with them. It was so well done, so calm and matter of fact, I don't think half those kids realized they were learning something important."

At Derek's expense.

Once more grinding her teeth, she acknowledged Mrs. Gandy's promise to let her know what kind of volunteer opportunities came up before she went outside to walk off her rage. She barely noticed the other people on the sidewalk as she silently seethed.

How *dare* he? Making Derek the center of attention while he was having breathing issues? Talking about him like he was some damn classroom project?

Bastard!

By the time class ended, she'd grappled her temper back into some semblance of control. Mostly, anyway.

Waiting outside the meeting room as the boisterous kids streamed out, she forced herself to take a few deep breaths. Confrontation always made her stomach a little woozy. But when it came to her kid, she'd never backed down from one before, and she wasn't about to start now. No matter how good looking the jerk was.

"Mom, is everything okay?"

The worry on Derek's face told her she wasn't doing as good a job as she thought of covering her temper. After glancing at the last of the kids pounding up the staircase, she asked, "Is there something you forgot to tell me, young man?"

His expression turned wary. "What do you mean?"

Disappointed at his evasiveness, she shook her head. "Never mind. We'll talk about it when we get home. First, I need to talk to your instructor before he leaves."

"What? Why?" The first hint of panic—and maybe a little guilt—colored his words.

"Just wait here. This will only take a minute."

"But Mom—"

"Wait. Here." She hated pulling out the "I've had enough, don't test me" voice, but she was all out of patience.

Pushing through the heavy door, she spied Mister Rick at the front of the room, bending over a black gym bag as he pushed a towel inside and zipped it shut. She didn't give herself time to second guess. Or to ogle his ass. She walked toward him with purpose in her step.

"I'd like a word with you before you go."

Straightening, he slung the strap over his shoulder as he watched her approach. "I'm sorry, if you're looking to enroll your kid in the class, you'll need to speak to—"

"My son is already in your class." From the way he raised an imperious eyebrow, she realized she'd very rudely interrupted him. Well, tough.

"And who might that be?"

"Derek Lovett." She waited for the recognition and guilt to hit him. Unfortunately, she only got one out of the two.

"Ah, Derek." He nodded with a small smile. "He's doing really well. Even though he's only a beginner, he's got a natural aptitude for the movements."

"I, ah, thank you." The reflexive pleasure at hearing her son praised threw her off for a second before she refocused. "But that's not what I wanted to talk to you about."

"Okay." He glanced at his watch and readjusted the strap on his shoulder. "I was on my way out, so…"

Irritated by the hint to make it quick, she tilted her chin up, fighting to ignore the pull of his incredibly gorgeous brown eyes. "I just found out my son had some breathing problems during one of your classes."

"That's right, he did." He frowned. "Wait, did you say you *just* found out?"

"Yes. And I also found out that instead of excusing him from the class, you made him sit there while everyone else watched what he was going through."

"Now, wait a minute. That's not how it happened."

"Oh, no?" She crossed her arms. "Then how did it?"

Looking a little flustered at her demanding tone, he ran a hand through his wavy hair, sending it into further disarray. Her fingers itched to do the same before she shut down that line of thought.

Think with your head, Amber Lee, not your hormones.

"When Derek started wheezing and having trouble breathing, I had the class keep practicing their kicks while he got his inhaler and—"

"He needed to use his inhaler?"

The look he gave her for interrupting this time was impatient, bordering on annoyed.

"Only as a precaution. Once I saw he wasn't in any danger of it turning into a full-blown attack, I decided it was the perfect situation to instruct the rest of the kids about what they should do if one of their friends or family members has an asthma attack. Or, at the very least, to keep them from thinking of it as some kind of freaky, scary thing. Kids tend to shun and make fun of things that are different or they don't understand."

Much as she hated to admit it, he was right about that. Kids could be vicious little shits to one another. But it still didn't give him the right to make that decision for her son.

"Did it ever occur to you that by bringing attention to his condition, you might have been making things worse for him, not better?"

Those gorgeous eyes narrowed, spearing her with a wilting glare of disapproval. "Are you embarrassed by your son's condition? Is that what this is about?"

"What?" Shock at the accusation left her momentarily speechless. Then indignation flooded in to fill the void.

"Of course not! How dare you even say something like that? I'm upset because I don't want my son held up as a classroom aide in front of a roomful of his friends because *you* decided it was the perfect teachable moment."

They stared at each other like two knights facing off on the field of battle, neither willing to be the first to yield. The tension sparking between them was off the charts, sending little prickles along her skin that, if she wasn't so angry, she might have confused for arousal. Which would be the absolutely *wrong* thing to be feeling at this moment, with this man.

Then, to her surprise, he gave a slow nod. "Okay. You're right. I might not have taken that into consideration. I was just trying to help." He sighed. "I'm sorry."

It was obvious how much those two little words pained him to say, but she appreciated them anyway.

"Thank you."

Giving another glance at his watch, he said, "I'm sorry, I really do need to go. Are we good here?"

She nodded. They were done, but there was still round two to have with Derek when they got home.

"Okay, then. You have a nice night, Mrs. Lovett." He turned to go, then turned back. "I hope you'll allow Derek to continue attending class. He's doing very well, and I'd hate for him to miss out because of my poor judgement."

"As long as he wants to come, I won't stop him."

With a nod, he walked out the door. Amber stood in the empty room for a long moment. Even with him gone, she could still feel the sparks dancing along her skin, fizzing in her veins. Anger, she assured herself. Just anger.

Oh, sweet baby Jesus, let it just be anger.

The ride home was done in tense silence. Derek refused to even look at her, staring out the passenger window the entire way and bolting from the car as soon as it was in park. Amber let him go. The more time she gave him to stew in his own guilt, the easier it would be to get him to acknowledge he'd been wrong and apologize.

She hoped, anyway.

As she climbed to the second floor of their apartment building, she wished for the thousandth time she'd been able to afford to rent somewhere with an elevator. Or at least gotten a ground-floor apartment.

"At least it keeps my thighs in shape," she muttered as she unlocked her door.

The tiny living room and even tinier kitchen were empty, which meant Derek had retreated to his bedroom. She sighed. "Derek, could you come out here, please? I want to talk to you."

After a wait long enough to make her wonder if he might just push that extra inch tonight and ignore her, he came slinking out to the living room with all the reluctance of someone heading for the electric chair.

He dropped onto the sofa, not meeting her eyes. "What?"

Refusing to be baited by the sulky question, she crossed her arms. "Why didn't you tell me you had breathing problems during your karate class a few weeks ago?"

One thin shoulder came up in a sullen shrug. "I dunno."

"You don't know?"

"It wasn't a big deal, all right? I used my inhaler, and I was fine."

"Any time you have problems breathing is a big deal." He might not have been looking at her, but she could see the eye roll he gave. God, she hated that. "Darn it, Derek, I can't have you hiding things from me. I need to know what's going on with your health."

"Why, so you could tell me I can't keep taking the class?"

She looked at him in surprise. "I wouldn't have done that."

"Right." Another eye roll.

Okay, she might have.

"Even so, you can't keep this kind of thing a secret from me. And you can't hide notes the people in charge at the center send home with you." At last, a flash of guilt crossed his face. "They have rules they have to abide by, you know. By not giving me the note, you put both Mrs. Gandy and your instructor in a terrible position."

He fidgeted in his seat. "I'm sorry, okay? I didn't think it would be a problem. Besides, Mr. Rick handled it just fine."

"Oh yes, I heard how Mr. Rick handled it." She perched on the sofa beside him and ran a loving hand over his hair. It was overdue for a cut, the long dark-blond locks flopping over his forehead and shading his eyes. "Don't worry, that won't happen again."

He reared back, dislodging her touch. "What do you mean? What did you do?"

"When I spoke with him tonight, I made sure he understood that using you as a teaching tool was the wrong thing to do. He might have meant well, but he had no right to make the decision for you and put you in such an uncomfortable position."

"But he didn't!"

"Didn't what?"

"He didn't make me uncomfortable. And he didn't make the decision for me. I was over at the side of the room with my inhaler, and when he came over to check on me, he *asked* if I would be okay with him explaining to the rest of the class about what an asthma attack was."

"He asked?"

Uh-oh.

"Yeah, Mom, he asked. Unlike you, who just assumed you knew what was going on and rushed in like you always do to try and protect me, even when I don't need your help!" He popped to his feet and stalked a few paces away before turning back to face her, small fists clenched at his sides, agitation written in every tense line of his body.

Feeling off-balance when a second ago she'd been standing on firm, righteous high ground, she shook her head. "Why would you let him do that to you? Make you a spectacle?"

"Because he said he understood about how it feels to be looked at funny because you sometimes can't breathe as well as everyone else. To not be able to do everything your friends can. To have them look at you like you're some kind of freak."

Oh, she knew what that felt like, too. But maybe her own experiences were a little different from what her son was going through.

And maybe she'd let them color her reactions without taking that into consideration.

She looked at her son. So young, and yet it seemed a whole lot smarter than she was about some things. "So, did it help?"

"Maybe, yeah." He shrugged. "At least it didn't hurt. No one treated me any different after."

Amber rubbed her forehead and the ache starting there.

"Then I'm sorry. I jumped to a conclusion when I didn't have all the facts." She gave him a pointed look. "Which wouldn't have happened if you'd told me the truth weeks ago when all this occurred." No way was he getting a pass on that just because she'd screwed up how she handled things tonight.

"Fine, whatever. I said I was sorry. It won't happen again. Can I go take my shower now, please?"

And they were back to sullen again. She stifled a sigh. His teen years were definitely going to kill her dead.

"Sure, go ahead."

Once the water in the bathroom went on, she selected the next day's work outfit from the closet in Derek's bedroom. She transferred it to the miniscule coat closet in the living room to take with her into the bathroom in the morning. They'd pretty much perfected their morning routine of getting ready at the same time in the small space. But she still counted the days until she could afford an apartment with a second bedroom.

Having a bed that didn't fold up was second only to the idea of having a little personal space and privacy.

But for now, they worked with what they had. Which really wasn't too terrible. The place might be small, but it was clean, the building well maintained, and, most important, it was in a good school district.

For that alone, she'd sleep on the floor for the next eight years if she had to.

But even as she went through the familiar motions of her nightly routine, her mind was spinning in twisty circles as she replayed the entire evening in her head.

Yes, Derek lied to her, if only through omission.

And yes, she'd jump to conclusions she probably should have thought through a bit more carefully before acting on them.

But then, hadn't Rick gone and confused the issue by letting her believe he'd made a unilateral decision, when the truth was he'd sought and obtained Derek's permission?

Although, was it really fair of him, as an adult, to ask such a thing from a child? Especially one in the throes of a health crisis, mild or not?

With a groan, she dropped to the sofa and covered her face. There were too many wrongs in this mess to figure out who was right. Everyone involved was guilty of some form of poor judgement. Bottom line, though, she'd accused someone of something he hadn't done. Like it or not, she owed the man an apology.

And how pathetic was she that a tingle of anticipation lit in her belly because she had a reason to talk to Mr. Rick of the biteable ass again?

Chapter 2

"So, how did things go with Kitty last night?"

Wincing at his brother's sardonic question, Richard Beaumont signaled to the waiter standing discreetly nearby for another sparkling water, wishing it was dinnertime rather than lunch so he could make it a scotch instead.

"About as well as you thought." His ears were still ringing.

Theo smirked. "Told you so."

He had. Richard just hadn't been inclined to listen. Not that he would have done anything differently, despite the end result. Life taught him being proactive was a hell of a lot better than being taken by surprise later on. "I thought it wouldn't matter to her."

"It" being the prenup agreement he'd handed his girlfriend over dessert after a gourmet dinner-for-two in his penthouse condo.

He winced again. Perhaps that hadn't been the best time to bring it up. But then, there never seemed to be a right time. Whenever he'd tried to edge the conversation in that direction over the past few weeks, Kitty found a way to distract him. Usually with sex.

And what kind of fool wouldn't have let her?

"Just because she comes from money doesn't mean you can't insult her."

Richard gave his younger brother a sour look as he cut into his salmon. "It's because she comes from money that she should have been a little more understanding. Do you really think her father wouldn't be handing me one to sign the second I put a ring on her finger?"

"But you haven't put a ring on her finger yet, have you? Or even really talked to her about marriage?"

"Why would I go to the trouble and expense before getting all the legal details nailed down first?"

Theo chuffed out a laugh. "Wow, you hopeless romantic, you. No wonder you have women swooning at your feet. Oh wait, that's right. You don't."

Deciding to ignore him, mostly because he was right, Richard attacked his meal with focused intent. He had things to get back to at the office. He didn't have time to sit around rehashing the debacle of his relationship with Katherine Carlyle.

Former relationship.

That was one of the few coherent things to come out of the stunning brunette's mouth before she'd stormed out the night before. They were through. Finished. Over.

It should probably bother him that all he felt was mild disappointment. But Theo was right. He wasn't a romantic. He couldn't afford to be. Not when all people saw when they looked at him were dollar signs. Everyone wanted something from him. It was simply a matter of parsing out what it was.

With women, prenups usually did the trick. There hadn't been a single one who stuck around after showing her the papers, no matter how generous the terms it laid out.

He might be cynical, but it didn't mean he was wrong.

Kitty was a bit of a surprise, though. He'd put a lot of thought into what went wrong in his previous relationships and decided he needed to find a woman who was his equal as far as family net worth went. Not as easy as it sounded, since the Beaumonts had graduated into the rarified air of the billionaire club.

The investment firm his father founded was reaping the benefits of Richard's savvy strategies. As Chief Operating Officer, he enjoyed the challenge of keeping the firm on the fast-track to bigger and better things. The money he made everyone—including himself—doing it was a very nice fringe benefit.

One far too many women wanted to get their greedy little hands on.

Since Damien Carlyle was a billionaire himself, Richard assumed his daughter wouldn't be one of them. A miscalculation on his part. It seemed no matter how much money some people had, it was never enough.

After lunch, the valets outside the restaurant almost rioted to be the one to grab his ticket. Not that they needed it to retrieve the right vehicle. The metallic blue Ferrari 488 Spider was entirely memorable. Not to mention a dream to drive.

A wet one.

After tipping the lucky valet, he took off, fully aware of the appreciative stares that followed. He grinned and revved the engine with a throaty growl, showing off a little for his audience before pulling into traffic.

His sister Lillian called him a car whore.

She wasn't wrong.

If it was powerful and sexy, he wanted to drive it. Over the last few years, he'd leased a half-dozen different high-end sports cars, just because he could. But the Spider... He wiggled his ass in the butter-soft leather seat and nearly groaned out loud. This car was a contender to be a keeper.

Maybe.

Because really, why settle when there might be something even better out there waiting to be discovered?

As the elevator opened on the fourth floor of their company's building, they parted ways. Theo turned right toward his office, and Richard left. There were three other executive suites on this level besides his own. Theo's as Chief Financial Officer, their father's, and the one which would have been Lillian's when she finally got around to joining the family business like she was supposed to.

Only, she never had. In usual Lillian fashion, she'd managed to dodge her responsibilities for years, until finally she'd sprung it on everyone last year she wanted to be an artist, not an executive. Or, as she put it, a nine-to-five suit-zombie.

Typical Lil.

But even he had to admit her paintings were pretty spectacular. And there was a part of him that was actually relieved he wouldn't have to deal with her on a daily basis at the office. He and his sister shared a loving yet contentious relationship. Sometimes more contentious than loving, if he was honest. Working together—or, rather, her working for him—would have been a nightmare.

In the end, the only person who'd really been disappointed by her decision was their father. He'd already conceded defeat once when Lil's twin, Peter, joined the Boulder police department years ago. Having another of his children desert the ship he'd always planned to pass on to all four of them to steer into the future caused a bruise to his pride the old man was still nursing almost a year later.

Not that the office had stayed empty for long.

Once it became clear Lillian was determinedly forging her own off-beat path, the head of the company's philanthropic arm had claimed the space. Who, in the keeping-it-all-in-the-family spirit, happened to be his mother, Patricia.

What began as a handful of scholarships a dozen years before had grown into the Everbrite Foundation, offering much-needed services and programs throughout Boulder and the surrounding areas. It was a job his mother thrived at.

Unfortunately, she had no qualms about taking advantage of that family tie to rope Richard and his siblings into helping out at her various fundraising events.

Taking the stack of phone messages his assistant Nan handed him as he walked by, he barely repressed a shudder at the memory of the bachelor auction he wasn't able to talk his way out of over the summer. Standing on stage and having women bid obscene amounts of money for the pleasure of dinner with him was an experience he never wished to duplicate.

The only up-side to that night was the fact he'd brought in a higher winning bid than either Theo or Max, a fact he had yet to let either his brother or best friend forget. Of course, gloating rights barely made up for an interminable evening with the winner, who seemed to think she'd paid for a lot more than dinner and conversation. It had taken all his willpower not to write her a check to reimburse her for her bid and walk out.

A man could only take so much objectification and innuendo.

He was deep in a report on one of the stocks he'd been watching when the intercom buzzed. "Mr. Beaumont, Mrs. Beaumont is here to see you if you're free."

Speak of the devil herself.

"Send her in, Nan." He rose and went to greet his mother with a kiss on the cheek, breathing in the familiar floral scent of L'Eau Bleue.

"So, to what do I owe the pleasure?" As if he didn't know.

Despite the touch of gray that had crept into the temples of her stylishly arranged brown hair over the past few years and the laugh lines edging her eyes, his mother was still an attractive woman.

And a determined one. That much he could tell from the gleam in her eyes as she smiled up at him.

"Can't I just stop in and say hello to my hard-working first-born son?"

"You could," he said as he led her to a chair before retaking his seat behind the desk, "but I'm pretty sure you didn't." He grinned at the chiding look she gave him.

"You think you know me so well." She huffed when he raised a brow and waited her out. "So like your father, I swear. All right, yes, I might have wanted to talk to you about the charity ball next month. I wanted to see if you and Katherine had decided on your costumes yet."

Since he'd never committed to the event one way or the other, he saw the question for the trap it was.

The masquerade ball right before Halloween couldn't possibly be as bad as the bachelor auction, but it still wasn't his idea of an evening well spent. Grown adults playing dress-up just seemed asinine.

"Why can't Pete and Lil step up to represent the family this time around? I think Theo and I more than did our duty at the last event."

"They will be. And Theodore and yourself will be there representing the company, showing its support for such a worthwhile cause." She nailed him with a steely stare. "Won't you?"

He wanted to say no. Oh, how he wanted to.

But since this fundraiser would generate the next year's funding for projects including the community center, he couldn't find it in him to refuse. He'd been getting a first-hand look at the people the center helped these past few weeks. Especially the kids. For them, he supposed he could put up with a few hours of boring small-talk and silly costumes.

Unbidden, the image of the blond avenging angel who'd blistered his ears two nights ago sprang to mind. God, she'd been a surprise. All fire and fury for what she'd seen as his mishandling of her son's breathing problem.

And maybe he had handled it poorly. At the time, trying to help normalize the poor kid's condition in the eyes of his peers seemed logical.

Lord knew he wished someone had done the same for him when he'd been Derek's age. Choking and wheezing in the middle of gym while the rest of the class stared with varying degrees of fear and morbid fascination wasn't one of his fondest memories. And being bundled off to the nurse had only reinforced the stigma of "weird sick kid" that hung around his neck from the very first day of school until he'd finally outgrown the asthma right before his senior year.

He'd felt a kind of kindred connection with Derek and wanted to help. But the kid's mother had been pissed about it, so what the hell did he know? His only experience with kids was when he'd been one himself.

And he tried really hard not to think about those years when he could help it.

But aside from her anger, or maybe because of it, the mom had been magnificent. He couldn't remember the last time a woman had gone toe-to-toe with him like that. Usually, they simply smiled or pouted, depending on what they wanted. But her? She let him know exactly what she thought of him, no holds barred.

It had been refreshing. And a little arousing. A reaction he'd quickly put the brakes on when he remembered there was most likely a Mr. Lovett lurking in the wings somewhere.

He might be a lot of things, but an adulterer wasn't one of them.

Funny how *her* taken status had been his reason for taking a step back from the instant attraction, and not his own. Which said a lot about why he wasn't more upset when said relationship imploded in spectacular fashion less than twenty-four hours later. Which brought him back to the question his mother was still waiting for him to answer.

"Fine, I'll be there. But you can cross Kitty off your list. She won't be attending."

His mother barely registered surprise at the announcement.

"She lasted longer than most, but I can't say I'm surprised. She really wasn't right for you, you know. But don't worry, the right woman is out there, Richard. You'll find her when you least expect it. Trust me."

Since matchmaking seemed to be his mother's second-favorite hobby lately—and a successful one, judging by his sister's recent engagement—he felt a justifiable prickle of unease raise the hairs on the back of his neck. "I'm not in any hurry."

He could have sworn he heard her mutter under her breath, "*You* might not be," before she smiled and stood.

"Well, let me know what costume you decide on. It would look silly if you came wearing the same thing as one of your brothers, and you know how you all tend to think alike sometimes."

"Really? That's the only reason I'd look silly?" He laughed when she rolled her eyes, looking for a second like her daughter despite the gray. "I'll have to think about it and let you know."

Maybe if he waited long enough, he could claim there were no more costumes left to rent anywhere in driving distance, and he could simply wear a tux and say he was James Bond or something.

As always, his mother seemed to know exactly what he was thinking.

"I'll be sure to reserve you something, in case you can't decide."

Richard gave a wry grin. "Thanks."

She returned the smile. "You're very welcome."

He waited until she was at the door before asking, "By the way, have you found a replacement for Steve yet?" From the way she froze mid-reach for the doorknob, he was pretty sure he had his answer.

Turning back, she gave him a puzzled look he knew to be totally fake. "Is there some kind of rush? I thought you were enjoying teaching his karate classes."

"I am, but that's not the point. My taking over was only supposed to be a stop-gap solution until you could get an actual replacement."

"Yes, well, it's not as easy as you might think to find someone qualified to teach children, and who's willing to commit so much time to an unpaid position, and who isn't—"

"So...no."

"There are background checks, and interviews, and insurance—"

"Mom." He gave an apologetic smile when she narrowed her eyes at his second interruption. "I don't mind helping out. You know that. But I didn't plan on it being long term, either. It could be five or six months before Steve is able to take over again. I do have a life, you know. You need to find someone. Soon."

She gave a beleaguered sigh.

"Fine. Since you're *so* busy with your life, I'll try a little harder to scrape up someone who knows at least *something* about martial arts and try to convince them it wouldn't be a complete waste of their time to give something back to the kids who need it the most. Kids who are there because they're being bullied or don't have anywhere else to go. Who will have to start over again getting used to yet *another* new instructor, after they were probably just beginning to get comfortable with you."

She waved a hand as though he'd said something, which he hadn't.

It was too much fun watching his mother when she got on her high horse to interrupt.

"No, no, it's okay," she continued in the same martyred tone, "it's not your problem. They're resilient at that age. I'm sure they won't feel *too* badly being pawned off to someone else so you can go live your life. Probably, anyway."

When it was clear she was done, he gave a slow clap. "You should consider putting on a play for your next fundraiser. You obviously missed your calling for the stage."

She sniffed. "You're a horrid child."

"I know. But you love me anyway."

He tilted his head back with a sigh. His mother's guilt-inducing soliloquy aside, she did have a point. It had taken time for some of the kids to warm up to him. He didn't know any of their backgrounds or family situations, but judging by the guarded look in some of their eyes, he had a feeling more than a few of them weren't very good. Might even be pretty bad.

That was part of why he'd gone in there as Mister Rick, everyday working guy. It was a safe bet none of the kids would have come back for a second class with Richard Beaumont, scion of the obscenely rich Beaumont clan.

Only Mrs. Gandy knew who he really was, and that was because there'd been no getting around it. When it came to the welfare of those kids, the center couldn't ask for a better gatekeeper.

The kids accepted Steve's departure without too much animosity because he hadn't had a choice. There was no good way to teach karate with a cast and crutches. But if Richard left, even if it was so a more qualified instructor could take over, what message would that send? That he didn't care about them? That they weren't worth his time? That he was a selfish asshole?

Damn it.

Leave it to his mother to know exactly which buttons to push to get her way. It was how she'd been able to keep control over the chaos of three rambunctious sons who were probably more than a little responsible for that touch of gray in her hair.

Just like her daughter, Patricia Beaumont looked all sweet and innocent on the outside. But underneath all the smiling mom goodness was a puppet master on par with Machiavelli himself.

Not wanting to cave completely, because it would set a dangerous precedent for future power struggles, he put on what he hoped was a convincingly reluctant expression.

"Fine. I'll keep teaching the class. For now. But if you should find someone more qualified—"

"Of course, dear. Whatever you think is best." She glanced at her watch. "I have to go. Love you!" With a sunny smile, she sailed out the door in an exit worthy of a Barrymore.

He chuckled, shaking his head. He might as well resign himself to the fact he'd be teaching that damn class until Steve got back on both feet, however long it took. Not that he really minded. It was only two hours out of his week, after all. As busy as his schedule could be, he could spare that much.

Especially now that he didn't have to worry about making time for Kitty and her constant need to socialize. As of last night, his evenings had gotten a lot less full.

And rather than feeling bad about it, all he could think about was whether the avenging angel would be there after class again tomorrow night. It was all kinds of wrong to get a buzz thinking about her. Especially when she was off-limits. But as long as he remembered she was in the look-don't-touch category, he could indulge without too much guilt. Kind of like looking at a live-action pinup. All pouty lips and curvy hips, and a pair of great big—

"Mr. Beaumont, your two o'clock is here." Nan's brisk voice over the intercom yanked him back from the brink of totally inappropriate workplace wood.

Jesus.

What was he doing, thinking about a woman—especially *that* one—at work? He'd never had a problem keeping his professional and personal lives compartmentalized before, and it annoyed him he'd let one spill over into the other, however briefly.

He scrubbed his hands over his face before answering. "Thanks, Nan. Send him in."

Shoving all thoughts about the curvaceous Mrs. Lovett from his mind, Richard focused on work for the rest of the day. And into the next. But by the time he'd changed into sweats and headed to the community center on Friday evening for class, he'd have been lying if he didn't admit to feeling more than a little sense of anticipation putting a zing in his step.

Which was ridiculous, but true. It was like he was a teen again, hoping Maddy Clark with her short little cheerleading skirt and clingy top would finally look his way.

But, like his dorky younger self, Richard was doomed to disappointment, because neither Derek nor his mother bothered to show.

Chapter 3

Pulling into the lot behind the community center Tuesday evening, Amber put the car in park but didn't shut off the engine. Instead, she turned to her son, who practically vibrated with unspent energy in his seat. "Are you sure you feel up to this, sweetie?"

"For like the thousandth time, Mom, *yes*. I'm fine. Now, can I go?"

"Missing one more class won't—"

"Mom!"

She sighed. "Okay, okay. But I want you to take it easy..." And she was talking to air.

Shutting off the car, she followed Derek inside at a slower pace, dreading what she had to do next. Much as she would have preferred to put her already overdue apology off until after class was over, recent events meant she'd have to forgo that extra hour's reprieve and talk to Rick now.

Hovering inside the basement room's open door, instead of looking for Rick habit had her scanning the room to locate Derek first. He was talking with a couple of the other kids as they took off their sneakers, preparing for class. One of them said something and gave Derek's arm a shove, but before she could react, Derek laughed and gave the larger boy an even harder push back. Uncertain, she wavered with one foot up to go to him and the other firmly planted to stop herself.

"They're fine." The deep voice from beside her sent unwelcome shivers through her insides. She turned her head to look at the man who'd trespassed through her dreams for the past week.

Dayam.

He was just as yummy as her memory had painted him. Even more so, now that she wasn't seeing him through a haze of fury.

She cleared her throat. "Are you sure? It looked like a fight might be brewing."

Rick leaned one strong shoulder against the wall. "Nah, they're just horsing around. Typical guy stuff." When she didn't look convinced, he said, "I have two brothers. I know what I'm talking about. Trust me, if there looked like there might be any problem, I'd take care of it before it became one."

Trust me. Probably the two worst words he could have chosen to say to her.

Unwanted attraction effectively squelched, she gave a curt nod. "If you say so." But it didn't stop her from looking back to where Derek was now doing warm-ups next to his shoving partner. He seemed okay. Maybe Rick was right.

She held back a sigh. Everyone said women were so hard to understand, but as far as she was concerned, it was boys who were the really confusing ones.

"Derek was missed on Friday."

Her head whipped around to stare at the softly spoken words. His expression was neutral, but there was something in his eyes...

"Actually, I, ah, wanted to talk to you about that."

"I thought you might have decided to take him out of class after all."

"What? No! I told you I wouldn't do that." It shouldn't have bothered her he'd think it of her, but it did. "Derek was in the hospital."

The neutral expression immediately turned to concern as he straightened from the wall. "The hospital? Why, what happened?"

"He had an asthma attack after school, at the park. He and some of his friends were throwing a Frisbee, and..." She shrugged, feeling the familiar tightness in her chest that came with thinking about her baby in danger. "It was a bad one. I had to take him to the ER for a nebulizer treatment."

The worst two hours of her life, standing there, helpless, as Derek struggled to get air while they waited for the drugs to take effect.

Rick put a hand on her shoulder, as though sensing her distress. "He's obviously okay now."

She tried to ignore how good the warmth of his touch felt. "It could have been a lot worse. To tell you the truth, I think he was more upset about missing your class than he was about being in the hospital."

His mouth quirked up in a half-smile, showing her a dimple she'd previously overlooked on the left side of his face.

Oh, lordy, could he get any more attractive?

She licked suddenly dry lips and tore her gaze away from the adorable dent. "I, ah, wanted to thank you, actually. It was because of what you said to the class, about what to do if someone's having an asthma attack, that kept it from being a real emergency. When he started having trouble breathing, one of the kids knew to run back to where they'd left their backpacks and get his inhaler for him, and to call for me and an ambulance when it didn't help."

She didn't even want to consider what might have happened if any of those things hadn't occurred as quickly as they did.

Rick must have felt the involuntary shudder the thought caused, because his hand tightened on her shoulder. That was it. No "I told you so" or any other smug recrimination. Which only made her feel worse.

"I also wanted to apologize."

"Oh?"

"I was wrong to accuse you of not thinking about Derek. I was so worried about his feelings, I didn't stop to consider you were thinking about his welfare. *And*," she added with a hint of disgruntlement, "he told me you asked his permission first, which you neglected to mention the last time we discussed it."

"There didn't seem to be a point." He crossed his arms and leaned a shoulder against the wall again. She felt the loss of his touch immediately, then got annoyed at herself for even noticing. "At the end of the day, you were right. I was the adult. It was my call, and I made the wrong one."

"No, you didn't. That's what I'm trying to tell you." With a sigh, she broke eye contact to help focus her thoughts, which the man seemed to have an uncanny knack for scrambling. "Even before what happened at the park, I knew I needed to apologize. I tend to be a little overprotective when it comes to my son." Her gaze sought Derek out again, a smile touching her mouth as she watched him go through his stretches. "I know what it's like to be the butt of other kids' meanness."

"So do I. That's why I did what I did."

She looked at him in surprise. From his expression, he hadn't meant to let that detail slip. "Oh, come on, *you* were picked on? For what, being too good-looking and athletic?" The second the words were out of her mouth, she wanted to groan. What the hell was wrong with her filter tonight?

Lips curving into a devilish grin, he asked, "You think I'm good-looking and athletic?"

"Fishing for compliments?"

"No, just surprised you're offering them."

Amber winced. She *had* been kind of a bitch to the guy.

"Sorry. I'm usually a very easy-going person." When he raised a dubious brow, she added, "I am! Ask anyone."

"If you say so."

"Are you laughing at me?"

"I wouldn't dare."

But he *was* laughing, damn him. She could see it in the way his eyes crinkled at the edges, softening his entire face into boyish charm. Instead of being annoyed, though, she found herself laughing at her own expense with him.

"Okay, fine. I might be a little less easygoing when it comes to protecting my family."

"Understandable." Rick straightened from the wall and looked at his watch. "I need to start class. You're welcome to stay and watch if you want."

A little confused by the sudden shift in his demeanor from teasing to all business, she shook her head. "It would only make Derek self-conscious. I'll wait upstairs. But if you could keep an eye on him, make sure he doesn't overdo?"

"Don't worry, I'll take good care of him."

Amber watched as he strode to the front of the room. The kids all fell into their lines without him having to utter a word. She hovered for a few seconds, waiting for...what? Him to look at her and smile again?

Ridiculous. His smile didn't mean anything to her. So what if it made her tummy fizz and her heart kick an extra beat? He was an attractive guy. There was nothing wrong with admiring attractiveness.

Admiring from a distance would probably be safer, though. Where she couldn't see that damn dimple, or the flecks of green she'd noticed in his lovely brown eyes. Or the subtle scent of sandalwood she'd caught when he'd touched her shoulder in sympathy.

Oh yes, she needed to be far, far away from all of that, before she ended up doing something incredibly stupid. Like licking him. Or biting that incredible ass, once more pointed in her direction as he led the class in their first drill.

Amber Lee, you are a naughty, naughty woman.

No, she admitted as she trudged up the stairs and found a quiet corner to read her book in. What she was was a lonely, lonely woman. One who hadn't allowed a man into her life—or her bed—in a very long time. Not since she'd realized Derek was getting more torn up about her break-ups with them than she was.

She hadn't considered how quickly a fatherless child might bond with any man she brought into their lives. Or how much it would hurt him when the relationships inevitably didn't work out.

And they never did.

Much as she wanted to say it was their fault, she was honest enough with herself to admit most of the blame lay with her. As nice as any of them had been, they just couldn't seem to break through the layer of mistrust that had encased her heart for the past ten years. She'd liked them well enough. Some more than others. She just hadn't been able to work up enough interest to love any of them.

But Rick...

Rick woke up parts of her she'd thought long dead. Dangerous, hopeful parts that wondered *what if?* What if she tried again? What if Derek was old enough now to understand the difference between dating and staying forever? What if she could finally have a little something just for herself?

It was an incredibly selfish, whiny thought, but she let herself have it, if only for a moment, before packing it away again. No. She'd have plenty of time for herself once Derek was eighteen and went off to college. Hopefully on a full scholarship, because God knew how else they were going to afford it. But she'd find a way. She always did.

Until then, her strict rule of "friends only" with men would have to continue. Even with the delectable Mister Rick.

Oh, but she could still dream.

RICHARD BREATHED A SIGH of relief the moment the door bumped shut behind the distracting woman. He didn't know what it was about her, but just being in her presence seemed to suck all the discipline and good intentions right out of him.

He'd been annoyed as hell at her on Friday when he thought she'd pulled her kid from the class over what happened. Then he'd decided it was her right to do whatever the hell she wanted. Right before he'd stomped up to the office after class to ask Mrs. Gandy for Derek's contact information so he could give the fickle woman a piece of his mind.

The gods that watched over impulsive idiots must have been looking out for him that night. Mrs. Gandy had been on the phone when he'd gotten there, and by the time she hung up, common sense returned. He'd left without asking for the phone number, deciding it was really none of his business, anyway.

And then she'd gone and shown up tonight with not only a perfectly logical explanation for Friday—one that still made his gut squeeze, because he remembered exactly how harrowing those ER trips could be—but with an apology as well.

A grudging one, perhaps, but still genuine. Not at all what he'd expected. That, coupled with the honest pain he'd seen in her eyes when she talked about Derek's stint in the hospital, had stirred something inside of him. Something that might have been admiration.

Which only stoked the simmering desire he'd been trying to suppress. And before he knew it, he'd been flirting with her. He didn't mean to. He wasn't even sure she realized he'd been doing it. Which he could only be thankful for, since she'd reminded him with one word exactly why he shouldn't be.

Family.

It was the slap in the face he needed to remember all the reasons he'd given himself to steer clear of her if they crossed paths again, no matter how much she appealed to him. She was taken.

Which made her off-limits, in all capital letters and flashing neon.

For the next hour, he managed to push her out of his mind, concentrating on the kids as he ran them through first kicking drills, then punches. As promised, he kept a close eye on Derek, but if he was still feeling any ill effects from last week's asthma attack, it didn't show. If anything, the kid looked determined to out-do everyone in the class.

Something he nipped in the bud as soon as he noticed.

As he corrected the angle of Derek's outstretched leg so he didn't hyperextend the sidekick, he said, "Don't push so hard." He met the boy's eyes and waited until Derek gave a quick nod, showing he'd understood the second meaning in the instruction.

After class, he zipped his bag and slung it over his shoulder, trying to work up some enthusiasm for heading home. Since Kitty stormed out of his life, his evenings had been a little empty. Not that he missed *her*, specifically. He missed having something to do other than retreat to his home office and research stocks and market trends.

Oh, he still enjoyed the anticipation of the hunt. But it didn't seem to be enough to satisfy him anymore. Which was why he'd started thinking about finding someone to settle down and start a family with in the first place.

Clearly not one of his best thought-out plans, given the result.

Turning off the lights as he left the room, he wasn't too surprised to see Derek lurking at the bottom of the stairs. The kid had lingered at the end of class, dawdling while he got his sneakers on and hanging back when the small pack of boys he usually hung around with pounded out of the room.

He'd obviously been trying to work up the nerve for something. Richard thought he'd lost it when he'd finally slipped out of the room.

It would seem he'd found it again.

"Derek, what's up? Everything okay?"

"Yeah, sure. I, ah...could I talk to you for a minute?"

The poor kid looked uncomfortable enough to jump out of his skin, so Richard took pity on him and gestured to the steps. "Sure. Let's have a seat." He picked the step one down from Derek to help keep from towering over him. "So, what's on your mind?"

"What did my mom say to you?" he blurted, looking equal parts embarrassed and determined.

"Normally I'd say it was none of your business, but in this case, I guess you have a right to wonder, since it concerned you." He fought back a grin at the kid's pained expression. "All she did was tell me why you weren't in class on Friday."

The pained look morphed into disgust. "Yeah. Me and my weak-ass lungs had to get hauled to the stupid hospital. Again."

Deciding it wasn't his place to call Derek on his language, he asked, "Again? Does that happen often?"

Derek lifted one thin shoulder. Damn, the kid really was scrawny.

"Not as much as it used to. The doctors say my lungs are getting stronger as I get older, and I try to stay away from as many things that can trigger an attack as I can, but..." He shrugged again.

"But who wants to live their life in a bubble," Richard finished for him.

"Exactly." Derek gave him a suspicious look. "How would you know?"

Because twenty-five years ago *he'd* been the scrawny ten-year-old with the weak-ass lungs.

"I spent my fair share of time in the emergency room when I was a kid, too. I wasn't any better about avoiding triggers than you are," he added with a conspiratorial grin.

"*You* have asthma?" The question came out on a squeak.

He nodded. "Had it, anyway. I finally outgrew it in high school."

Derek's eyes took on a wistful look. "The doctors say that could happen with me, too." He didn't need to say the rest. There were no guarantees with childhood asthma, no way to predict who would beat it, and who wouldn't. All he could do was wait and see.

He gave Derek's knee a quick nudge with his. "Being in this program will help your body get stronger. That's the best thing you can do. Aside from not pushing your luck on your triggers."

"I know," Derek muttered. "I didn't know they'd just cut the grass in that part of the park, or I wouldn't have gone."

At least he wasn't stupid. Or reckless.

Something Richard had been more times than he should have, trying to keep up with his healthy, able-bodied younger brothers. It had killed him to see them doing things he was forbidden to, like skiing and tubing on Copper Mountain, where the cold air would have seized his pitiful lungs up like a rusty engine with no oil. It was why his parents ultimately enrolled him in his first karate class.

"Now you know to keep your inhaler close by next time you go to the park, just in case."

Derek nodded and ducked his head. "Thanks."

He wasn't sure what the kid was thanking him for, the advice or taking the time to talk, but Richard found himself glad he'd done both. Sometimes hearing the same thing everyone else was saying from someone who knew firsthand how frustrating it was could make all the difference.

"We should get going," he said, glancing at his watch. "Your mom's probably wondering where you are."

"Probably. Listen…" Derek hesitated, grimacing. "I'm sorry my mom gave you a hard time the other day. I had no idea she'd get all crazy about it when she found out and blame you. It was totally lame of her."

"Okay, first off, your mom being concerned about you isn't lame. It's what moms do. You should be glad you have someone who cares so much about you. And second, your mom already apologized."

Derek's eyes widened. "She did?"

From the surprise in the boy's tone, it seemed admitting she was wrong wasn't something his mom did very often. He should probably feel flattered.

"Yeah, she did. Not that she needed to, though. She didn't do anything wrong. We did."

Throat working as he swallowed hard, Derek managed to hold his gaze on Richard's face. "You're right. I'm the one who should apologize. If I'd just told her the truth right from the start, she probably wouldn't have gotten as mad as she did. I'm sorry."

Brave kid, owning up to his mistakes.

"It's okay, but why didn't you tell her?"

Derek pulled a face. "Are you serious? You saw how she gets. My mom's crazy overprotective sometimes. My first day of kindergarten, she sat in her car outside the school the whole morning, just in case I needed her. Who does that?"

"Moms who worry about their kids."

Although it did sound a little extreme.

"Yeah, I guess. She probably can't help being that way, since it's only the two of us."

"The two of you?" Now that piqued his interest enough to keep him from looking at his watch again. "So, ah, no brothers or sisters, or…anyone?"

Like a dad or stepdad or wanna-be dad?

"Nope, just me and Mom since Meemaw died, and that was when I was little. I don't really remember her." He got a wistful look in his eyes. "I used to wish I had a brother, though, or a sister even. At least then there would have been someone else for her to worry about besides me."

"Sorry to disillusion you, champ, but it doesn't work like that. Your mom will always worry about you, and stick her nose in your business, and think she knows best, no matter how many brothers or sisters you have, and no matter how old you get." He shrugged, thinking about his own mother's constant meddling. "It's just the way it is. Better get used to it."

He laughed when Derek gave a dramatic groan. Slapping his hands on his knees, he stood. "Let's go before Mrs. Gandy turns all the lights out on us."

That earned another groan, this one more heartfelt. "I guess I should apologize to Mrs. Gandy before I go, too," Derek said with a sigh.

"It would be the right thing to do."

"That's what my mom said." He gave Richard a shy smile. "Thanks, Mr. Rick. For, you know…everything."

"Sure, kid. Anytime." He slung the strap from his bag over his shoulder as Derek bounded up the stairs two at a time, only to freeze when he heard him say "Hi, Mom" after he made the turn to the second half of the staircase. That was followed by "going to see Mrs. Gandy, meet you outside!" and more footsteps pounding up the rest of the stairs.

Then, silence.

Caught between embarrassment, annoyance, and a sense of the inevitable, Richard started up the stairs. Sure enough, Derek's mother was standing about halfway up the second part of the doglegged staircase. He stopped with his foot propped on the bottom step and cocked his head, trying to decide the appropriate thing to say.

The best he could come up with was, "Hi."

"Hi."

He cleared his throat as he readjusted the strap that suddenly felt like it was choking him, even though it was nowhere near his neck. "So, um, I guess you heard us talking."

"Some of it, yeah." She offered a smile, small but warm. "Thank you."

"I didn't do anything."

"Oh, but you did! Derek obviously looks up to you, and taking the time to talk to him like that, well, I'm sure it really meant a lot to him. I know it did to me."

Wondering how much, exactly, she'd heard, the tips of his ears started to burn. Jesus, was he *blushing*? "Yeah, well, I guess I should be going."

"Yeah, me too."

And still, neither of them moved.

"So, um, I'm taking Derek and his friends down the block for some pizza. Would you maybe like to join us?" The offer was hesitant, as though she expected him to refuse.

And judging by the way his body was leaning in her direction like a lodestone, that's exactly what he should do. It was the safest way to fight the tug of attraction once more threatening to make him do something stupid. And then he remembered.

There was no husband. No boyfriend.

No reason to say no.

He smiled like a cat handed a bowl of cream. "I'd love to."

Chapter 4

What had she been thinking?

Sitting in a booth across from the man she'd already decided was *exactly* the wrong person for her to do anything more than fantasize over, Amber was still kicking herself for the impulsive invitation. Because the more time she spent with him, the more she liked him.

And she couldn't *afford* to like him.

Not if she was going to stick to the no-man plan.

Which had seemed like such an easy thing to do, right up until she'd accidentally overheard part of his conversation with Derek. Okay, maybe accidentally was overstating it a bit. She'd eavesdropped, plain and simple.

Not that she'd planned to. All she'd wanted to do was find out what was taking Derek so long. She'd never expected to walk in on such a serious conversation. But once she had, wild horses couldn't have pulled her away.

Of course, she also hadn't planned on being caught.

The invitation to join them for pizza was an olive branch of sorts. An apology. That was the only reason she'd asked. And if she kept telling herself that enough times, she might even start to believe it.

No, she wouldn't. She'd invited Rick because she'd wanted to.

It was stupid, selfish, and totally self-defeating since nothing could come of it. But even if they couldn't have a relationship, maybe, just maybe, they could become friends.

Maybe with benefits?

Shushing her inner hussy, she tried to focus on the conversation raging around the table as everyone devoured the large meat lover's pie she'd ordered, only to sigh. They were *still* discussing video games. She'd tuned out over Minecraft versus Portal 2. Now it seemed they'd moved on to one that was coming out in a few weeks. Zombie mutant something.

Derek and his two friends—and more surprising to her, Rick—seemed to know everything there was to know about the thing, right down to the release date and expected price tag. The number made her wince. She'd better start working some extra shifts at the restaurant if she was going to be able to put it under the tree for Derek in December.

It was easy to zone out of the conversation again while the four of them fanboyed on and on. And on. She was practically in a coma by the time the last crumb was consumed and the kids—the little ones, anyway—all bounced up out of their seats, staring at her expectantly.

She blinked. "Uh..." Clearly, she'd missed a question somewhere. Something Rick confirmed when he mouthed the word "arcade" to her.

"Oh, sure. You can have"—she glanced at her watch—"twenty minutes. Then we have to get Mitch and Jesus home." She reached into her wallet and pulled out a five-dollar bill, which Derek snatched with a wide grin.

"Thanks, Mom!" With the bill held over his head like a battle flag, he led the charge toward the back of the building.

"I'm surprised he didn't ask for more," Rick said as he watched the receding horde.

Amber stiffened. "He knows what we can afford to waste on video games."

He stared at her for a long second. "More *time*."

"Oh." Wanting to sink under the table, she busied herself cleaning up the debris from their meal so she wouldn't have to look at him. "It's a school night. I promised the boys' mothers I'd have them home no later than nine." She went and dumped everything in the garbage before forcing herself to go back to her seat.

What was it about this man that made her so damned defensive?

"You know, I never realized there was an arcade in this place."

More grateful than he would ever know for the casual change of subject, she nodded. "It's pretty small, really, maybe a dozen or so machines, but the kids love it." She gave him a teasing smirk. "Are you sure you don't want to go check it out? You seemed pretty into the whole video game thing."

"And you definitely didn't," he teased back.

She laughed. "Noticed that, did you?"

"The eyes glazing over kind of gave it away."

She laughed again. "Guilty. You lost me on all the M&M stuff." Rick actually winced, so she knew she'd gotten it wrong. "Okay, smart guy, what's it called?"

"MMORPG. Massively Multiplayer Online Role Playing Game."

"Well, I was close."

"Not even a little."

"Whatever. I told you it wasn't my thing. But I'm still sorry you got stuck talking to a bunch of ten-year-olds, even if it was something you understood. That probably wasn't what you had in mind when you agreed to come."

"No, it wasn't." The intense look in his eyes sucked the laughter right out of her and left her a little bit breathless. Then it was gone and he grinned, showing her that damn dimple again. "But I still had a good time. I had no idea kids that age could be quite so hardcore."

"Are you kidding? They're like rabid badgers when it comes to that stuff. Derek practically inhales those gamer magazines as soon as I bring them home." Which might have been a waste of money put to better use somewhere else in their tight budget, but it was totally worth it for the pleasure on her son's face when she handed them over every month.

That, and the library book Derek had agreed to read for every magazine he got. It sucked she had to blackmail him into it, but she wasn't above doing it, either. Ruby Lovett didn't raise herself no fool.

Use what you can to get what you want, Amber Lee, because sure as spit you know everyone else will. There are no real nice guys left in this world.

"Hey, where'd you go?"

"Hmm?" She looked up into Rick's curious eyes and realized he was talking to her. "What do you mean? I'm right here."

He tapped his temple. "Up here. You looked, I don't know, a little sad all of a sudden."

Damn.

She was usually better at not showing what she was thinking. God knew she'd had to be, especially at work. She decided a half-truth was better than a lie.

"I guess I was, kind of. I was thinking about my mom."

"Ah. Derek mentioned she passed away. I'm sorry."

"Thanks, but it was a long time ago. I'm just sad Derek never really got a chance to know her. Or her him."

"He's a great kid."

She grinned. "Thanks. I think so, too." Checking the time, she saw they still had almost ten minutes to kill. Feeling absurdly awkward without knowing why, she groped for something to talk about. "Thank you for telling him about your asthma."

Oh, real smooth. Way to remind the man he caught you eavesdropping.

"I mean, I know it must have meant a lot to him to know someone with it can end up like you."

"Like me?"

"You know." She waved a hand. "Healthy. Strong. Virile."

One dark brow winged up. "Really?"

She groaned when she realized what she'd said. "God, I need to stop talking."

Rather than letting her off the hook, Rick leaned forward on his elbows, eyes alight with keen intent. "No, no, this is getting interesting. You think I'm virile?"

"Oh, please. Fishing for compliments again, Mr...." She frowned. "You know, I just realized, I don't think I know your last name." Derek had talked her ear off about *Mr. Rick*, but she couldn't recall him ever mentioning his surname. Or if he did, it hadn't stuck.

Rick stared at her for a long moment, the strangest expression on his face. Before she could even begin to decipher it, he leaned back in his seat, resting one long arm along the back of the booth.

"How about I trade you my last name for your first, Mrs. Lovett?"

"What? Oh! It's Amber. And it's Miss, not Mrs." Why she felt she needed to add that distinction, she had no clue.

Or maybe she did. Most of the time when people used Mrs. she welcomed the incorrect assumption, since it helped keep unwanted interest at bay. But with Rick, she found the thought of him believing her married oddly distasteful.

"Amber," he repeated, as though rolling it around on his tongue. "That's a beautiful name for a beautiful lady."

A little off-put by the rote sounding words, she shrugged the unexpected compliment—if that's what it was—aside. "Well, I had nothing to do with either, but thank you." Her abrupt dismissal seemed to surprise him, judging by the way his gaze narrowed. She waited. Then waited some more, before prompting, "Mister...?"

"Bowman." This time he was the one who seemed to be waiting, so she extended her hand over the table.

"Well, Rick Bowman, it's nice to meet you."

He hesitated, then took her hand, giving it a soft press. "The pleasure's all mine."

This time, the words didn't feel rote. They felt more like a promise. A shudder of something hot and exciting moved through her belly.

Good lord, was he potent.

Even after she took her hand back, she could still feel the warmth of his fingers wrapped around it like an invisible caress.

Oh, she was in serious trouble.

"S-so, um, are you a full-time martial arts instructor like Sensei Steve?" Aside from the small stutter, she was proud of herself for being able to string together an actual coherent sentence.

"No, but I have my black belt and I'm qualified to teach. The center wouldn't have hired me otherwise."

"Oh, I wasn't questioning your qualifications," she said quickly, realizing she must have sounded like she was. "That was just me, making small talk. Badly, it seems." She gave him a wry grin. "Let's try this again. So, Rick, what do you do for a living?"

There was another of those odd looks before he answered. "I mostly do the computer work for the family business."

"Oh, me too! The computer work, I mean, not the family business part. I do data entry at Boulder General."

"Oh. That sounds, uh..."

"Boring as hell, I know. But the medical benefits are great, and the hours mostly line up with when Derek's in school, so it all balances out." It would balance even better if she got the promotion to supervisor she'd interviewed for.

But getting her hopes up about things was something she'd stopped doing to herself years ago.

"Sounds to me like Derek is pretty lucky to have you for a mom."

"Actually, I think I'm pretty lucky to have him for a son." Her gaze went unconsciously in the direction of the arcade. "He's my everything."

"Does that mean there's no room for anyone else?"

The question was asked in a low voice, forcing her attention back to him. Her breath caught at the intense focus in his eyes. "There hasn't been."

"Could there be?"

Mouth dry, she flicked the tip of her tongue out to moisten her lips. She tried to form the word "no" but instead, somehow, what came out was "Maybe."

Panic beat in her chest. Or maybe it was anticipation, which ratcheted even higher when Rick's serious expression split into a satisfied smile.

"Good."

Good? No, not good. Definitely bad. But nothing she tried to tell herself could make her take it back. There was something about the man's animal magnetism that seemed to have taken full control of her rational brain and left her rioting hormones in charge.

Damn hormones.

A panicked glance at her watch told her it was finally time to collect the kids and run. There was no shame in retreat when you knew you were fighting out of your league.

"I have to get the boys home." She grabbed her purse and got up, almost cursing when he did the same.

"Thanks for asking me to come. This was fun."

Ignoring the—hopefully invisible—happy dance of her hormones, she flashed him a quick smile. "Yeah, it was." Realizing she was standing there staring like a smitten ninny, she fisted her hand around her purse strap, anchoring herself back to reality.

"Well, I don't want to keep you waiting while I gather the kids up, so, um, have a nice night."

Refusing to feel like a coward, she tossed him a little wave and bolted.

It took a few minutes to wrestle the boys away from the machines, but she finally got them moving toward the front door. For some reason, seeing Rick waiting on the sidewalk outside didn't surprise her as much as it should have.

So much for a clean getaway.

"You didn't have to wait."

"But I did."

Thank you, Captain Obvious.

"Well, thanks, but you don't have to walk us back to the car."

"Yeah, I do."

All the fizzing sexual attraction went flat at his 'I'm the big, strong man, I'll protect you, you poor, weak woman' attitude.

"No. You really don't."

It was only three blocks, and while they weren't in the best of neighborhoods, it wasn't exactly the worst, either. She might not know any cool martial arts moves the way he did, but the pepper spray in her purse was a great equalizer.

That, and a swift knee to the nuts.

"Since my car is parked there, too, I kind of do."

"Oh." Right.

Way to keep jumping to those conclusions, Amber Lee.

"Unless you want me to wait and give you a five-minute head start?"

She knew he was teasing, but it still made her feel like an idiot.

"Don't be silly. I was just..." Suddenly aware of their nosy audience listening to the exchange with keen interest, she started walking. "Never mind."

Rick fell into step beside her as the kids ranged ahead like a pack of over-eager puppies. "I'm not the guy," he said finally.

"What guy?"

"The one who made you so prickly about accepting help from anyone."

Her back stiffened. "I'm not prickly."

"Like a cactus. Or maybe a hedgehog."

She shot him a dirty glare, which was wasted because he wasn't looking at her. "Just because I can take care of myself doesn't make me prickly. And I am not a hedgehog," she couldn't stop from adding, not sure if she was more offended or amused by the comparison.

"I don't know, I think they're kind of cute. In their own prickly way." He looked over at her and winked.

Damn the man!

She let out a huffing laugh, the last traces of her annoyance disintegrating. "You're horrible."

"So my mother tells me."

"Well, she's right."

The rest of the short walk was made in silence, but it was the comfortable kind that didn't demand to be filled. She couldn't remember the last time she'd had that with a man. Or anyone, really.

When they reached the almost empty parking lot at the rear of the community center, she stopped and smiled at him. "Well, thanks for the company. This was nice."

"Yeah, it was. Thanks again for inviting me to tag along."

There was a split second where she wondered if he was going to try and kiss her. Then the kids crowded around to say their goodbyes to him, shattering the moment. Caught between being relieved and disappointed, she gave him another smile and a wave as they headed for the car.

After making sure everyone was properly buckled in, she gave in to the desire to look for Rick and see what car he got into, but he'd already been swallowed by the darkness.

She sighed.

It was just as well. Nothing good could come from her fascination with the man. He was too much for her. Too handsome, too virile, too confident, too...everything. All the things she'd sworn she'd stay away from.

She might have been fooled once by someone who seemed too good to be true, but she'd be damned if she'd let herself make the same mistake twice.

❦

STANDING IN THE SHADOWS next to his car, Richard watched with a frown as the ancient-looking Ford Escape pulled out of the lot. The ominous rattle that accompanied its departure was a pretty good sign the exhaust pipe's brackets were rusted out. Not uncommon after a few harsh Colorado winters, but the car aficionado in him cringed at the obvious lack of maintenance. If Amber wasn't careful, she'd end up losing the whole muffler in a snowbank before spring.

Amber.

The name tasted like rock candy on his tongue as he rolled it around a few times in his mind. Unusual, but it suited her.

With her wild honey-blonde mane that flowed in loose waves over her shoulders and the generous splatter of freckles on her face, she was all country girl innocence. But add in those incredible curves and a mouth so obviously meant for sin, and she was a combination no man with blood in his veins could resist.

He knew he couldn't.

As he slid into the bland beige sedan on extended rental for the duration of his community center stint, he found himself frowning again, this time at himself. Was it wrong to want to seduce a woman who was also a single mother?

It wasn't a situation that had ever come up before, so he'd never needed to consider the ramifications. Then again, was it simply seduction he had in mind, or something else?

Ridiculous.

Driving back to his condo, he refused to even consider his interest in the delectable Amber Lovett as anything other than a deep, dragging need to get her underneath him in bed.

Kitty had been generous with her body, but stingy with her enthusiasm. Amber, though...there was something about the way she kept herself so tightly wrapped and under control that hinted at something inside desperate to break free. He had a feeling once she let go of that control, *really* let go, she'd be a wildcat in the sack.

Of course, there was still the kid to consider.

Strangely enough, he found he liked Derek. He reminded him a lot of himself at that age, all awkward arms and legs and an illness that kept him from ever really being able to join in all the fun things his friends were doing. Richard had gotten deeply into gaming as a result, determined to be the best at *something*.

It was likely Derek's reasons were similar.

Punching in his security code at the entrance to the parking garage under his building, he grinned. He'd expected to spend an hour laying the groundwork with the mother for a second, more grown-up get-together. Instead, he'd spent it having a zealous discussion about the new MZA game with a trio of enthusiastic pre-pubescents.

And damned if he hadn't enjoyed himself.

That reminded him, he needed to call Max. His friend had been worried how the follow-up game would be received since it'd been almost four years since the original Mutant Zombie Apocalypse released. If tonight's fervid interest was anything to go by, he wouldn't have any issues on that front.

Not that Richard had thought he would. When he'd helped beta test the game six months ago, he'd known it was another winner.

After working out a few bugs and tweaking some graphics, it was set to be the biggest launch in Woodbow Entertainment history.

The little company started in a college dorm room was finally poised to give the big boys a run for their money.

Parking in the open slot next to his Spider, he grabbed his gym bag and walked to the private elevator in the corner. Using his keycard to unlock it, he entered his security code and rode to the fourth-floor penthouse, where soft light bathed the living room as motion sensors detected his presence.

Turning off the alarm, he dropped the bag and started for the kitchen to grab a beer, then reconsidered and headed for his office instead. He needed to think, and he did that better with a tumbler of scotch.

Taking it out onto the wide terrace, he settled into one of the comfortable chairs with a contented sigh. The tang of freshly mown grass from the park across the street flavored the air. During the daytime, the Flatirons loomed large and majestic to the southwest, but right now, they were silent shadows backlit by the still darkening night sky.

The view had been the key selling feature when he'd purchased the condo, which encompassed the entire upper floor of the building. The amenities were impressive, but the view was killer.

And if the place sometimes felt a little large and empty lately, so what?

He preferred it to the crowded parties Kitty insisted they host there, with dozens of people he barely knew invading his personal space, drinking his expensive liquor and making the same small talk he heard at every single social function she dragged him to. The men would compare the size of their portfolios, and the women would sharpen their claws on some unsuspecting victim behind her back, all the while smiling to her face.

He wasn't going to miss that, he mused as he took a swallow, letting it burn down his throat with a satisfying bite. He stared into the glass, rolling the amber liquid around and around.

Amber.

Who was she, really? Overprotective mom? Sexy ingenue? Prickly hedgehog? Whatever else she might be, she was a puzzle, and puzzles were one thing Richard couldn't stand to leave unsolved. His analytical brain wouldn't allow it.

It was still hard for him to believe she didn't know who he was. Surprised when she'd asked for his last name, he'd given her the one he was using at the center. The one for when he was trying to fly under the radar.

His conscience, dusty thing that it was, gave a twinge, but he brushed it aside. It wasn't like he'd actually *lied* to her. Just...fuzzed the truth a bit. Bowman was a legitimate alias. He even had ID and a credit card in that name for when he traveled.

If she honestly didn't know who he was, he could always apologize later.

If she did know, however, and was faking her ignorance to try and find a way to exploit their acquaintance, then he had absolutely no qualms at all about the deception. Liars and gold diggers got what they deserved.

He thought about her expression when she'd asked what he did for a living. There hadn't seemed to be anything duplicitous there.

Of course, look how wrong he'd been about Kitty.

Obviously, he still wasn't the best judge of women and their underlying motives.

You'd think after all these years he would have developed some kind of sixth-sense or something. Unfortunately, his only super-power in regards to women seemed to be getting suckered in by ones who wanted his bank account first, and him second.

Not this time, though.

This time, he was going to be the one in control of how things went. If she was amenable, Amber would have just as good a time as he did while he explored how to get past those prickly thorns of hers. And once they'd had their fun, they'd be done. No fuss, no muss, no expectations of anything more than total sensual combustion.

He gulped a mouthful of scotch as his body tightened at the prospect.

This was exactly the kind of distraction he needed after the disaster with Kitty. The thrill of the hunt without the worry of getting caught in any of his own snares. Amber might be built like a dream, but the reality was she wasn't the kind of woman a man like him considered for more than a good time.

Hell, a *great* time.

Swallowing a growl of anticipation with the last of his drink, he put aside the empty glass and grabbed his phone. He hesitated, though, as he pulled up Max's private number.

Involving Derek in the game of chase he was about to put into motion felt a little underhanded. But hell, the kid was going to get the thrill of a lifetime out of the deal. If it helped advance Richard's cause at the same time, where was the harm?

Dusty conscience fully gagged, blindfolded, and thrown into the closet of rationalization, he put the call through, ignoring its muffled whimpers.

"Hey, buddy, sorry to call so late. Listen, I have some good news about what the kids on the street are saying about the new game, but first, I have a huge favor to ask. You know the big launch party you're throwing next weekend? Do you think you could add a few last-minute names to the guest list?"

Chapter 5

"Incoming."

The whispered warning as one of her coworkers zipped past her cubicle was all Amber needed to know who was approaching. There was only one person in the data processing division who provoked such wary animosity in the staff. Unfortunately for her, it was also the same person who held her possible promotion in the palm of his moist, pudgy hand.

Fate had a pretty twisted sense of humor sometimes.

"Miss Lovett, hard at work as always, I see."

Willing herself not to gag on the nuclear cloud of Versace Eros that enveloped her space, she managed a smile over her shoulder while continuing to enter information into the computer. "Good morning, Mr. Hollingsworth."

She mentally willed him to keep on walking, but it seemed fate planned to screw with her a little more today.

"Your work ethic is, of course, appreciated, Miss Lovett, but surely you can take a minute to give me your full attention."

Damn, damn, damn.

"Of course, sir." She saved her work, marked her spot on the patient file she was entering, and swiveled her chair to face him, a fixed smile on her face. Despite her conservatively cut blouse, experience had taught her not to give him a side view if she could help it. "What can I do for you?"

She knew as soon as she said it, she should have chosen her words more carefully. The glint in Hollingsworth's eyes told her exactly what he was thinking, and it had nothing to do with work.

With every ounce of her being, she wanted to tell him to take his dirty thoughts and offensive cologne and go to hell, but she couldn't. Not until he actually did or said something she could take to human resources to file a complaint over.

Unfortunately, Horny Hollingsworth, as he was not-so-affectionately known among the female staff, was too smart for that. He knew exactly where the line lay, and he was very careful never to put so much as a toenail over it.

"Well, now that you ask…" The tip of his tongue flicked out to moisten his lips. The resemblance to a lizard was so strong she almost couldn't catch back the snort that wanted out. "You can have lunch with me."

Panic drained the amusement right out of her.

"Oh, um, I was actually going to…" Her frantic gaze landed on the single yellow rose in the bud vase on her desk. Inspiration struck. "I'm sorry, but I already have lunch plans with someone." She should probably be polite and thank him for asking, but she just couldn't make herself do it.

Hollingsworth's pale green eyes narrowed on the flower, his expression pinching in displeasure. "From your boyfriend?"

"We're…dating." Okay, that was stretching the truth. A lot. They'd shared a pizza with three game-crazy boys as chaperones the night before. If anything, it had been more of a testing-the-waters thing.

Although after a restless night filled with dreams of Rick and his dark chocolate eyes and all his very biteable parts, she'd decided over a large double-shot coffee it had probably been more of a one-time thing. Despite his question about whether there was room for someone other than her son in her life, she had no illusions Rick was in a hurry to fill that spot.

Not many men would be.

And then the single, perfect rosebud, half unfurled, with leaves and thorns intact, had been delivered to her department this morning with a handwritten note that read, *Roses are prickly, too, but only because they're guarding something precious.*

She'd stared at the note for a good ten minutes, trying to figure out what the heck it meant. Was he calling *her* precious? Or saying he understood she was so prickly—and okay, she admitted she could be, with him at least—because she had a good reason to be?

She had no more answers now than she'd had then, but the flower certainly kept her thinking about him all morning.

It was both annoying and arousing as hell.

Hollingsworth made a noise of displeasure.

"I'll be talking to both applicants who made the final cut for the supervisor's position. I simply thought it might be less stressful for each of you to get out of the office environment while we did, seeing as how much is at stake on the outcome of my interviews. But if you already have plans, we can always do this in my office at the end of the day."

She'd made the final cut for the promotion?

The surprise of that news momentarily overshadowed everything else he said. Long suppressed excitement burbled up, making her skin tingle.

It might actually happen!

She wanted to punch the air in triumph.

Then the rest of Hollingsworth's words sank in. A meeting in his office? Alone? At the end of the day when everyone else was leaving? Not a good idea. Lunch in a public place was decidedly the lesser of the two evils.

"No, that's okay. I'm sure Rick will understand me cancelling, since it's for business." She laid a little more stress than necessary on the word. No harm in reinforcing there was absolutely nothing personal about this lunch meeting. At. All.

Hollingsworth made a little frowning moue. "Well, if you're sure it won't be a problem for him."

"No problem at all."

Especially since there'd been no lunch plans to begin with.

The frown disappeared, replaced by a smug look of satisfaction that had her grinding her teeth. "Excellent. Meet me at quarter of twelve at my office."

She blew out a relieved breath as he left, taking his toxic cloud with him. Lunch with Horny Hollingsworth. Fate didn't just have a sense of humor. She was a fucking bitch.

"What did he want?" Peeping like a curious prairie dog over the top of the beige wall separating their cubicles, Belinda's whispered question made Amber jump.

"To do an interview with me for the supervisor's spot."

"You got it?"

"Not yet, but it's down to me and someone else. He didn't say who, though. He wants to talk to each of us again before making his final decision."

"Oh my God!" Belinda's restrained squeal echoed the one Amber refused to let out. "Do you have to go now?"

"No. At lunchtime."

"Oh. *Oh*." Belinda gave her a commiserating look. "Lunch with the toad. That sucks."

"It beats the alternative of his office after hours with the door closed."

"Very true. Good luck!" Belinda shot her crossed fingers.

"Thanks." Turning back to her computer, she forced herself to concentrate on the words and numbers in front of her and not on the upcoming interview. Even so, she double checked every bit of work she did before hitting enter, just to be sure.

At eleven-thirty, she shut down her station, slid on the lightweight cardigan hanging off the back of her chair, and grabbed her purse from the bottom desk drawer. After touching the rosebud once for luck, she made a quick stop at the restroom before taking the elevator up one level to where the administrative offices were located.

Where she was left cooling her heels for almost twenty minutes outside of Hollingsworth's office before he finally emerged, shrugging on his suit jacket. His mouth tightened in disapproval as his assessing gaze took in the loose sweater that now hid her breasts from view. Then his lips switched direction and swung upward in a patently false smile.

"I hope you're hungry. I know I am. Let's get going, shall we?"

That was it. No apology for keeping her waiting. No explanation of where they were going. Just one of his thinly veiled double entendres that wasn't even worth getting annoyed about.

It was going to be a *long* lunch meeting.

The short cab ride to the restaurant proved a trial on both her nerves and her nose. Surprisingly, though, there were no attempts to use the confined space to "accidentally" brush against her, no more innuendos or lecherous looks. By the time they were seated at the small table for two at the edge of the trendy restaurant's outdoor dining area, she was starting to think maybe, just maybe, Horny Hollingsworth was actually going to act like a professional for the duration of their interview.

"So, Miss Lovett, tell me. How badly do you want this promotion?"

Or maybe not.

"Being promoted will be a tremendous help to me financially, of course," she replied, choosing her words carefully as she concentrated on buttering a roll. "And the hours would still line up almost perfectly with the time my son is in school, so I won't have to rely too much on other people to watch him when he gets home."

"That's right, you have a son." He took a roll and cut into it. "It must be difficult for you, being a single parent, raising a child all by yourself with no one to turn to if things were to get rocky."

The hairs on the back of her neck started to stir. The words had been spoken with almost careless disinterest, but they felt dangerous all the same.

"We do perfectly fine, thanks." Looking at the warm, flaky roll in her hand, she found she'd lost her appetite and put it down. "The promotion to supervisor would just give me a little added security."

That was all she wanted. For once in her life, to have the security of knowing she wasn't one piece of bad luck away from losing her job, her home, her family. Was that really so much to ask?

Thankfully, the waitress came to take their order, offering a reprieve. Going with a salad since she didn't think her knotted stomach could handle anything else, she sipped her water, willing herself to ignore the trickle of sweat that rolled down her spine.

Now she knew why Hollingsworth asked to be seated outside despite the sunny September day. But she'd let herself melt into a puddle before she'd oblige him and take off her sweater the way he'd stripped off his suit jacket and loosened his tie as soon as they'd sat down.

Stupid oversized boobs.

They'd caused her more trouble than she could keep track of over the years. What she wouldn't give to have them *not* be the first part of her to arrive whenever she entered a room.

"So, Amber." He made her wait while he chewed a large bite of his roll. "What do you think makes you uniquely qualified to get the position?"

Ignoring the fact he'd started using her first name, creating a false sense of intimacy between them, she concentrated instead on her answer.

"Well, I've worked in the data entry department for over two years now, so I have a solid understanding of both the job and the people there."

"You don't worry that you might have problems with your coworkers if you suddenly became their boss?"

"Not at all. I get along well with everyone in the department. And I think they'd like having one of their own in charge."

Hollingsworth chuckled. "They might like you now, but trust me, nobody likes you once you're the boss."

Only if that boss happens to be an asshole.

"I don't see it being a problem for me, sir. Or for them."

"No need to 'sir' me when we're not in the office. This is just us, getting to see how well we might rub along if you were to get the position."

And there it was. The one massive pitfall to getting the promotion. It would mean she'd be reporting directly to him as her immediate supervisor. But compared to everything else she'd gain, it seemed like a trade-off she could live with.

Hopefully.

Dabbing as discretely as possible at the sweat beading her upper lip, she willed the food to arrive. "Um, I also believe my work record speaks for itself as far as my qualifications. My reviews have all been exemplary, and the last supervisor even added a note saying she felt I would be an excellent candidate for promotion."

"Yes, I was looking your records over right before we left. Where I also saw that you've had to leave work to go deal with 'personal matters' on more than one occasion."

Her stomach cramped.

"That's true. My son has asthma, so there have been a few times I've needed to pick him up from school after he had a particularly bad attack. But I've always made up the hours I missed, either by coming in early or working through lunches," she added, hoping it didn't sound like she was making excuses.

"Hmm." Shoving the rest of the roll into his mouth, Hollingsworth stared at her with a considering expression as he chewed. He dabbed at his mouth with the napkin after swallowing. "You're clearly an excellent mother who would do anything for her son. I like that."

The hairs on her neck stirred again. "Thank you."

"I hope that...what's his name?"

Something in her rebelled at telling him, but there was no good reason she could find not to. Derek's name was in her file, after all. Hollingsworth could easily look it up himself anyway. "Derek."

"Derek. That's a good, strong name. And he's how old?"

Amber's fingers tightened over the linen napkin she was squeezing in her lap, finally seeing the train wreck looming straight ahead. "Ten."

"Ten. Really." He cocked his head and studied her. "Oh, come on now, you look much too young to have a son that old. You're what? Barely thirty yourself?" There was something much too calculating in his expression to carry it off as the compliment it was supposed to sound like.

"Twenty-seven." Something he damn well knew if he'd been reading her personnel file half an hour ago.

Bastard.

"Twenty-seven." He paused as though doing the math.

Like he hadn't already.

"So, you were...*very* young when you became a mother."

It wasn't the first time someone felt it necessary to point that out. But it had been a long time since she'd been in a position where she couldn't tell them to mind their own damn business and walk away. If she did that now, she'd be all but guaranteeing she wouldn't get the promotion.

Which was exactly why he'd said it.

Hating the helpless, boxed-in feeling slowly creeping over her, she simply gave a non-committal smile and reached for her water again, wishing it was something stronger.

She wasn't ashamed of having Derek when she was basically still a kid herself. A little embarrassed she'd once been such a gullible, trusting fool, but never ashamed. Not of him. Derek was the best part of her life, no matter how he'd come to be in it.

Or when.

"That's a lot of responsibility to have so early in life," Hollingsworth said, running a pudgy finger around the rim of his glass as he looked at her. A small smile played at his lips. "I can see why you'd be looking for that extra security you mentioned. Especially when the boy's father isn't in the picture." The statement turned to a question at the end.

Rather than answer, she took a breath to steady her racing heart. "Mr. Hollingsworth. Sir. I believe in my qualifications for this job. If you'd just give me the chance to prove it, I know you won't be disappointed."

The small smile became a satisfied grin, making her skin crawl. Hollingsworth lifted his glass toward her in salute.

"My dear Miss Lovett, you just might be right."

⟨O⟩

"WHAT A SLIMEBALL!"

Feeling ten pounds lighter after having unloaded her afternoon of horror onto her best friend, Amber dropped her head back against the sofa with a whoosh of expelled air. "He is. He really, really is."

"How dare he bring Derek into the discussion! Why would he even do that, other than to be an ass?"

"If I had to guess? He was making a point." And making it very well.

"About what?"

The ball of impotent fury sitting in her gut all afternoon twisted even tighter.

"That as a single mother, I'm in a very precarious position, financially. And he has the power to either help me or hurt me."

On the other end of the chocolate brown sofa in the NoBo apartment she shared with two roommates, Elena Moustakas bolted upright in outrage. "He was threatening you? Are you sure?"

"Pretty sure."

"Then report his ass to Human Resources!"

Amber gave a humorless laugh. "If only it were that easy."

"But—"

"He didn't actually come right out and say anything that was a threat. It was all innuendo and 'wink-wink, nudge-nudge, you know what I'm really talking about' kind of stuff." She shuddered. "It's how he's gotten away with his crap for so long at the hospital. He's really careful about what he says, how he says it, and who he says it in front of. Everyone knows what he really means, but there's no way to prove it."

"That's bullshit."

"That's life." And sometimes it sucked big hairy donkey balls.

"Well...what are you going to do?"

She lifted her hands and let them fall back to her lap in defeat. "What *can* I do? He's got all the power. All I can do now is wait and see what happens next."

The all-too familiar feeling of helplessness was practically choking her. She hadn't done anything wrong, but once again, she found herself at the mercy of someone with the power to destroy her life. It just wasn't fair.

Life's not fair most of the time, Amber Lee. Best you get used to it.

Her mother had been brutally honest about that cynical fact from the time Amber could remember. But it was still a lesson the universe seemed bent on teaching her again and again.

"There has to be someone you can tell who can do something."

She gave her friend a weary smile. "It's not like the restaurant, El. I don't have a Mrs. P to go to with my problems."

Parthenia Papadopoulos and her husband Minos owned the restaurant where Amber spent her first few years in Boulder waitressing alongside Elena. Her husband handled the business side, but Mrs. P was the one who kept the staff in line, and her word was law. She was the sweetest woman in the world unless you stepped out of line. Then she became four-feet-eleven of pure Greek fury.

Even her husband was a little terrified of her.

Amber sighed and drained the last of the sweet wine in her glass. Normally, she didn't indulge during the week, but today had seemed like a pretty good reason to break her rules. Derek was having dinner at a friend's, and she didn't have to pick him up until nine. Plenty of time to indulge in half a glass of cheap rosé.

Although half a bottle probably still wouldn't be enough to erase the slimy feeling she got every time she thought about Horny Hollingsworth and his lizard tongue and the way he'd managed to say the word "position" at least a dozen times over the course of their interminable lunch. Only he could infuse such a simple word with so much disgusting innuendo. By the time the check came, she'd been ready to vomit.

"So, what now?"

"Now I guess I wait and see if I get the job." She looked longingly at the wine bottle on the coffee table but didn't reach for it. "Enough about my crappy day. What's up with you? How's Nik?"

Elena made a face that was half-pain, half-resignation. "Mrs. P set him up with another of her friend's daughters last weekend. They had dinner at the restaurant."

"Ouch." She winced in sympathy for her friend. Unrequited love sucked.

Especially when you worked every day with the object of your desires.

Elena had been pining for Nikolas Papadopoulos since before Amber started working at the restaurant. Amber thought she'd seen signs he returned the sentiment, but he'd never acted on it. Probably because he knew his mother wouldn't approve.

Despite her last name, Elena was far too American to suit Mrs. P's very Old World ideas of a suitable bride for her only son.

Amber felt for both of them, in a Romeo and Juliet kind of way. But if Nik didn't have enough balls to stand up to his tyrant of a mother about something as important as the rest of his life, then he didn't deserve Elena, anyway.

"Yeah." Elena swirled her wine before bolting the remainder down in a large gulp. She coughed. "Sucks to be me."

"I know you hate when I say this—"

"So don't."

"—but what you need to do is move on and find yourself a man who's willing to treat you the way you deserve."

Elena snorted as she poured more of the pale pink wine into her glass. "Right. Great advice, coming from the queen of not moving on. *You're* the one who needs to find herself a man!"

"We're not talking about me." Especially not when she could feel her cheeks heat up as a picture of Rick flashed through her mind. "We're talking about you."

The slightly inebriated sneer turned to disbelief as Elena studied her face. "Oh my God, there's a guy!"

"There isn't any guy."

"There's so definitely a guy! You don't blush like that for nothing."

"It's the wine," Amber muttered into her glass. Empty.
Damn.

She chased the last stray drops out of it anyway.

"Bull. Now dish. Who is he? How did you meet? Have you taken him for a test ride yet?"

"That's it, no more wine for you." Amber moved the almost empty bottle out of her friend's reach. Then she sighed. "Okay, there might be a guy."

"I knew it!"

"It's just...it's complicated."

"The good ones always are." Settling against the sofa cushions like she was getting ready for a bedtime story, Elena gestured with her glass, barely keeping the wine from sloshing over the rim. "Okay. Tell me everything."

"There's not much to tell. He's filling in teaching Derek's karate class at the center."

"So, he's athletic. Nice. Go on."

"He works for his family's company doing computer stuff." Although he'd been kind of vague about what, exactly.

"Which means he's gainfully employed, *and* you have something in common. Better and better. What else?"

"His name is Rick. And Derek really likes him."

"Definitely a plus, but the real question is, do *you* like him?"

Like was much too mild a word for what she felt whenever she allowed herself to think about the man. *Lust, hunger, desire.* Those were closer to the churning emotions the man evoked in her. Emotions she wasn't sure she wanted to let free.

"He's...nice."

"Don't say nice," Elena groaned. "Guys hate being called nice."

"Okay, fine. He's..." *Charismatic. Confusing. Scary.* "Different."

Elena's dark brows pulled into a frown. "Different how?"

"Well, he actually talked to my face instead of the girls, which was a really nice change," she said with a wry grin. "And he spent an entire meal discussing video games with Derek and his friends, and it was because he wanted to, not to score points with me."

She might not have understood most—okay, any—of what they'd been talking about, but that much at least had been obvious. He'd truly been into the discussion.

"Wait, you've already been to dinner with him?"

"It was just pizza."

"Did you both eat?"

"Obviously."

"Then it was dinner."

"It wasn't...okay, technically it was dinner. But I only asked him to come with us as a way of apologizing."

Liar, liar.

"For what?"

"I might have, uh, jumped to a few conclusions and yelled at him the first time we met." Not her finest moment. Thinking about it still made her want to cringe.

After staring at Amber for a long second in disbelief, Elena burst out laughing.

"It's not funny." But a smile tugged at her lips anyway.

When the laughter finally ran out, Elena wiped the tears from her cheeks and shook her head. "Oh, sweetie, I think you're going to need to start at the top. I'm obviously way behind on what's been going on in your love life."

"I don't have a love life." Not outside of her dreams, anyway.

"Sounds like that might be changing."

Ignoring her friend's smirk, Amber gave a quick rundown of her first, embarrassing meeting with Rick, right up through the delivery of the single rosebud at work that morning. When she was done, Elena wore a thoughtful look on her face.

"From yelling to flowers in a little over a week. I'm impressed."

"Flower," Amber stressed. "Just one."

"Which makes it all the more meaningful."

She happened to agree. Which was why she was struggling so hard to find a flaw in Rick's gift. Any flaw.

"It was a joke. Because of the hedgehog thing."

"Ri-ight. The guy went to a florist, picked out a single perfect flower, wrote you a note about it, remembered where you said you worked, and sent it to you, all for a joke."

"It can't mean anything. I've only known him for nine days. *Nine*. And we were annoyed with each other for seven of them."

"So what?"

"So..." She spluttered to a halt. "It's moving too fast."

"For a sloth, maybe. For a man and woman? I'd say you're right on track." Putting her glass down, Elena reached over and clasped Amber's hands. "Sweetie, I love you to pieces, but I'm going to tell you this for your own good. You need to get the hell out of your own way. This could be a really good thing."

"Or it could be a major disaster."

But her friend's words echoed in her mind.

Was it true? Was *that* the reason none of her relationships had worked out over the years? Had she been subconsciously sabotaging things with any guy who'd shown the slightest potential of breaking through the ice around her heart, just to save herself the pain of having things fall apart later on?

What a depressing possibility.

"Okay, for argument's sake, how would I go about getting out of the way?"

With a squeal, Elena squeezed her hands and bounced, making the sofa springs squeak. "This is going to be so much fun!"

Doubtful. But the half glass of wine was just enough to mellow Amber's internal cynic to where she thought it might not be too awful, either.

Chapter 6

SHE WAS WAITING OUTSIDE of the meeting room after Friday night's class.

Richard felt an almost savage burst of satisfaction when he saw her leaning against the wall near the bottom of the stairs as he came out. Sending the flower and then not following up had been a calculated risk.

But it looked like it was about to pay dividends in a big way.

Derek wasn't waiting with her, which meant she'd sent him upstairs on his own. Another good sign. Either that, or she didn't want the kid's tender ears to be scorched when she gave him hell for overstepping.

But he already knew what she looked like when she was pissed, and this wasn't it. This seemed more like nervous. And maybe...a little anticipation?

Better and better.

Careful to keep his expression neutral, he walked toward her, not surprised when she met him halfway. Whatever else she was or wasn't, Amber Lovett had backbone. He liked that almost as much as he liked the way she filled out the dark blue t-shirt she was wearing.

Forcing his eyes to stay northward, he gave a small smile. "Hi."

"Hi." Her hands fidgeted on the strap of her purse. "I got the flower. Thank you."

"You're welcome." It was difficult to tell if she was being polite or sincere. Not that it should matter, but...damn it, it did. "I hope I didn't overstep by sending it. The last thing I wanted to do was make you uncomfortable."

"Oh, no, you didn't. I was just surprised." A smile finally curved those luscious lips. "Pleasantly. It's been a long time since anyone's sent me flowers." A look of panic flashed across her face. "Not that I think you meant anything by it," she added hastily. "I meant, you know, it was a nice gesture, and you were nice to do it, and..." She groaned and shook her head. "I'll stop talking now."

Fighting a laugh because it would only embarrass her more, he said, "Every woman should have someone who sends them flowers once in a while." He waited a beat and lowered his voice. "And for the record, I didn't send the rose to be nice."

She swallowed. "Oh?"

"I sent it because I wanted to make sure you were thinking of me."

"Oh."

"Is that all you can say? Oh?"

Damn, he loved teasing her. Hell if he knew why, though.

"No." She rolled her eyes and laughed. "I mean, I'm not sure what else to say. I honestly don't know what this is."

"This?"

"You know." She gestured between them. "*This*."

"Ah. *This*. Well...I guess it's whatever we want it to be, don't you think? We're two consenting adults. We're both otherwise unattached. And we obviously have some kind of chemistry happening between us."

Amber gave a nervous laugh. "Just a little."

"So why shouldn't we explore where *this* might go?"

She was silent a long moment, chewing her lip and practically strangling her purse strap as she mulled it over. Finally, to his immense satisfaction, she nodded. "I think I'd like that."

Yes!

He wanted to roar in triumph. Instead, he smiled, careful to keep it from being smug. "Great. In that case, what would you think about going to dinner tomorrow?"

"With you?" Again, she rolled her eyes. "Obviously with you. I swear, I'm not usually this verbally challenged."

"Good to know." Because that meant he was the reason she was all flustered and tongue-tied. If he was already affecting her without even touching her, getting her into bed would be a piece of cake. "So, what do you say?"

"I wish I could, but I have to work tomorrow night."

The excuse made him pause. "I see."

But he didn't.

What just happened? She'd already told him she worked weekdays at the hospital. Not weekends, and not nights. So why would she lie?

She must have picked up on his confusion.

"No, really, I do. On any weekends when Derek stays overnight at a friend's, I pick up shifts at the restaurant where I used to waitress. With Derek's birthday coming up and then the holidays right after, I have to make whatever extra cash I can, when I can. I'm sorry."

She looked and sounded like she meant it. Richard mulled over her words.

Money. Everything always came down to money. Pushing aside his knee-jerk annoyance at that fact, he tried to consider Amber's situation objectively.

Even if Derek's father wasn't in the picture, he should probably be paying child support, so money shouldn't be *that* tight. Unless, for some reason he wasn't paying what he should. He could be a deadbeat dad. Or maybe just dead. And if that was the case, then working a second job seemed not only plausible, but an unfair necessity.

Deciding she was probably telling the truth, he shrugged one shoulder. "No problem. There's no rush, right?"

Looking relieved at his easy acceptance of being turned down, she smiled. "Right."

Time to move on to Plan B.

With a casual glance at his watch, he said, "I was thinking of hitting that pizza place again. I never did get a chance to check out the arcade. Want to tag along for a slice? My treat," he added, thinking about this new insight into her money situation. No wonder she'd been so prickly about how much cash she forked over to be wasted on video games last time.

"That would be nice, but Dutch is fine," she countered.

Prickly to the end.

"Whatever you want."

They collected Derek from upstairs and walked down to the pizza parlor. Being a Friday night meant the sidewalks were more crowded than the last time they'd made the trip, forcing them to walk a little closer, their arms occasionally bumping.

By the time they got in line to place their order, Richard was cursing himself for telling her there was no need to rush. Every accidental brush of her skin against his had been like a stroke to nerve endings that led straight to his groin.

True to her word, Amber refused his attempt to pay for her and Derek's food. The look she shot him could have frozen molten lava. It would have been amusing if he hadn't been in so much pain. Thank God he was wearing loose sweats. No way would he have been able to hide his body's reaction if he'd been in jeans.

Even so, he kept his hands casually clasped in front of him until he could will his body back under control.

They grabbed a table as it was vacated by a bunch of noisy teenagers. He and Derek held the food and drinks while Amber did a quick wipe-down of the table with a damp napkin to clean up the crumbs and smears of sauce left behind.

The long-suffering expression on Derek's face led Richard to believe this was a normal occurrence, and not just for his benefit.

"So, is this a waitress thing or a mom thing?"

"It's an I don't want to eat in someone else's mess thing." Opening her purse after they were finally seated, Amber rummaged around until she pulled out a little bottle of hand sanitizer. She squirted some onto her palm and gave her hands a brisk rub, releasing the subtle and not unpleasant aroma of cucumbers and melon.

Richard bit into the steaming slice on his paper plate, savoring the spicy heat of the buffalo chicken generously heaped on top even as it scorched his tongue. He'd loved pizza as a kid. But as he'd gotten older and started moving in more sophisticated circles, first for work, then with his own social group, his palate had changed.

Or maybe just his perception had. People who ran Fortune 500 companies dined at five-star restaurants with award-winning chefs and white-glove service. They didn't eat pizza and tacos.

Christ, when had he become such a food snob?

Taking a long drink of his soda—another thing his taste buds had forgotten the enjoyment of—he decided the time was right to pull out his ace. "So, listen. I kind of had an ulterior motive asking you to come here with me tonight."

The immediate wariness on Amber's face, her sapphire blue eyes filling with distrust, left him silently cursing. Bad opening gambit when starting negotiations, putting the other side on the defensive.

Rookie move, Beaumont.

"Okay, that came out wrong. What I meant was, I wanted to talk to the both of you about something, and this seemed like a good way to do it."

"Okay." The wariness hadn't abated, but at least she was listening. "Talk to us about what?"

"You remember that game we were talking about? The one coming out next week?"

"Kind of hard to forget."

He bit back a grin at her wry tone. "Well, there's a launch party next Saturday for when it goes live at midnight, and I was wondering if the two of you might be interested in going with me?"

"Are you kidding?" Derek yelped. "A launch party for MZA2? That would be so freaking awesome!"

"Language."

"Sorry, Mom, but it would! Can we go? Please?"

Amber looked pained. "I don't know..."

Time to sweeten the pot.

"It's actually not just *a* launch party. It's *the* launch party. There's going to be media, maybe even some celebrities." Neither one of them looked impressed, so he pulled out the big gun. "And they'll have copies of the game in the swag bags they give away."

The breath Derek sucked in almost sounded like a wheeze. He looked sharply at the kid to make sure he was okay, but Derek was too busy aiming a pleading look at his mother to notice.

"Mom?" It came out as a squeak.

Looking resigned, she asked, "How much do the tickets cost?"

"Nothing." He raised his hand when she glared at him. "I swear. Max is a friend. I was already going, and when I asked him if I could bring a few friends along, he said no problem." She still didn't look convinced. "Not everything has to have a price tag, you know."

The look in her eyes called him a liar. "Everything comes with a cost."

Too excited to pick up on his mother's cynicism, Derek practically bounced in his seat. "Max? You know Max Woodward?"

"We went to college together."

Derek's eyes grew larger. "For real?"

"For real."

"Okay, who's Max?" Amber looked between them, a pucker creasing her forehead.

"He created Mutant Zombie Apocalypse," Derek said before Richard could, "and he owns Woodbow, the company that distributes it. And Mr. Rick knows him. That is so frea—ah, darn cool!"

"I guess it is." Although she only sounded mildly impressed.

Probably because she didn't realize how much money being the owner of Woodbow translated into. He was pretty sure she'd be impressed by *that*.

And why did that thought irritate the shit out of him?

"I know video games aren't your thing, so I can take Derek myself if you don't want to go." He was banking on her maternal instincts making her turn down the offer, though. The last thing he wanted was to spend the evening in charge of a kid.

Although, as kids went, Derek wasn't so bad.

"I'm not sure..."

"Mom, *please*?" The poor kid looked like he was going to cry if she said no. Which was probably why she caved.

"Okay. Yes, we'll go."

"Awesome!" Derek squeezed his mother in a quick hug, his eyes shining with excitement as he looked across the table at Richard. "Thank you! This will be the best day ever! And now I won't have to wait until my birthday to get the game!"

Shit.

The last thing he wanted was to upstage Amber's gift plans for her son. That would be a death knell for any goodwill he might have built so far.

"There's nothing wrong with having to wait for what you want, sweetheart," Amber said, smoothing her hand over Derek's hair with such affection Richard felt a little twang in his chest. "But you're right, it's definitely an amazing opportunity. Now, finish your slice so you can go to the arcade."

As they ate, Derek peppered Richard with questions about the game, the party, Max, and anything else he could think of. By the time he grabbed the handful of quarters Amber dug out of her purse and took off to conquer space aliens in the arcade, Richard felt like he'd been through the Inquisition.

He must have looked it, too, because Amber gave him a sympathetic grin.

"Sorry, but you did kind of bring that on yourself, you know."

"I guess I did," he replied with a laugh. "Look, I'm really sorry if I screwed up anything you already got for his birthday."

"You didn't. I was actually saving up to get the game for Christmas." She made a wry face. "At least now he won't be disappointed when his birthday gets here."

Double shit.

"I didn't mean to step on your toes."

"I know. And it's fine, really." She smiled. A real, honest one. "And it's not just about the game. This is something he'll remember for years as one of the best days of his life. Thank you for making it happen."

"You're welcome."

He thought about the second part of the plan, wondering if he needed it, then decided what the hell.

"There's one other thing." He paused as Amber's expression immediately turned closed and guarded. "Damn, lady, you don't give a guy a chance, do you?"

She blinked at his rough tone. "What do you mean?"

"You're always expecting the worst, aren't you?"

"I..." She sighed. "Maybe I am. I'm sorry."

"Hey, like I told you last time, I'm not the guy, okay?"

"Okay."

He thought he heard her mutter 'get out of the way' under her breath before she jammed her straw into her mouth and finished her soda with a rattle of ice.

"What I was going to say was, your names weren't the only ones I got added to the list. There are tickets for Derek's two friends as well, if they want them. I didn't want to bring it up in front of him, in case you didn't think it was a good idea."

Amber stared at him for a long second, her mouth hanging open before she finally snapped it shut. "Are you kidding? They'd be over the moon about going. Not to mention making you a hero to all three of them. Not like you aren't halfway there already."

The idea made him squirm inside. He was nobody's hero. He was a man on a mission, and this was a piece of strategy to help him close the deal, just like any piece of business he put his mind to.

"What about their parents? I guess I need to get their permission first."

"I can check with their moms for you if you want. They should be okay with it, since I'll be there to ride herd on them all."

That was when the drawback to his plan hit him square in the face.

He'd been so focused on giving her a reason to attend, he'd completely overlooked the fact that with any of the kids there, she'd spend the night playing babysitter. Hell, they both would.

Not just a rookie move, dumbass. A fatal flaw.

Well, too late to change anything now.

Resigned, he nodded. "Thanks."

"No, thank you. This is really great."

She stared at him long enough to make him uncomfortable. "What? Do I have sauce on my face or something?" He swiped at his chin.

"No. It's just...you did this amazing thing for my kid, even after I turned down your dinner invitation, and it's kind of blowing me away."

The baffled amazement in her expression almost hurt to see. How much crap had life thrown at this woman that it was so easy to expect the worst of people, but so difficult to accept a kind gesture?

Even if it had been a calculated one.

He reached across the table and put his hand gently over hers. "I told you—"

"You're not the guy." She offered a tentative smile. "Yeah, I think I'm starting to get that."

He squeezed her fingers even as his conscience gave a faint kick to the closet door he'd locked it behind. "Good."

"So, um, dinner on Saturday might be out, but what would you think about lunch on Sunday?"

"The three of us?"

She shook her head slowly. "The two of us."

A triumphant smile threatened to break free. Holding it under rigid control, he stroked his thumb over the back of her hand and watched with primitive satisfaction as her pupils dilated and her breath caught.

"I think it's a date."

◆◇◆

"THIS PLACE IS BEAUTIFUL!"

Where to take Amber for lunch had been a more problematic decision than it should have been. He didn't want to insult her by going too cheap, but he also couldn't bring her to one of the usual restaurants he wined and dined women at, either. He was enjoying the undemanding anonymity of being plain old Rick Bowman too much to give it up yet, and "Rick" wouldn't be able to afford that kind of luxury.

Not to mention he stood the chance of running into people who knew him.

A picnic in the park seemed like a safe middle-ground choice. And judging by the smile on Amber's face, the right one.

Score one for Team Rick.

Shading her eyes, she looked down the hill toward the small lake, where a few kayakers were puttering around in the late morning sunshine. "I can't believe I've never been here before. It's so far north of the city, I didn't even realize it was here."

"I'm glad you like it. I wasn't sure how you'd feel about dining *al fresco*. Some women aren't a fan."

Something odd passed over her expression, then was gone. "It all depends on the company." She paused. "So, I guess you bring a lot of your dates here, then?"

If the woman ever played cards, she'd lose the shirt off her back. She had no poker face whatsoever.

"I can say with total honesty you're the first woman I've ever brought here on a date. Or to any park, for that matter."

Because none of the other women he was usually involved with would be caught dead sitting on a blanket on the ground eating food bought at a downtown deli.

Which was too bad, because it smelled *amazing*.

With a flick of his wrist, he opened the lid of the wicker hamper he'd borrowed from his sister the day before. That decision had almost turned into a disaster, since the request piqued Lillian's infamous curiosity. In hindsight, it would have been easier—and safer—to just go buy one somewhere. With luck, Lil would be too distracted by her wedding plans to have time to stick her nose into his business.

The thought of his baby sister getting married still gave him a jolt of the uneasies.

Or maybe it was her choice of husband. Raphael Delgado wasn't the man Richard would have chosen for her, but they seemed happy, so what the hell did he know?

Rafe seemed a decent enough guy. But they were never going to be best friends or anything. Not after Richard had conspired with the rest of his brothers to try and keep him away from Lil last year and nearly broken them up.

Probably not his most shining moment, he acknowledged as he doled out the sandwiches and drinks. But in his defense, he'd only had his sister's best interests at heart. There'd been too many men more interested in her bank portfolio than in her heart over the years. Rafe's blue-collar background as a cop made him seem like one more of the same.

He could only hope Lil hadn't been suckered in by a handsome face.

Especially since she'd threatened to shove the prenup he'd had his lawyers prepare for her into a very uncomfortable place if he didn't drop the matter and never bring it up again. She loved Rafe, she'd told him, and you couldn't love without trust.

Although as far as he was concerned, trust was a useless commodity if you couldn't put it to the test.

He slanted a look at Amber, who was shooing a persistent bee away from her soda. Had she passed the test yet? He wasn't sure. He was ninety-nine percent convinced she didn't know who he really was.

It was that niggling little one percent still holding him back.

He'd tell her after the launch party. He made the snap decision as he unwrapped his sandwich and bit into the pastrami on rye that oozed melted cheese everywhere and exploded onto his taste buds with mind-blowing flavor. *Heaven.* If he didn't have proof she was playing him by then, he'd let her in on his real name.

But in the meantime, he'd enjoy being just Rick. Rick didn't work eighteen-hour days. Didn't have employees pecking him to death for minute after minute of his time, or feel the responsibility for the finances of hundreds of clients entrusting his company with their life savings weighing on his shoulders like Sisyphus's boulder.

He honestly loved his job, but he was finding it oddly liberating to not be himself for a little while.

"Oh, I meant to tell you. I spoke to Jesus and Mitch's mothers, and they're on board with the boys going with us to the launch party."

"You make it sound like they might actually have said no."

"Well, they were a little suspicious at first." She nibbled at her sandwich.

His head snapped up. "What? Why?"

"Come on. You have to admit, this isn't the kind of thing that just drops into a person's lap on a normal day. It's only reasonable for them to be cautious where their kids are concerned. Neither of them has even talked to you since you took over the class, so you're just some stranger who wants to take their kids out on a Saturday night to some video game party."

He winced.

"Okay, yeah, I can see that."

He should probably rethink his plan to pick everyone up in the limo. No need to raise any more red flags with the parents than were already flying. Especially not if he was going to finish out his time at the center with his anonymity intact.

Amber grinned at him. "The kids, on the other hand, just about lost their minds when they found out. Don't be surprised if they treat you like a god at class Tuesday."

"It's not that big a deal." He crumpled the paper from his sandwich and tossed it into the hamper. "All I did was make a phone call to a friend."

"It *is* a big deal, at least to them." She reached out and placed a hand on his arm. "Rick, you have to understand. These kids come from very little, where luxuries are few and far between." She swallowed. "Derek included. So for them, getting to go to this party is like Christmas, Hannukah, and Kwanza all rolled into one. And you made that happen. So, thank you."

He wasn't expecting her to lean over and kiss his cheek. Good thing, too. If he had, he might have turned his head and captured her lips with his own and dragged her down beneath him on the red-and-black checkered blanket the way he'd been wanting to since they first sat down on it.

Instead, she retreated and started cleaning up the remnants of their meal before his brain and body got in synch to react.

"You're welcome." He hated that his voice sounded gravelly. It was just a damn kiss. Barely even one. Stupid that he could still feel the warmth of her lips against his skin.

Stupider to wish she'd do it again.

Clearing his throat, he sucked down the last of his soda and added the empty plastic bottle to the refuse in the hamper. "Would you like to take a walk around the lake?"

After a moment's consideration, she shook her head. "After being on my feet last night at the restaurant, I'd rather just sit here and relax, if you don't mind."

"Sure." He moved the hamper aside to make more room and was surprised once again when Amber stretched out on her back with a sigh of contentment. His body flexed at the obvious invitation.

"I used to do this with Derek all the time," she said on a dreamy sigh.

Okay, not an invitation.

Shoving the surging lust back down his deep well of steely control, he leaned on one elbow beside her. "What, go on picnics?"

"Sometimes. But I meant laying on a blanket under the open sky. Listening to nature. Watching the clouds. Being still. Being thankful. Just...being."

"Sounds a little Zen for a kid."

"You should try it before you knock it." She patted the blanket beside her. "Come on. Relax a little. It won't hurt, I promise."

Tell that to his aching groin.

Rolling onto his back, he made a show of getting comfortable, which not-so coincidentally moved him closer to her. "Okay. Now what?"

"Just...relax."

"Right, why didn't I think of that?" He bent first one leg, then the other, then put both back straight out flat where they'd started.

"My God, you don't know how to, do you?" she asked finally.

"I know how to relax." It was just impossible to do while lying flat on his back less than a foot away from her. Not when the light scent of lilacs drifted from her sun-warmed skin to tease at his senses with arousing effect.

"Okay, let's try this." Using the hand closest to him, she pointed upward. "See that cloud? What does it look like?"

He squinted. "Like...a cloud?"

"Try again."

"Like a big cloud?" He grinned at the sound of annoyance she made.

"This isn't about using the left side of your brain. This is about letting your mind kind of unfocus and make abstract connections with the changing shape of the cloud. Let your right brain take over for a little while."

"Is this like a Rorschach test? Are you going to psychoanalyze my answers?"

"Only if you start seeing decapitated bunnies. Now." She pointed again. "What about that one, there, a little to the right of us?"

How had he forgotten how tenacious she could be?

He sighed, but followed the direction of her finger to the cloud in question. It was just a big, freaking cloud. White, with some wispy gray around the trailing edge. The wind was blowing it from right to left overhead, changing the shape as it moved, pushing it higher, making it taller and less flat on one part, and almost...like...

"A dog," he said, surprising himself. "It looks like a dog. One with a thin body and a little tail. See, right there." This time he was the one who pointed, only to be distracted when she leaned in closer to look, her floral scent charging his imagination like no cloud formation ever could.

"I see it."

He cleared his throat. "So, I got it right?"

"There's no right or wrong. It's just a fun way to let your brain slip its leash for a little while."

Something else was threatening to slip its leash. Richard held it back, but he did let his hand fall over hers on the blanket between them. He waited a heartbeat. Two. Three. She didn't protest or move away. Triumph surged through him.

One more small victory.

They spent the next ten minutes studying the sky, arguing over the shapes of different clouds. He might be new to the game, but there was no way that last one could be a fish. Not even close.

"How can you not see a horse? See? Right there. Head. Body. Tail."

"I think I should know what a horse looks like," she replied with a snort, "and they usually have legs."

"I thought we weren't supposed to be so literal in our interpretations?"

"There's literal, then there's just plain anatomically incorrect."

The last thing he wanted was to risk disrupting the teasing camaraderie that had sprung up between them, but he couldn't pass up the clue she'd just dropped.

"So, you know horses, huh?"

"I'm from Texas. Of course, I know horses." She tagged an unspoken "duh" at the end of her statement.

"Then I guess I should bow to your greater equine wisdom on this one."

"You definitely should."

They lay in silence for a minute as he digested that tidbit. There was a slight twang in her speech every once in a while that definitely wasn't Colorado. But it was so infrequent, like something she'd worked hard to scrub from existence, that he hadn't been able to place it. Texas sounded about right.

"Is that where Derek's father is from, too?"

Amber's hand went stiff in his. "Why does it matter?"

Since he had no idea why the hell the question popped out of his mouth in the first place, he had to grope for an answer. "I was just wondering if he might show up at any point, maybe have a problem with me being around his kid." He risked a glance over.

Her lips were pinched in a tight line.

"He's not," she said after a long moment. "Going to show up, I mean. He hasn't been a part of Derek's life since before he was born."

Unexpected anger flashed through him on Derek's behalf. "Then he's a jackass who doesn't deserve a great kid like him."

Laughter bubbled from her lips as the tension leaked out of her. "You're right. He is a jackass." She gave his hand a squeeze. "Thank you."

"For what?"

"For saying that. For being so good to my kid. For...everything."

A whisper of guilt dampened the pleasure of her words since 'everything' also included a big, fat fib, but he ruthlessly squashed it. All's fair, and all that.

He squeezed her hand back. "You're welcome. And thank you for agreeing to have lunch with me today. This was really nice."

They both lapsed into a contented silence, still watching the sky, still holding hands, and Richard realized he'd spoken nothing but the cold, hard truth. It was stupid, and crazy, but he didn't think he'd spent a better afternoon with a woman in his entire life.

And that scared the hell out of him.

Chapter 7

AMBER HADN'T UNDERSTOOD EXACTLY what Rick meant when he said it was going to be *the* launch party. As in, the one the game's designer and company owner big shot Max Woodward would be attending.

Talk about a shock when she was introduced!

But not as big a one as when the man had greeted Rick with a huge one-armed guy-hug and a few pounds on the back. So much for them just being old college friends. They'd acted more like two long-lost brothers or something.

Rick Bowman was clearly king of the understatement.

Shifting her head to the left on the car headrest, Amber studied the man in question as he drove through the early morning darkness toward her home. The strobe flash of streetlights as they passed under them gave her brief glimpses of his profile, all sharp jawline and full lips. The intermittent light glinted off his metal-rimmed glasses, another surprise.

A good one, though. The fact there was at least one thing about him that wasn't perfect made him a little easier to like.

Hell, who was she kidding? He was far too easy to like.

Which was why she'd spent the entire evening wrestling with her hormones whenever he touched her back or took her hand as they moved through the crowd. They didn't care that she'd only known the man a little over two weeks. They didn't worry about repeating past mistakes. They just wanted to come out and party, preferably all over Rick's glorious naked body.

Down, girl.

Before she did something embarrassing like start to pant, she turned her head further to look into the backseat. They'd already dropped off the other boys. Derek was slumped against his seatbelt, out cold. She grinned. He'd had the time of his life tonight.

"Is he finally asleep?"

She brought her gaze back to Rick. "Yeah. He was so wired I wasn't sure he'd ever go under." Good thing she'd gotten him to nap earlier to make up for how late she'd known they'd be out. Otherwise, he'd have crashed hours ago.

"Did he have a good time, do you think?"

"Are you kidding? I'm going to have to pry that game out of his hands with a crowbar when I put him to bed." And it was only barely an exaggeration. Even unconscious, he was still clutching the gift bag like it held the Holy Grail.

Rick laughed. After a pause, he asked, "What about you? Did you have a good time?"

"You know, I actually did."

She'd expected a lot of computer nerds standing around spouting gamer techno-babble that would go right over her head like at the pizza parlor. But it had been a really pleasant party, with interesting people, excellent finger food, and—thankfully—enough video game stations set up to keep the kids entertained.

Especially when they'd gotten to play against the game's creator himself. Talk about being star-struck.

"Your friend Max wasn't what I expected."

For a second it looked like Rick was annoyed by her words, but in the next flash of illumination, his expression was back to normal. Probably just a trick of the ever-changing streetlights.

"How so?"

"Well, he's obviously smart, and a pretty big deal in the gaming world right now."

"Don't forget rich."

The edge to his tone confused her. Was he jealous of his friend's success?

"Rich isn't always a good thing," she said with equal sharpness. "Sometimes having money can make you a very sucky person."

Like all the kids who'd given her shit all her life back in Perrytown for being poor trailer park trash. Like Hunter King and his condescending parents and their absolute belief that money gave them the ability to do whatever they wanted and get away with it.

The hell of it was, they'd been right.

Tearing her thoughts away from the whirlpool of anger and helplessness she'd promised to leave behind when she put Texas in her rearview mirror, she got back to her original train of thought.

"I just meant it was very kind of him to spend as much time as he did with three kids he doesn't even know. Especially when there were lots of other, more important people there who wanted a piece of his time."

"Are you kidding? He would have much rather spent the whole night hanging out with the kids than talking to the media. He may be a 'big deal', but Max is still just a computer geek at heart. These kinds of functions give him hives."

Judging by the way Max seemed more interested in dissecting some aspect of the original game Derek asked him about than in answering any of the reporter's questions, he probably wasn't wrong.

"Even so, I'm still grateful to him for making the kids feel a part of things. Including them in the publicity pictures made them feel extra special."

She was even more grateful to Rick for making *her* feel that way, too.

From the second they walked in the doors of the swanky downtown hotel the party was held at, she'd been so far out of her element she'd felt the immediate pinch of panic. But Rick had kept her grounded. Engaged. It wasn't anything overt. A question to draw her into the conversation. A shared look when one of the kids did or said something amusing. The solid warmth of his body as he stood at her side.

A position, she realized with a jolt, he hadn't relinquished the entire evening.

A quiver of something warm and hopeful filtered into her chest.

He'd made her feel like she belonged. More importantly, he'd made her feel wanted. And he'd never understand how much that meant to her after a lifetime of always being left on the outside looking in.

When they pulled into the parking lot of her apartment building, there was a pang of remorse that the night was finally over. Like Cinderella, midnight had struck, and it was time for her to leave the fancy ball behind and go back to the ordinariness of her real life.

Unhooking her seat belt, she noticed Rick doing the same. "Oh, you don't have to walk us in. It's late."

"Which is precisely why I do. Besides"—he cast a look into the backseat—"I don't think you're going to be able to wake him to walk in on his own. I'll carry him for you."

She bit her lip. Much as she'd like to argue, he was right. When her son went out this hard, he was a bear to wake up again. And carrying Derek's dead weight up a flight of stairs in three-inch heels wouldn't be the smartest choice.

But having Rick do it for her meant having him actually come inside her matchbox-sized apartment and see the shoestring budget lifestyle they lived.

Her stomach knotted at the thought.

On the other hand, if something like that could scare him off, better to have it happen now before Derek got any more attached to him.

And yeah, before *she* got any more attached.

"Okay, yes. Thank you."

Leading the way inside and upstairs, she couldn't keep from checking over her shoulder. But Rick had an easy, firm hold on Derek despite his boneless state. His face pressed against Rick's shoulder, arms and legs dangling, his expression was so peaceful and innocent she had to turn away and blink against the wave of confused emotions suddenly swamping her.

No man had ever carried her son before. Ever. Not even when he was a baby. Seeing him in this man's arms now seemed so perfect it terrified her.

With an unsteady hand, she slipped the key from her purse and unlocked the apartment door. Turning on the light, she led Rick to the bedroom, where she snapped on the desk lamp before he placed her gently snoring son on top of his clean but faded Star Wars comforter.

"That's fine. I'll come back and get him into his pj's in a minute."

Rick stood there a second, dwarfing the already cramped room, taking in the sparse furnishings with an unreadable expression before retreating back out into the living room.

Her tummy did a small dip as she pulled the door closed and followed. Derek probably wouldn't wake for anything short of a nuclear blast, but she wasn't taking any chances. Whatever Rick might have to say, she didn't want him overhearing it.

Rick was looking around the small living room the same way he'd done in the bedroom, his eyes hooded and assessing.

She knew exactly what he saw and refused to be embarrassed by it. So what if the sofa and chair were a little old and faded and completely mismatched?

Or that the end table holding the butt-ugly lamp Derek picked out at a garage sale of a cowboy riding a bronco had a few magazines under one leg to keep it level?

Or that her grandmother's ancient Singer sewing machine sat on top of a pretty wooden dining table with old cigarette burns scarring the surface at one end?

Even the frames on the photos hanging above the sofa were from the thrift store. The pictures inside were the only things in the room that weren't second-hand.

As she came to a halt a few yards from him, Rick turned that assessing gaze on her.

"There's only the one bedroom?"

The familiar starch of pride stiffened her back. "Clearly."

"And you gave it to your son."

"Of course."

"Then where do you sleep?"

The answer was obvious, but she gestured to the sofa anyway. When his brows drew downward in a scowl, she said, "It pulls out into a bed."

Wow, defensive much?

"This can't be a very comfortable living arrangement for you."

"I've had worse." Like living in her car, back in the desperate months after her mother died and she was suddenly left homeless and afraid, with a toddler to care for and no idea how she was going to do it.

But she had. And she thought she'd done a damn fine job, despite everything life kept kicking into her path along the way.

Including the man who just a few short hours ago had treated her like a princess, but was now looking at her like he'd never seen her before. Or maybe like he never wanted to see her again.

Damn it.

It pissed her off that he'd turned out to be one of the judgmental assholes. Yes, she was poor. So what? She had nothing to be ashamed of. This was her life, and she wasn't about to apologize for it.

To anyone.

Spurred on by her pricked pride, she spread her arms out wide. "So, yeah, this is home. What do you think?" She half expected him to say "see ya!" and head for the door.

She didn't expect him to step right up in front of her and stare down with those incredible, long-lashed eyes in a way that deflated her annoyance and made her insides go all squishy.

"What do I think? I think you're the most confounding woman I've ever met. You keep surprising me at every turn, and I can honestly say that rarely ever happens anymore. I usually know all I need to about a person the first time I meet them. But you...every time I think I've got you figured out, you go and prove me wrong. That's what I think."

Wait, what?

"Um...oh." She had no idea what else to say to *that*.

His long fingers framed her face. "I also think that I'll regret it if I don't kiss you right now."

Her heart gave a little stutter. "I think I would, too."

Where she expected fierce hunger, his lips descended on hers with exquisite gentleness. But it only took a second to realize the hunger was there, right below the surface of the kiss, being held in tight restraint. Though it didn't take long for that control to slip, especially when she ran her hands up his chest, digging her nails lightly into the silky material of his shirt.

With a growl, he deepened the kiss, his mouth demanding entrance to hers, which she freely gave. His fingers trailed along her cheek, her jaw, down her neck and over her shoulders, leaving a line of awakened nerve endings in their wake.

God, she was on fire, and it was still just a kiss!

Somehow, they made their way to the sofa without their mouths breaking contact. She found herself half under him, her back pressed to the soft cushions as Rick's rock-hard body rubbed along her front, creating eddies of sensation that shot straight to where she was suddenly wet and ready.

Too soon! some small voice of reason screamed through the lust fogging her thoughts. *Too fast! Too much!*

But reasonable Amber wasn't in control at the moment. Right then, her hormones were at the wheel, and they were enjoying the ride too much to hit the brakes just yet. They wanted to revel in the deliciousness of Rick's touch, his kiss, his obvious desire urgently prodding against her thigh.

Oh, yes!

The damp spot between her legs pulsed with equally urgent need. What if she gave in, just this once? Would it be so wrong? It was obvious he wanted it as much as she did. As primed as they both were, it wouldn't take long. Certainly quick enough that they wouldn't have to worry about—

"Derek." She gasped the name as she ripped her mouth from his. How could she have forgotten, even for a second, that her son was asleep in the next room?

Furious at herself for such an unforgivable lapse, she pressed her hands to Rick's shoulders. Thankful he moved without argument, she ran a trembling hand down her face. The combined heat of arousal and shame scorched her cheeks.

"I'm sorry." The gravelly words from the man she'd been two seconds away from jumping surprised her into looking at him. He appeared as shell-shocked as she felt. "That was supposed to just be a kiss. I didn't mean for it to get so out of hand." He dragged a hand through his rumpled hair, and it reassured her it was as unsteady as her own.

"It's okay. I'm just as much to blame. That was…" *Amazing. Incredible. Terrifying.* "Incendiary."

Rick let out a rough laugh. "That, and more." He stood in one swift movement. "I should go."

She followed him to the door, trying to come up with the right words so their wonderful evening didn't end on such a jarring note.

Before he opened the door, he swung around toward her so abruptly it forced her back a step. "To be clear, I'm not sorry about the kiss. I've been thinking about doing that since I picked you up tonight. And not as any kind of payback for the party, either. It was because I wanted to. Because I wanted *you.*"

It startled her to realize the thought of what just happened between them being payment had never crossed her mind. Her, the woman who saw a price tag attached to everything.

Something inside of her eased.

She smiled. "Just to be clear, I wanted you, too. It's just…"

"Too soon?" When she nodded, he took a deep breath and let it out slowly before nodding himself. "I can live with that." He hesitated. "Can I kiss you goodnight?"

"Yes, please." She was moving as she spoke, her arms slipping around his neck as their lips met once, twice, before breaking apart with reluctant longing. It took a lot for her to step back and let him open the door. "Be careful driving home."

An odd smile curled his lips. "Call you later?"

Not trusting herself to speak for fear she might end up sounding like a giddy teenager, she simply nodded. Rick opened the door, then turned back and stole one last kiss before seeming to force himself to leave. When the door clicked shut behind him, she collapsed against it with a whoosh of air, fighting the insane urge to giggle.

"You were wrong, momma," she whispered, hugging herself tight. "There are still some good, honest men out there, and I think maybe I just found one of my very own."

———◆———

"What's going on with you?"

"Hmm?" Glancing up from his menu, Richard frowned at his brother, who was studying him from across the table, a puzzled look on his face. "What do you mean?"

"You've been staring at that menu for the past five minutes and barely blinked once."

"So?"

"So, you never take this long to decide what you want. About anything." Theo gave a derisive snort. "If it were anyone else, I'd say you were daydreaming."

Daydreaming? No. More like fantasizing.

It had been happening all week. He'd be going through his day, and suddenly *poof!* There she was, filling his thoughts when he should be analyzing stock trends or listening to reports from his staff.

Or deciding what to eat at his weekly lunch with Theo.

"I'm just thinking about work." At least, he should be.

Theo looked like he was considering the excuse, then shook his head. "You don't smile like that when you're thinking about work."

He was smiling? "Like what?"

"I don't know. Kind of...goofy. Like you just got—" Theo's eyes widened. "Son of a bitch. Please tell me you didn't get back together with Kitty."

What did it say about his failed relationship with Katherine that the mere thought sent a shudder of revulsion through him?

"God, no. Why would you even think that?"

"I don't know. You just have this cat-in-the-cream smirk lately. Unless you're working some big deal you haven't let the rest of us in on, the only other option is a woman. And since you were planning to marry her—"

"Considering."

"—she seemed the logical choice." Theo winced. "No offense, but the thought of facing Katherine Carlyle over the dinner table every Thanksgiving..."

"Yeah, I know." She would have never fit in with his family. In hindsight, that should have been obvious from the start. For all the money the Beaumonts had, they were still, at their core, a tight-knit bunch with pretty down-to-earth values. Kitty pitching in to help put together the annual family turkey-day dinner was an image he couldn't even conjure.

Although it didn't take too much to imagine Amber elbow-deep in turkey and stuffing with his mother and sister, joining in the perennial debate of in-the-bird versus on-the-stove.

With a silent groan, he thrust the image away. This was the problem. The more time he spent with her, the more it felt like she fit into his life, like tab A slipping into slot B, and not the ones he'd originally planned on. But she shouldn't.

She couldn't.

She wasn't supposed to be anything more than a short fling. It was only supposed to be about the sex. The challenge. The conquest. The mutual sensual satisfaction.

But here he was, two weeks out from the decision to seduce the woman as a way to get rid of the bad taste his derailed almost-engagement left in his mouth. And instead of plotting to advance that cause, he was taking her and her son to play mini-golf on Saturday.

What the hell was happening to him?

Thankfully, the waiter came to take their order before he had to answer his own question, because he didn't have one. Their salads arrived almost as soon as the waiter retreated, a testament to the impeccable service provided to the restaurant's elite clientele.

And yet, he found himself wishing it was a deli sandwich served on a picnic blanket with a certain blond angel at his side for company.

"There!" Theo pointed at him with his fork, a glistening cherry tomato impaled on the tines. "That's the look. What were you thinking about right then?"

Not about to splay his inner thoughts—or anything else—open for his younger brother to gleefully dissect, he shrugged. "Food."

"Uh-huh. Maybe if 'food' is a new euphemism for leggy blond goddesses." He crowed when Richard's head snapped up. "I knew it!"

"There's nothing to know."

"Oh, yeah?" After slipping his phone from an inner pocket in his impeccably tailored Armani suit jacket, Theo swiped the screen a few times before holding it out for Richard to see. "So, that's not you, skulking in the background playing Clark Kent for the paparazzi?"

A chill raked down his spine as he took the phone and looked at the image.

It was one of several attached to an article on MZA2's launch. In the foreground, Max was mugging for the camera with his arms around Derek, Mitch, and Jesus. In the background, Amber smiled as she watched them. And beside her, barely in the picture, was himself. He was turned away, his face not really visible, at least not on the phone's small screen. But on a computer...

"Shit."

"Then it *is* you."

"*Shit.*" He scrolled through the article, skimming quickly, but didn't see any mention of his name. One minor miracle, at least.

But then he saw another picture at the bottom of the piece. This one showed Max and Amber laughing at something, Derek tucked in between them, grinning madly, the coveted video game clutched in both hands like pirate booty.

Richard was on Amber's other side, his face turned away like he'd done every time the photographer had been within a dozen feet of him. His name wasn't in the caption under the picture with the others, but enough of his profile showed that someone who knew him well would probably know it was him, despite the glasses.

Theo clearly had.

"Who is she?"

Richard stared at the picture of Amber and Max laughing, an unfamiliar burn of jealousy souring his appetite. He thrust the phone back at his brother. "No one you know."

"Obviously, or I wouldn't have to ask." Theo waited.

Richard let him, calmly eating his salad. Inside, though, his thoughts were racing like they were being chased by the game's mutant zombies. There was always the chance of some other business publication picking up the story, especially with how the sales had been breaking records since the weekend. Which meant the possibility of someone, somewhere, figuring out who he was, what his connection was to Woodbow Entertainment, and outing him in one or both of the pictures.

Which meant he needed to seriously reconsider his decision to hold off on telling Amber the truth. Again. He'd planned to do it Sunday. But as they'd spent the afternoon window shopping through the Pearl Street Mall, eating hot pretzels and listening to some buskers play, there'd never felt like a right time to bring it up.

Maybe because that annoying little one percent of doubt had still been nibbling away at him like a hungry mouse.

He wanted to blame it on seeing Amber wrapped in that expensive-looking dress, glammed up with makeup and heels, getting along so easily with Max and his millions. That image, juxtaposed with her standing in her little cracker box of an apartment with its thrift store cast-offs, was a jarring enough example of extremes that his warning bells had once again sounded off.

But the truth was, he was a wuss, plain and simple. Things were so good between them he didn't want to do anything to change it.

"She doesn't know who I am," he found himself saying after the waiter delivered their entrées and discretely melted away.

"Ah...come again?"

"Amber. The woman in the pictures. She doesn't know me as Richard Beaumont, COO of Beaumont Investments. She thinks I'm Rick Bowman, part-time karate instructor and full-time computer geek for the family firm."

Theo laid his fork and knife down. "Okay, once more, from the top?"

He listened with an expression of growing incredulity as Richard poured out the details of the past few weeks with Amber, from their contentious first meeting to their plans to take Derek to mini golf that weekend.

Theo was shaking his head by the time he finished.

"You're completely screwed, you know that, right? *Rick*."

He'd been coming to the same sickening conclusion himself, but he wasn't ready to admit it yet.

"The fact I'm rich and not just some middle-class worker drone will take the sting out." He wished he felt half as confident as he sounded.

"Right. Because money fixes everything." Theo shook his head and took a large bite of his steak. "What were you thinking?"

"In the beginning? That I couldn't be sure if the attraction was me or my money."

"And now?"

"That I want it to be me."

"But you're still not sure." Theo sighed when Richard shook his head. "Do you want my advice?"

Did he? He supposed he did, considering he'd never opened up about his personal problems to his brother before. "Hit me."

"Tell her the truth. She's going to be pissed either way, but better she hears it from you than from someone else. At least then you can break it to her in private, where no one can hear you begging for forgiveness."

"Ha-ha." But he had a point. There was a tactical advantage to being the one to control the where, when, and how of things. Basic business strategy.

"I'm serious. The longer you wait, the worse it's going to be."

That's what he was afraid of.

"I'll tell her Saturday."

Theo looked at him like he was an idiot. "When you're out with her and the kid?"

"No. After." He scowled. "Wait, she's working at the restaurant again that night. Damn it. Sunday. I'll tell her Sunday night. She's got some volunteer thing with the community center in the afternoon." Which bought him one more weekend of being Rick.

And it still didn't feel like enough.

"You need to stop making other women pay for Maryanne Alcott being a greedy, grasping bitch back in high school. Not all of them want you for what you can give them the way she did."

It was faint now, barely a ghost of the old hurt. But it was still there, lodged somewhere deep inside with barbed hooks where it could remind him about not repeating old mistakes whenever he started to forget.

"Don't kid yourself. Everybody wants something." Including Amber Lovett, even if he didn't know what it was yet.

"Okay. If that's true, what do *you* want?"

Good question.

A few months ago, he would have said a comfortable marriage with someone of his own social standing, who wouldn't make any waves in his life. A few weeks ago, he would have said a blazing affair to burn off the lust Amber instilled in him every time she was nearby.

Now?

He just wanted Amber, whatever way he could get her.

Chapter 8

"THANKS FOR A REALLY great day. I had a wonderful time."

Tired but happy, Amber leaned back against her apartment door and looked up at Rick. After mini golf, they'd dropped Derek off at Mitch's for his sleepover. Then Rick had insisted, as he always did now, on walking her from the car to her door.

Not that she was complaining. It was a sweetly chivalrous thing to do. It made her feel...special. Cherished. When was the last time she'd felt like that?

"Of course, you did. You and the kid both beat the pants off me." He put a hand on the door over her head, leaning in, bringing the scent of fresh air and warm man with him. "I want a rematch."

Feeling the ever-present sizzle whenever they got within five feet of each other, she barely resisted the urge to crawl up his tall, muscular body and devour him right there in the hallway.

"Any time." She owed him that much, since she knew for a fact he'd been playing far below his potential for Derek's sake.

Plus, she'd take any excuse to spend more time with him.

Which, unfortunately, wouldn't be tonight, since she had to be at the restaurant for her shift in two hours. An unfamiliar bubble of resentment welled up, and for the first time ever, she considered calling and saying she couldn't come in.

Just as quickly, she shook the urge aside. Much as she'd love to have some quality adult time with Rick, she had commitments and responsibilities, and she wasn't about to boot them for a man.

Not even this one.

"So, I guess I'll see you tomorrow?"

"Dinner. Here. Six o'clock." He'd offered to take the three of them out to eat—again—but she couldn't in good conscience let him keep spending his money on her and Derek. It was her turn to do something for him.

Since he hadn't run away when he'd seen where they lived, she'd sucked it up and invited him over, figuring a bachelor who probably ate takeout or frozen dinners most of the time would enjoy a home-cooked meal. Her mother taught her how to do a lot with a little. So, while it wouldn't be fancy, she knew it would be good.

"Can I come early to help?" He leaned a little closer. "Or maybe get in the way?"

Heat erupted down low, causing her to bite back a groan. "Yes. I mean, no."

"Which is it?"

His wicked, knowing grin should have annoyed her, but the promise in his eyes made her pout instead.

"I don't know how long I'm going to be at the center. Mrs. Gandy wasn't real forthcoming with details about what she volunteered me for." The only thing she'd promised was it wasn't anything in front of a crowd. Since that was the only condition she'd given, she couldn't complain about whatever she ended up with. "But if you want, I can text you if I'm done early."

"Sweetheart, you don't know how much I want."

He leaned the rest of the way down and pressed his lips to hers, the tip of his tongue rimming the seam until she granted him entry. Both of them sank into the kiss, Rick's body pressing hers against the door briefly before he tore himself away with a rough sound. "You'd better go before I see how late I can make you for work."

Lips still tingling from the taste of him, she ran her fingers down Rick's firm chest, reluctant to let him go but knowing he could easily make good on his threat if she didn't. "Okay." Opening the door, she turned back to find him looking at her with a pensive expression. "What?"

He looked indecisive for a second, then shook his head. "Tomorrow." After one last stolen kiss, he strode away down the hallway.

As she listened to the receding drum of his feet on the stairs, she wondered about that look. Had he been about to ask if he could come over after she got off of work? She'd have said no if he did, but it would have been harder than it should've been.

Closing the door on a sigh, she touched her slightly swollen lips. "Tomorrow."

She hurried through getting ready so she'd have time to check for any last-minute things she needed for tomorrow's dinner. As she was putting a few more pins in her hair to catch the flyaways escaping the French braid taming the unruly mess, there was a knock at the door.

Cursing under her breath as she jabbed her scalp with the last pin, she put a mental dollar in the swear jar. If the super was finally coming to look at the leaky faucet in the shower, she was going to have a fit. He was supposed to call first, not just show up at his convenience. Which never managed to be convenient for anyone else.

Then again, maybe Rick decided to come back and make good on his promise to make her late after all. Buoyed by that possibility, despite how irresponsible it would be, she almost skipped to the door and yanked it open with a smile.

"Did you—" Her words dried up at the sight of the man standing on the other side.

Tall. Handsome. Muscular. Looks of a god, morals of a barn cat.

"Hunter." She almost choked on the name.

Ten years. She hadn't seen him. Hadn't talked to him. Hadn't tried to have any contact whatsoever, just the way his parents demanded when they'd made their threats the last time she'd been to their ranch.

Seeing him now was like suddenly being shot back to the past. To when she was young and in love and naïve enough to believe any lie that came out of the rutting bastard's mouth.

No, *stupid* enough to believe it.

The reminder helped unlock her from the paralysis the shock of seeing him had frozen her into. "What are you doing here?"

"I came to see you, of course." When he smiled, she saw some of the eighteen-year-old charmer who'd sweet-talked away her virginity in the backseat of his daddy's Cadillac. But there was an oily quality to it now that hadn't been there before. Or maybe it had, and she'd just never noticed.

"Really? Why now, after all this time?"

"Let me in, and I'll tell you."

Her stomach rebelled at the idea of this man in her home. She crossed her arms and stood firm in the open doorway. "No. You can tell me right here."

Something tightened around his cornflower blue eyes before he cranked up the wattage on his smile. "Amber Lee, we have lots of catching up to do, you and me. Do you really want to do that out here in the hallway where anyone can listen in?"

Hell's bells.

She didn't know what he wanted to talk about, but there was nothing about their shared past she wanted her neighbors getting an earful of.

Bowing to the lesser evil, she ground her back teeth and opened the door wider. The still familiar scent of leather and cigarettes clung to his clothes, and she forced herself not to flinch when he purposely brushed against her on the way by. Shutting the door felt like closing a cage, with her locked on the inside with a dangerous animal.

And he *was* dangerous. Maybe not physically, but this was the man who'd torn her life apart once before with his cavalier indifference and sense of entitlement. She couldn't—wouldn't—believe he'd suddenly grown a conscience after all these years.

With that in mind, she stayed next to the door.

Just in case.

Hunter took in the cramped apartment with a condescending smirk but didn't comment. Instead, he raked her from head to toe with an expression she remembered far too well from high school.

"You have ten minutes. I have to be at work soon." Not that soon, but the faster she got this over with, the better.

"Amber Lee, honey." Hunter's eyes were firmly fixed a good foot below her face. "Still looking good."

What was it with men and boobs? It didn't matter how young or old. Show them a set of breasts and they'd forget their own name.

"You didn't come all this way to tell me that. And don't call me honey."

It was the pet name he'd whispered in her ear when they'd made love. Except, she'd realized later when she'd taken to dissecting their infrequent, furtive assignations in the long, depressing months after he'd gone off to college, it hadn't been love for him. Just sex.

And it was much more likely it was easier to use 'honey' than remember the name of the girl he was currently screwing.

"Aw, baby, don't be that way."

"Nine minutes."

That tight look entered his eyes again. He didn't like that his usual flirtation wasn't having the desired effect.

Good.

"Still haven't learned how to play it smart, have you?"

Ah, there he was. The arrogant ass she'd once known and loved.

"I'm plenty smart, Hunter. I just don't have time for whatever game you're playing."

"Right. Work." His gaze flicked over her waitress uniform. "I see after all these years you're living up to your full potential. Mother always said you'd end up working in a greasy diner somewhere."

Actually, the woman said she'd end up working the street *outside* a greasy diner.

Every meeting with the intimidating Monica King had left her with another strip of skin sliced off, courtesy of the woman's razor-sharp tongue. Much as she'd prefer to forget every soul-shriveling encounter, some things were impossible to erase.

Resisting the temptation to tell Hunter waitressing was only a part-time gig, because that would mean she cared what he thought, she reached for the doorknob. "I think we're done here. You need to—"

"Where's the kid?"

The question froze her in the act of turning the knob. "What?"

"The kid. My kid. Is he here?"

"No." *Thank you sweet baby Jesus for that.* "Why do you care?"

"Why wouldn't I? Like I said, he's mine."

"Derek is *my* son," she half-shouted before getting hold of her temper. And her panic. "You said you wanted nothing to do with him."

It, actually. Hunter had always referred to the baby he'd put in her belly as "it."

As in, *Why would I want it?*

You'd better get rid of it.

Stop bothering me, it's your problem now.

He shrugged. "Maybe I've changed my mind."

And maybe she'd start farting rainbows out of her butt.

"After ten years? You just suddenly decided hey, I wonder how my kid turned out, let me go find him and see? Right." Her breath caught at the import of her own words. "How did you know where we lived?"

Because she sure as hell hadn't left a forwarding address with anyone back in Perrytown. Especially not the Kings.

"It wasn't hard to track you down."

Not when you had money, anyway. The reminder hit her like a slap. It probably took a private investigator all of ten minutes on the internet to get her home address. It wasn't like she'd been hiding. Not really. But she'd really thought putting two states between them would keep them safe from ever crossing paths with a King again.

Clearly, she'd been mistaken.

"Hunter, cut the bull. Why are you here?"

"I told you. To see my kid." He gestured to the large group of framed photos on the wall behind the sofa, documenting Derek from the day he came home from the hospital to the flume ride they'd gotten soaked on over the summer at Water World. "He looks like me."

God help her, he did. The same dirty-blonde hair, the same soft blue eyes. Derek even had the same small dent in his chin. The worry sprang up a time or two over the years if she might feel some animosity toward her son as he blossomed into a pint-sized replica of his sperm donor.

But no matter what, no matter who he looked like, Derek was her baby boy, and she couldn't love him more.

Unlike the man frowning at the photos of him, who couldn't possibly love him at all, because he didn't even know him.

"That was taken this year?" he asked, pointing at the water park picture.

Since the souvenir photo had the date stamped right on it, it was a stupid question. Still, she nodded.

"Kind of a scrawny thing, isn't he?"

"He's a little small for his age, but nothing to be concerned about," she answered stiffly. Typical Hunter. His first comment about Derek was vanity, and the second criticism.

"I dunno. Looks to me like he might not be getting all the right foods and things to help a young boy grow strong." He gave the apartment another disparaging study. "What with your current circumstances and all."

A trickle of fear started to seep into her belly. "Derek has never wanted for anything. He's a perfectly healthy boy."

Hunter wagged a finger at her. "Now, see, that's not entirely true now, is it, honey? My guy turned up some interesting information when he was tracking you down. Seems my boy has been in the hospital a lot more than what most folks might consider normal. That could raise some serious concerns about how well you're taking care of him."

"Derek has asthma. Anytime he's gone to the hospital it's been because he had a severe attack and needed to go in for a treatment. That's all. He's never had a broken bone or stitches or anything." Thank God. The asthma attacks were bad enough. She didn't think she could handle seeing her baby's blood.

"Maybe. Or a judge might think the boy was in an unsafe environment, with a mother who barely makes enough waiting tables to keep a roof over his head, much less see to his welfare."

The trickle of fear became a tsunami. If not for the door at her back, she would have slipped to the floor under its force. "Did you just *threaten* me?"

Hunter smiled, and for the first time she really saw the changes the past ten years had made in him. The face that had gotten the panties off of half the girls at their high school wasn't as lean and angular as it had once been, or as stunningly handsome. There was a slight puffiness around the jawline and eyes that came from spending a little too much time with a bottle, and the lines beside his mouth seemed carved deep by more than just being outside running cattle on his daddy's ranch.

But it was the look in his eyes that shook her the most. They were cold. Frigid. Totally devoid of kindness or empathy. She remembered seeing eyes like that on one other person before in her life.

His mother.

"I don't need to threaten you, honey. Not when I have the law on my side."

"The law? What law?"

"My rights as a father. The ones you stole from me when you took my son out of state without my permission."

"You bastard." Her fists clenched at her sides. "You're the one who gave up those rights when you walked away from us. You told me you wanted nothing to do with the baby. That I should get rid of it."

"But you didn't, did you? That means he's half mine now, and you've been keeping him from me. You even left my name off his birth certificate."

"Because your mother threatened to make my life hell if I didn't!"

"Says you." Hunter shrugged away her excuse.

She stared at him and had a bizarre thought. Was it possible he didn't know what his parents had done ten years ago? He'd already been sent off to early admission at Texas A&M the last time she'd gone to the ranch that summer. Maybe they'd never told him about her attempts to get in contact with him, or about the threats they'd wielded to guarantee her silence about Derek's paternity.

Foolish to entertain even a sliver of hope he wasn't the total bastard she'd believed him to be. But if he was honestly upset about being cut out of his son's life, didn't she at least owe him the benefit of the doubt to find out?

"Hunter, listen to me. I went to see your parents before Derek was born, after you'd already left for school. I wanted you to know you were having a son, to try one more time to get you to change your mind. But they made it clear you weren't interested in being a part of his life. Of our lives." She swallowed the memory's familiar bitterness.

"You went because you were looking for money."

"No! They're the ones who brought up money. They said if I went looking for child support, or ever told anybody you were the father, they'd sue me for custody on the grounds I was an unmarried teenage mom with no job, no means of support, and no prospects since the school said I wasn't welcome back for senior year because I was pregnant, so I couldn't graduate and get my diploma."

She'd never been as terrified in her life as when Monica King had sat behind that grand old hand-carved desk in the ranch house office and issued her threat without a single flicker of emotion.

Who do you think the judge will think the better guardian for a baby? The stupid little whore who got herself knocked up looking for a payday, or the baby's rich, pillar of the community grandparents who can give him every advantage trailer trash like you never could?

Not that she'd believed for a second the Kings wanted Derek, or had the slightest interest in his welfare. It was blackmail, plain and simple. Leave us alone and keep your mouth shut, or we'll take your child away from you.

And they could have, too. She'd never had any doubt of that. No matter what, money always won over truth. Always.

"I only wanted you to be a part of your son's life, Hunter. You have to believe that." Hands clasped in front of her to keep them from shaking, she waited.

Please let him believe me.

But when his mouth twitched as though holding back another of those smirks, she knew she'd been played. He'd known the truth all along. Had just been taunting her like a cat with a wounded mouse.

The small kernel of hope she'd been nursing shriveled and died.

Hunter shook his head slowly, the smirk still threatening to break free. "See, the problem with your little story is you don't have a lick of proof. Where I, the wronged party, can easily show a judge how much better a life I can give the son I never knew I had than the no-account trash who stole him from me."

Panic began to beat at her, making her heart thrum in her chest at hummingbird speed. This couldn't be happening. Not again.

"Why are you doing this?" she choked out, horrified to hear a sob in her voice.

"Doing what? Laying claim to my flesh and blood?"

"Don't! Don't pretend you actually give a flying fuck about Derek." Forcing her back straighter so she didn't feel so much like she was cowering against the door, she stared him in the eye. "What do you really want?"

"You mean besides my son?"

"*Hunter*!"

The bastard laughed.

"All that sass. I forgot what a little firecracker you could be, Amber Lee honey." His lips rolled together as he gave her another of those indecent once-overs. "Maybe we could work something out that would give us both a little of what we wanted."

Her stomach rebelled at the thought of him touching her. "You didn't come all this way to find me just for sex."

"No, but it might put me in a more generous frame of mind if you gave me a little sugar to help sweeten the deal."

"Not. Happening."

He sneered at her flat refusal. "That's okay, honey. I'm not much for well-used goods, anyway."

Ignoring the sting of the insult, she said, "Last time, Hunter. What do you want?"

"Well, since you asked...the ranch has hit a small rough patch lately. Beef prices are dropping, feed prices are going up, and everybody wants organic everything. Like good old US Grade-A prime beef isn't good enough anymore." He snorted in disgust.

Confused, she stared as if he were speaking tongues. "What does that have to do with me?"

"I know you didn't graduate high school, darlin', but try not to be so slow. I need money."

"Money." She repeated the word like she didn't know what it meant.

"The ranch needs an infusion to stay alive. Things will turn around soon, they always do. But until then, I need some emergency capital to tide us over."

"I'm not..." She shook her head and started again. "You want money? From *me*?" She spread her hands out to encompass her small, sad, second-hand life. "Seriously?"

"Clearly you don't have what I need on hand." He gave her a knowing look. "But you can get it."

"How, by robbing a bank?" Her breath seized. Did he expect her to use her access to the computers at the hospital to embezzle funds? Then she remembered he didn't know about her job there. As far as he was concerned, she was just a waitress struggling to make ends meet.

But if not that, then what?

"Don't play dumb, honey. I know you've managed to hook another big fish with that sweet little honeypot of yours."

"What are you talking about?"

"Your new sugar daddy."

Her *what*?

"You've totally lost your mind."

"Although"—he glanced around—"by the looks of this dump, spreading your legs for him hasn't paid the dividends you were expecting yet, now has it? Maybe you need to put a little more effort into it."

"That's it! Take your filthy mouth and get the fu—"

"Uh-uh-uh." He waggled his finger again, making her want to grab it and snap it clean off. "You don't want to make me mad, now, do you, *honey*? Not with everything you've got at stake."

Reminded of the threat hanging over hers and Derek's heads, she subsided, struggling to control her temper when he gave her a smug look that said *I know you hate me, but you can't do a damned thing about it.*

Through clenched teeth she said, "You're wrong. I don't have, have *never* had, a 'sugar daddy,' so I can't help you."

He reached into the pocket of his Wranglers for his phone, swiping the screen to wake it up. "You can lie all you want, Amber Lee, but pictures don't."

She didn't want to move closer to look at what he held out for her to see, but curiosity and a swelling sense of dread forced her to leave the relative safety of the door and take the phone.

It was a picture from the launch party the week before. The one where the photographer who wouldn't leave poor Max alone had gotten the four of them to pose together, although Rick seemed to have looked away at just the wrong time, the picture only catching him in profile. She hadn't thought about the pictures being published anywhere. Stupid of her.

And there was her name below the picture next to Max's. Hers and Derek's.

No wonder Hunter had known where they were.

She shoved the phone back at him. "So? I was invited to a party. What does that prove?"

"It proves you've got your hooks into a pretty rich man, Amber Lee. And I need you to use those skills of yours to convince him to give you some money to help out an old friend. A real *close* friend, if you get my meaning."

Oh, she got it all right. But Rick, rich? He might work for his family's business, but he was a nine-to-fiver, just like her. Hell, he drove a boring beige four-door for pity's sake. What rich guy did that?

"You're wrong. He's not rich."

"Don't try to bullshit a bullshitter, honey. The man's got to be worth millions. With that new video game of his selling like they're giving it away? What I need is chump change to him."

Amber opened her mouth on another protest, then closed it as his words sunk in. *Video game?* Then it clicked. Max. He thought she'd been at the party with Max.

An almost giddy sense of relief washed over her.

"I don't 'have my hooks' in Max Woodward, so there's no way I can get you your money. Not that I would have, even if I could. Which means you can turn your shitkickers right back around and head on home, because there's nothing for you here."

A gasp of surprise escaped her as Hunter grabbed her by the shoulders and pushed her backward into the door. Pain exploded through her back as it made contact, dragging out another gasp, this one ending in a whimper.

"You fucking bitch!" He shook her once, hard, making the door rattle. "You think you can tell me what to do? Who the fuck do you think you are?"

Stupid, stupid, stupid!

Staring up into his furious eyes, his fingers digging into her flesh, she knew a moment of raw terror. So much for believing Hunter would never be a physical danger to her. She didn't even know this man.

Maybe she never had.

"You listen, and you listen good, Amber Lee. You're going to talk to your boyfriend, and you're going to do whatever it takes to get him to give me what I need, understand? Because if you don't, it won't take a judge a hot minute to grant me full custody of the brat. Hell, you might not even get the right to see him unless I say so."

"Bastard," she choked out, humiliated and furious when he just laughed.

"But I'm a bastard who plays to win, darlin'." He loosened his grip on her shoulders and let his hands skim down to her breasts. "Best you don't forget that." He laughed again when she shuddered and slid to the side along the wall to get out of his reach.

Yanking the door open, he paused to give her one last look, all humor gone from his expression. "Make sure you think long and hard about all you have to lose before you do anything stupid. I'll be back in a few days."

With a flinch as the door slammed, she wrapped her arms around herself and held on tight against the shaking that wracked her body. Tears flowed unchecked as the shock and disbelief of the past twenty minutes fully hit her. With a low groan, she stumbled to the sofa and collapsed.

"This isn't happening," she whispered over and over again.

But it was. And wishing this mess was all a nightmare wouldn't help get her out of it. Hunter would never believe she'd only just met Max Woodward the one time, because it didn't suit his purpose. He was a man on a mission, and he was willing to knock down and trample anything—or anyone—who got in his way.

Namely, her.

What could she do, though? Putting aside her instinctual impulse to grab up Derek and run somewhere far, far away from the long arm of the Kings, she was at a loss. She had no money for a lawyer, and if she went to the police, they were much more likely to believe Hunter than her, just the way he said. She had no proof. No one who would take her at her word.

Except maybe Rick.

The possibility slid into the turmoil of her brain and gave her something firm and safe to hang onto. He wasn't rich, and he wasn't a lawyer, but he knew her well enough to hopefully believe her if she told him what Hunter was threatening her with. Maybe, just maybe, he could help her come up with a way out of this mess without putting Derek at risk.

Derek.

Oh God. That was another nightmare waiting to happen. If Derek was home when Hunter showed up again...

No. One problem at a time. First, she'd talk to Rick after tomorrow's dinner about Hunter's threats. They involved his friend, so hopefully he'd be invested in helping her come up with a solution. Then she'd deal with keeping Derek from finding out the father she'd told him regretted not being a part of his life was really a cold-blooded bastard willing to use him as a bargaining chip for blackmail. No way could she let that happen.

She'd kill the son of a bitch first.

Chapter 9

Richard ran a hand down the soft curve of Amber's hip, relishing the silky warmth as she purred her approval, stretching her gloriously naked body out on his bed like a kitten who enjoyed being petted. His hand slid lower, down between her legs, which parted willingly.

Damn, she was so wet and hot, so ready for him. He stroked through the damp heat, finding her clit and circling it with his thumb, making her gasp.

He grinned. "Like that, do you?" Then it was his turn to suck in a sharp breath as soft fingers curled around the hard length of his penis, squeezing gently.

Biting her lower lip as she stroked him, Amber answered his question with one of her own. "What do you think?"

"I think...*God.*" The feel of her touching him, caressing him, was almost too much. He put his hand over hers lightly. "No need to rush, sweetheart. We have all the time in the world."

But something in the urgency with which she touched him made him edgy as well. Discarding caution, he met her stroke for stroke, groan for groan, as they both seemed to rush towards some invisible finish line he wasn't sure he wanted to reach.

"I want," Amber gasped.

"What, baby? What do you want?"

"I want...I want..." Her head thrashed on the pillow as her body tightened like a coil about to snap.

"Do you want to come, is that it?" One long finger slid into her heat while his thumb continued to work at her clit. "Then come, baby. I'll catch you."

A low wail escaped Amber's throat as her back arched. Even in the throes of her own climax, her hand still stroked his erection in a frantic rhythm that had him following her over the edge with a guttural groan…

…that yanked him right out of sleep.

Breath sawing in and out like he'd just run a marathon, Richard blinked up at his bedroom ceiling, trying to put the pieces of reality back together again. Dim light rimmed the curtains, telling him it was morning, but still early. The sheets and pillows were shoved half off the bed. His bed. One he was very much alone in.

A dream.

It had all been just a vividly intense, incredibly erotic dream.

Well, most of it was. The evidence of his very real release was cooling on the hand still loosely gripping his penis. With a laugh that was half groan, he closed his eyes and pressed his head back into the pillow. How pathetic was he? Reduced to servicing himself in his sleep by his own cowardice.

If he'd had any balls at all, he wouldn't have chickened out of telling Amber the truth about who he was when he'd dropped her at home yesterday. If he did, then he could have spent last night doing for real what he'd only been able to dream about. Because the two things were inextricably entwined for him. He couldn't take her to bed without first coming clean.

He might be ruthless, but he wasn't a total bastard.

By the time he showered, dressed, and dropped a bagel in the toaster, he'd already replayed the snippet of dream he could still remember a dozen times, savoring every nuance, every exciting breathy gasp and spine-tingling moan. He slapped some cream cheese on the bagel and took it and his coffee out onto the terrace despite the early morning chill.

Yup, it was official. He was pathetic.

Taking in the magnificent view as he sipped the smooth imported dark roast, he accepted the truth. It was time. Past time. He needed to come clean to Amber about his little deception tonight. It was the only way they could move forward with their relationship.

Because whether he'd been willing to admit it or not, somehow this thing that started between them as mere sexual attraction had become the very thing he hadn't been looking for. The very last thing he should want with a woman like her.

He might finally have accepted whatever she felt for him was based on the man rather than the money. But she was still worlds different from the kind of woman he'd expect to become a part of his life, even temporarily. And maybe that wasn't such a bad thing.

Look how well he'd done with the ones he thought were the kind that should.

Bringing a second cup of coffee into his home office, he did his best to concentrate on the information scrolling across his computer screen. But more than once he caught himself thinking instead of the soft, wet heat he wanted to explore, the silken curves and pink crested breasts, wondering if his imagination even came close to doing her body justice.

When he had to stand up to adjust the growing tightness in his jeans for the second time, he finally admitted defeat. No way was he getting any work done at home. Where had all of his vaunted self-discipline gone?

Right into a masturbatory wet dream, that's where.

Maybe he'd have better luck concentrating at the office, where he wouldn't be within steps of the bed that had hosted said dream.

Since it was Sunday, he went a little crazy and skipped the usual suit, heading down the private elevator to the garage as he was. What good was it being the boss if he couldn't dress casual on what was technically his day off?

Besides, it wasn't like there'd be anyone else at the office to see him. He was the only idiot who worked nights and weekends.

Far too often, according to Kitty.

And Greta.

And Charlaine.

Okay, maybe there was a pattern there he'd been ignoring, he conceded as he swung the Spider into his spot in the solar panel-covered executive lot. A pattern which might have more to do with the fact he'd never felt a greater desire to spend time with any of them than with his portfolios.

Amber, on the other hand...

He'd had no trouble at all leaving his work at work for her. Even today, he was only using it as a distraction to keep himself from ticking off the minutes until he could see her again.

"So pathetic." But he was grinning like a fool as he said it, amused at his own expense.

"What was that, Mr. Beaumont?"

Realizing the ginger-haired guard at the lobby security desk had heard him as he came through the glass door of the building, Richard gave him a wry grin. "Nothing, Vince. Just commenting on being the only one with nothing better to do than come into the office on a Sunday."

"Nothing wrong with a good work ethic, sir," Vince replied with a grin of his own. "But truth is, you're not the only one. Mrs. Beaumont came in, oh, about half an hour ago or so with a few of her people. Said they'd be here most of the day, working out the details for the big charity ball."

Damn.

Talk about bad timing. The last thing he wanted was to get trapped into another conversation about the party he was still trying to find a way out of attending. At least in costume. But other than turning tail and running, he had no choice but to go upstairs and hope his mother was too involved in whatever she was doing to notice he was in the building.

Ha. As if his mother ever missed anything.

With a nod to the guard, Richard rode the elevator up. Being so unnaturally quiet on the empty floor, he could hear the faint hum of voices coming from the direction of his mother's office, in the opposite corner of the building from his.

Thankful for the distance between them, he made a beeline for his own office and breathed a sigh of relief when the heavy door clicked shut behind him.

A few hours and several cups of coffee later, he sat back and stretched, feeling each pop as the tension from hunching over the computer released from his spine. Other than the classes at the community center, he'd been neglecting his usual workout routine for the past few weeks.

Ever since he'd found a much more enjoyable way to spend his free time.

Unable to stop the spontaneous grin at the reminder he'd be seeing Amber soon, he checked his watch. Almost one. No wonder his body was unhappy with him. It needed sustenance.

Since Amber hadn't texted to say he could come over early—he checked his phone again to be sure—it was time to stop being a pathetic wuss and say hello to his mother, and see if she wanted him to order in food for the troops.

Two birds, one lunch order.

As he walked down the thickly carpeted hallway to her office, he couldn't help but wonder what his mother would do once his father finally decided to retire. The Everbrite Foundation took up as much of her time as a full-time job. It would be pretty hard to get her husband to slow down if she didn't do the same.

And yet, he couldn't see her abandoning the charity to someone else's care, either. Not with how much each and every cause they helped meant to her.

For a tough-as-nails lady, Patricia Beaumont had a heart like a marshmallow.

Her office was empty, so he followed the voices to the small meeting room connected to it. There were a half-dozen people clustered around the table there. Several were hard at work on laptops. The others compared paper lists to a whiteboard filled with a diagram of the hotel ballroom where the event would take place. Based on all the little numbered circles, he assumed they were working on a seating chart.

He might not know much about charity events, but he was savvy enough about the politics of business to know where someone sat at an event they'd paid big bucks to attend was a major issue. The more money you spent, the closer to the front of the room and the power-players on the dais you got.

As with real estate, it was all about location, location, location.

He didn't envy his mother the task of placating all those egos, but he knew she'd do it. She somehow always did.

Straightening from where she'd been looking over a blonde's shoulder at something on one of the laptops, his mother turned around and noticed him in the doorway. After an initial expression of surprise, she smiled and walked toward him.

"Richard! What a lovely surprise." She presented her cheek for a kiss. "Have you come to help save the day?"

He chuckled. "If by save the day you mean order food for everyone, then yes. The rest I'm sure you have perfectly under control."

With a huff, she said, "Yes, well, I would have, if two of my key people hadn't suddenly backed out in the last week because of family emergencies. Normally it wouldn't be a problem, but with the ball only three weeks away..." She threw her hands up in a helpless gesture. "Chaos."

All thoughts of a fast escape evaporated. "I didn't realize you were so short-handed. What can I do to help?"

"You're such a dear." She patted his cheek the same way she had when he was a child. "Thank you, but I think we've got it under control for the moment. I got a last-minute replacement, and so far she's been a godsend."

Still feeling guilty he hadn't noticed how frazzled his mother was, he asked, "Then can I at least feed you?"

"Already handled. I had something sent over. It's being put out in the breakroom right now." Turning back to the men and women who were still hard at work, she said, "Lunch in five minutes, everyone."

"Well, in that case—"

With the prescience of knowing him too well, she looped her arm through his, preventing his escape. "I need to check and see everything's ready. Come and have a quick bite with me." They were already walking when she added, "Oh, and while I have you, I had a few ideas about your costume..."

Stifling a groan, he dutifully accompanied her down the hallway, careful not to make any noises that could possibly be construed as agreement to the ridiculous ideas being tossed at him. A pirate? Really? Maybe when he was five. Did his mother not know him at all?

The only place he was a pirate these days was in the stock market.

The delicious aroma of food smacked him in the face as he stepped into the large breakroom, ending all thoughts of leaving as soon as he could shake loose from his mother's hold. With the bagel nothing but a distant memory, he was willing to surrender thirty minutes of his freedom for a plate of whatever was under the tin covers on the table making his mouth water.

Then the woman putting out plates and napkins turned, and everything stuttered to a stop. "Amber?"

Shock, then pleasure marked her expression. "Rick!"

There was nothing anywhere near pleasure in his reaction to seeing her there. In the building where he worked. That his family *owned*. More like disbelief.

And betrayal.

Okay, wait. Maybe this wasn't what it seemed. Maybe she'd ended up going to work instead of to the community center. Maybe she'd been the one to deliver the food. He'd never asked which restaurant she filled in shifts at.

It would be a ridiculously huge coincidence for it to be the one his mother had ordered lunch from, but he grabbed onto the possibility with both hands.

Only to have it yanked away again when his mother said, "Richard, this is the young lady I was telling you has been such an enormous help today." She looked between the two of them. "But it seems you might already know each other."

Amber nodded. "We met a few weeks ago at the community center. Rick, I didn't know you were working for the Foundation, too."

With a small laugh, his mother patted his arm. "Oh, my son answers the call when I ask for his help, but he's not much for stuffing envelopes or making guest lists. I save him for when I need to pull out the big guns."

If he hadn't been staring at her so intently, he might have missed the way Amber's eyes narrowed as she cocked her head, glancing from his mother to him and back again. "Your *son*?"

"Yes. Oh, that's right, you might not have known Everbrite is a part of Beaumont Investments."

"No. I mean yes, I did know that, but not...Rick?"

Oh, she was good. Really, really good.

There was just the right amount of confusion in her expression, in her voice, as she looked at him for answers. Answers he knew damn well she already had. Had probably had for some time now.

Fuck!

He hated being wrong.

But worse, he hated being played.

Pasting on a smile that felt more like a grimace, he said, "Mom, would you mind if I borrowed your new protégé for a few minutes? We have some things to discuss."

"Oh, of course..."

He already had Amber's elbow in his grasp and was pulling her from the room before his mother could finish. She came with him easily, no resistance in her body as he marched them down one hallway and then another, ending in his office where he finally released her and closed the door. Turning to face the woman he'd only a few short hours ago thought he'd be making a part of his life, he now saw only the liar he couldn't get away from fast enough.

"Game over, lady. You lose."

⚬

AMBER BLINKED AT THE man glaring at her with such venom, trying to stop her head from spinning. Son? He was Patricia Beaumont's *son*? How was that even possible? And why was he looking at her like she was horse manure he'd tracked in on his shoes?

Stop the merry-go-round, I'm gonna be sick.

"Rick, what's going on?"

"Oh, we're going to pretend you don't know, is that how we're going to play it?"

Feeling like she'd been dropped into the middle of a soap opera she didn't have the script for, she spread her hands. "Play what? And who's pretending? I don't have any clue what's going on here. Why are you so angry?"

His lips thinned. "Because you lied to me."

"Lied? I didn't lie. I told you I was doing volunteer work today."

"At the community center."

"I assumed it would be. But when I got there, Mrs. Gandy said the charity committee that needed help was meeting here, so I came here." She'd been embarrassed by how casually she'd been dressed, in faded jeans and a long-sleeved Colorado Rockies t-shirt, when the guard brought her up to the luxuriously appointed top floor.

But Mrs. Beaumont—Patricia, she'd insisted—had put her completely at ease, thanking her with honest gratitude for giving up her Sunday to lend a hand. Everyone else followed Patricia's lead. Not one of them had made Amber feel the least bit out of place or uncomfortable.

Until Rick.

"How convenient."

"It's the truth! Why would I lie?"

Rather than answer, he walked past her, running a hand through his hair to clasp the back of his neck as he went. Turning back, he leaned on the front of the large granite and glass desk dominating the room, arms crossed, his expression as closed off as his body language.

"Was I taking too long? Is that it?"

"Too long for what?" Why was he talking in riddles?

Ignoring her question, he went on. "So, what? You decided to move things along by just *happening* to get yourself onto my mother's pet project, and then just *happening* to show up here where we could run into each other?"

"I didn't just happen to do anything! I told you, Mrs. Gandy sent me—"

"Don't blame Mrs. Gandy."

"Blame her for *what*?" The dull ache throbbing in her head since she'd rolled out of her sleepless bed increased in tempo. She rubbed at her temples, frustration and weariness leaving her on the verge of tears.

"For the love of God, just tell me what the hell is going on, because up until five minutes ago, I thought I knew, but clearly I don't know a damned thing."

The answering look of disgust on Rick's face was like a knife in her chest. She shifted her gaze to escape it, looking instead at the sleek desk he was leaning back against. Whoever sat there would be an intimidating presence to the poor peons he dictated to on the other side. In her experience, people with desks like that enjoyed using them as thrones for the petty despots they were at heart.

Then her gaze slid across the gold embossed mahogany nameplate.

Richard Beaumont.

Richard...Rick.

Richard Bowman? Or...Beaumont?

No. It couldn't be.

As she stared at that innocuous hunk of wood and metal, pieces clicked into place, while at the same time other parts of the past few weeks blew apart like tumbleweeds in a windstorm. Mrs. Gandy always stumbling over his name. Being friends with Max. Never once inviting her over to his apartment.

She didn't want to believe it. But it was the only thing that made sense. This wasn't just any empty office he'd dragged her into. It was *his* office.

He really was Patricia's son.

Which meant he'd been lying to her since the day they met.

For the second time in less than twenty-four hours, her world shattered around her. Only this time, she didn't think she'd be able to fit the pieces back together again. At least she expected Hunter to be an amoral bastard. Rick was supposed to be the rock she could lean on to get through dealing with him.

Except there was no Rick. There was just a man she didn't even know.

"Why?" She rasped out the question. "Why pretend to be Rick Bowman?"

"Oh, so now you've figured it out?"

She didn't bother trying to explain about the nameplate. Why waste her breath? It was clear he'd already decided she'd known his true identity before now. She didn't know why, but she also didn't care. The only thing that mattered now was getting some answers of her own.

And then getting as far away from here—and him—as she could.

"Can't you give me one straight answer? I think you owe me that much, at least."

Rick—Richard—drew back as though struck. "*I* owe *you*?" He gave a harsh bark of laughter. "Okay, fine. I'll play." He paced behind the desk and leaned his hands on the back of the tall leather chair. Classic power position.

"Richard Beaumont is a prize to be captured. A cash cow. One of the top-ten eligible bachelors in Colorado—along with both of my brothers. Rick Bowman is just a regular guy, with a regular job and a regular bank account. I wanted to see which one you really wanted."

She could almost see his point.

Almost.

If only it didn't hurt so much.

"That's fine for when we first met. I don't like it, but I get it. But you could have told me the truth any time in the last month." She sucked in a small breath. "You still didn't trust me? After everything we—" She shook her head. "God, I'm such an idiot. I thought you were different. I thought..."

"What? That I'd be your meal ticket? Your way out of that shoebox of an apartment and into my penthouse?"

Every word pounded at her like a hammer blow to the heart. So that's what he really thought of her and her life.

She swallowed the bile rising in her throat. "I thought I could trust you."

Rick—*Richard*—flinched before the sneer was back. "Funny. I thought the same thing. And yet, here you are."

Not for long.

"Were you ever going to tell me the truth? Or was this just some kind of sick game for you? See how long you can string along the low-rent bimbo before she figures out you've been lying to her?"

"I never lied to you. Except about my name," he amended with ill grace.

"Really? How about your job? What was it, working at the family business doing computer stuff?"

Something she realized she'd never bothered to clarify after he mentioned it that one time. Not even the name of the company, or what they did. It didn't seem important. Their time alone together had been too precious to waste talking about work.

More fool me.

"Not a lie. I do work for the family business, and I do handle most of my work on the computer."

"You're unbelievable. You have absolutely no guilt about any of this, do you? Of course, you don't." She threw her hands up in disgust. "You have money, so that makes it okay to do whatever you want and to hell with the people who get hurt along the way."

"Nobody here got hurt."

"No?" Tell that to her shredded heart. "What about Derek?"

"I'd never do anything to hurt him."

"What do you think it's going to do to him when he finds out you're not the guy he thought you were? That you've been lying to us because you didn't trust us enough to tell the truth?"

Thinking about how torn up her son would be helped her push past her own pain of betrayal and replace it with a burning ember of maternal fury. Bad enough he'd lied to her. But he'd screwed with her kid's feelings, too, and *that* she wouldn't let him get away with.

"What do I tell him when you just disappear from our lives?"

He looked stricken for a moment, but his expression quickly changed to something colder. More calculating. "Who said I have to go anywhere?"

"What?"

Seriously, *what*?

"We're both adults. Just because the game didn't turn out the way you wanted doesn't mean we can't change the parameters of the situation to suit our needs."

Situation. Not relationship. Amazing how one little word could take something beautiful and turn it into nothing more than a business transaction.

"And what needs would that be?" she forced herself to ask. Because as much as it was going to hurt, she needed to hear him say it.

"Everything else aside, the sexual chemistry between us has been off the charts from day one. I know it. You know it. So, why keep denying ourselves the pleasure to be had from a mutually satisfying arrangement?"

She couldn't help it. All she could hear was the echo of Hunter's *'maybe we could work something out that would give us both a little of what we wanted'* in Richard's words.

Was that all she was ever going to be worth to anyone? A good fuck?

Refusing to bend under the weight of grief trying to drive her to her knees, she tilted her chin up and gave him her best come-and-get-it smile.

"So, let me see if I have this right. After you lied to me about who you were, lied to my son, believed I was trying to date you for your money, and, let's see…" She tapped a finger to her chin. "Oh, right. Accused me of somehow finagling my way onto your mother's charity so I could manage to bump into you and get access to all that wonderful wealth of yours. After all that, you think it would be perfectly okay for the two of us to just skip the whole relationship part of things and get down to the screwing part. Is that it?"

The fact her tone and her words didn't match wasn't lost on him, judging by the wary confusion on his face. "I wouldn't put it that way, exactly..."

"No?" She dropped the smile and let him see the frustration and anger that was all but drowning her. "Then let me put it this way, Mr. Beaumont. The only thing around here you can go fuck is yourself."

She yanked the door open and stopped long enough to say over her shoulder, "Looks like we were both wrong. You *are* the guy, after all."

Heart pounding so loudly in her ears she couldn't hear if he said anything, she stalked down the hall. It didn't matter if he did. She wasn't interested in anything he had to say. Not anymore.

Grabbing her purse from the thankfully empty meeting room, she scrawled a quick note of apology for Patricia about having to leave for a family emergency. It was a sucky way to bail on a woman who'd been nothing but kind to her, but there was no way she could face her—or anyone else—and not lose the last tenuous grasp she had on herself. It wasn't like she could spill her guts to the woman if she asked what was wrong.

Nice or not, she was still the bastard's mother.

The elevator opened immediately when she hit the call button. Riding down to the lobby, she beat off the panic slowly rising inside her. Rick was Richard. Hunter was a blackmailer. And she now had absolutely nowhere to turn for help about either one.

Once again, the men with all the money were playing with her life.

And winning.

She straightened her spine. So what if they were? So what if she was once again left to deal with the mess of her life all on her own? She'd been alone since her mother died and look how far she'd come. Good job, great son. Dealing with her problems by herself was what she'd always done, and she'd damn well do it again.

Richard and Hunter wanted to mess with her life? Let them.

Bring it on, boys. And to hell with you both.

Chapter 10

"You said *what*?"

Acknowledging the incredulity in Rafe's voice with a sigh, Richard stared down at the sweating bottle of Corona cradled between his palms, wishing it was a glass of scotch instead. Four fingers. Neat.

"I admit, I may have miscalculated a bit with that offer." Something he rarely ever did, since making those kinds of mistakes in judgment could cost people millions.

This one, though, may have cost him far more.

"Miscalculated?" His future brother-in-law gave him a look that questioned his sanity. "Dude, what you did was fuck up. Royally."

The rebuke had him stiffening. Not that he didn't deserve it. But hearing it from Rafael Delgado made it doubly hard to swallow.

They'd never been on the best of terms. Things had started out rocky when Richard and his brothers found out he was sleeping with their baby sister. They'd gotten seriously worse when they conspired to break them up.

Something Lillian was still making each of them pay for.

But things had thawed enough between them in the ensuing months—or maybe Richard was just desperate enough—that he'd actually asked for Rafe's help. As a cop, he possessed the same keen intuition for analyzing people situations as Richard had for stocks.

Listening to his no-punches-pulled opinion, however, was turning out to be a lot harder than he'd expected.

"Okay, it may have been a mistake to suggest we could be adults and enjoy a physical relationship—"

"*Pinche idiota.*" Rafe squeezed the bridge of his nose between his fingers as he muttered the curse. "You told her she wasn't worth having as a girlfriend, but you were still willing to screw her. You treated her like she was just one more commodity for you to add to your portfolio. No, worse. You treated her like a whore." He shook his head. "What were you thinking?"

That no matter how angry he was at discovering Amber's duplicity, he was even more terrified at the thought of her walking out the door and disappearing from his life forever. The offer of an affair was the first thing that leapt to mind to stop that from happening.

In hindsight, he probably should have kept his big mouth shut and let her go.

I really am *a fucking idiot.*

"Okay, you're right. I was wrong to say it." He frowned when Rafe took a long look at his watch. "You have someplace to be? I thought you were off-duty tonight."

"Oh, I'm not going anywhere. I was just marking the time the great Richard Beaumont actually admitted he was wrong about something."

A few choice words came to mind, but he held them back. Lillian wasn't the only one still making him pay for previous bad behavior. He supposed Rafe deserved to get in a few shots of his own.

"So, now that we both agree I was wrong to suggest it, what do I do about it?"

"Why do you want to do anything? I thought you'd be glad to be rid of someone who was only getting close to you for your money."

He'd thought the same thing. He'd spent Sunday night demolishing a bottle of twenty-five-year-old Glenlivet to celebrate his near miss, Monday paying for it, and all of today burying his head in his work to forget it ever happened.

Through it all, he'd kept one certain blonde siren out of his thoughts.

Mostly, anyway.

But when Derek didn't show up tonight for class, the disappointment had been surprisingly painful. So much so he'd driven over and sat in the parking lot outside their apartment building afterward.

He never got out of the car. Never even opened the door. Just stared at the red brick structure for a good half hour as he struggled with the conflicting emotions battling inside him until finally, he broke down and called Rafe.

"I'm not sure," he admitted, rolling the bottle between his hands before taking a swallow. When Rafe looked at his watch again, he said, "Fuck you," but there was no heat to the words.

An answering grin flickered over Rafe's mouth, then was gone. "Is it possible you're thinking, deep down, you might have been wrong about more than just your sleazy proposition?"

Denial was swift, but not altogether certain.

That *was* the question he'd been struggling with ever since his mother had given him an earful on Sunday following Amber's departure. Suspicious of the timing of her sudden "family emergency" right after Richard all but yanked her out of the breakroom, she'd stormed his office and demanded to know what he'd done to upset "that very nice girl."

"I asked my mother about how Amber came to be on her charity ball committee." The admission stung.

"And?"

"And it turns out my mother called Mrs. Gandy in a panic last week for recommendations to help fill the spots left by the two people who dropped out." He'd wondered for a split second if it would have been possible for Amber to have somehow arranged those convenient openings, then been ashamed for even considering it. "Mrs. Gandy went through the available volunteers she had on file, sent her top three picks to my mother, and she chose Amber."

"So, she really had no part in what project she got assigned to."

"No." It happened just like she'd said. Even the part about reporting to the community center first and then being redirected to the Beaumont building. A simple miscommunication, according to his mother.

Who was less than happy with him since his questions all but confirmed her suspicions he was somehow at fault for Amber's hasty resignation.

Rafe got up from the kitchen table and grabbed two more beers from the fridge. "Since she was telling the truth about that, isn't it at least possible the rest of your assumptions were wrong, too?"

Rather than answer right away, Richard concentrated on pushing the lime wedge into the bottle with his thumb and taking a long swallow of the ice-cold brew. *Were* they wrong? That was the problem. He just didn't know anymore.

"She still could have known who I was." It always came back to that.

"Okay, say she did." Rafe thumbed his own lime down the long-necked bottle. "Does it really matter?"

"Of course it does."

"Why?" Rafe raised his bottle and drank, his dark eyes pinning him with the kind of intensity usually reserved for a suspect across an interrogation table.

"Because I'm...and she's...fuck." He ran an agitated hand through his hair.

"Because you're a Beaumont, and she's a nobody."

"She's not a nobody," he snapped.

Rafe shrugged. "Okay, she's not of your social standing, then."

That sounded snobbish even to him. He squirmed under the continued cop-stare. "No, she's not. But that's not the point."

"Isn't it?"

Was it?

Was he digging in his heels because deep down he was uncomfortable, maybe even embarrassed, by the wide gulf in their income brackets? He'd felt a twinge or two of worry when he'd escorted her to Max's launch party.

She'd comported herself well, but things had been low-key and casual there. Unlike a true social event, dripping with diamonds and haute couture. How would she fare at one of those? Amber might think herself tough, but women like Kitty and Greta would rip her to shreds with their dainty little society claws.

Son of a bitch. He *was* embarrassed.

Only not *by* her.

For her.

That realization must have showed, because Rafe dropped the stare and reverted to his normal casual posture. "Do you like this woman?"

"I did. I do," he amended, because damn it, he hadn't been able to stop.

"Do you love her?"

"I've only known her a month!" Twenty-nine days, to be exact. Not that he was keeping track. He was simply a numbers person.

Really.

"Sometimes all it takes is a day."

"Not for me."

Rafe rolled his eyes, a bad habit he seemed to have picked up from Lillian. "Because you always overanalyze everything to death. Love isn't about logic or timeframes or fitting into neat little boxes for you to check off on some imaginary list. It's about what you feel. Here." He thumped his chest. "When you think about her, what do you *feel?*"

Contented. Angry. Happy.

Confused. Off-balance.

Afraid.

If that was love, he wasn't sure he wanted any part of it.

Evidently tired of waiting for an answer, Rafe sighed. "You went out with that Kathryn person for how long?"

"About six months, give or take." Funny how he couldn't remember exactly. "Why? What does she have to do with anything?"

"How did you feel after you broke up with her?"

"Feel? Annoyed, I guess. And a little relieved." More than he was willing to admit to.

"No second guessing ending your relationship? No wondering if you made a mistake?"

"Hell no."

"So, don't you think the fact breaking up with Amber is twisting you up enough to come to *me* of all people for advice might mean your feelings for her ran a little deeper than just 'like'?"

"I don't *know*, damn it." He took an angry swallow of beer, trying to wash away the ever-tightening snarl of emotions threatening to choke him.

"You do know. You just don't want to, because it doesn't fit into your tidy little spreadsheet of what kind of woman Richard Beaumont should be with. And don't say it's not true." He pointed at Richard with his beer. "I've been on the receiving end of the same bullshit from you. I know it's how you think. And you know I know. Why else would you be here?"

He was right, damn him.

He'd chosen to talk to Rafe over Theo because if anyone could give him advice relevant to the situation and call him on his crap, it was Rafe. And if he was willing to come and spill his guts to the man he knew still held a grudge, then that meant he cared. A lot.

Maybe too much.

"Okay," he said slowly, decision made. "Let's say you're right." He sighed when Rafe raised a dark brow at him. "Fine. You're right. I more than like her. Happy?"

"Ecstatic." Rafe saluted him with his beer.

"Great. I'm officially in touch with my fucking feelings. Now, what do I do to put things back the way they were between us?"

"Oh, *mi hermano*, it isn't going to be that easy. Once you finish working your way past your own elitist prejudices, then you still have to worry about her forgiving you for what you did. Not just the indecent proposition. I mean all of it. And even then, things won't be the same as they were."

"Why the hell not?"

"Because you won't be the same guy you were pretending to be. You'll be you." Rafe shrugged. "I'm not saying that's any better or worse, but it does change things. For both of you. And I don't mean the money. I'm talking about all the other parts of your life. Your work, your friends, your family. There's a whole other side to you she has no idea about that you need to see if she fits into. Or if she even wants to."

A few days ago, the possibility she wouldn't prefer Richard over Rick seemed inconceivable. Now, it was like a fist being driven into his solar plexus. What if he'd been wrong about everything? What if she didn't want him? The real him?

"I'll find a way to make it right."

He had to.

"You wanted my advice? Here it is. Bring kneepads when you go to see her. You have some major groveling to do."

⸺◈⸺

"MS. LOVETT, A MOMENT?"

Jumping at her boss's unexpected voice behind her in her cubicle, Amber's fingers fumbled on the keyboard, sending a line of incorrect numbers into the patient file she was working on. Biting back a curse, she swiveled her chair to look at him, doing her best to seem composed and competent rather than frazzled and edgy.

"Sir?"

Hollingsworth's pale eyes did their usual tango over her chest, leaving her hyperaware her cardigan was hanging useless on the back of her chair and she was wearing one of her more figure-hugging dresses today.

Damn.

Nobody had given the warning he was on the floor.

Then again, they might have, and she just didn't hear it. She'd spent the past three days feeling mule-kicked. Worrying about when Hunter was going to show up again. Wondering if Richard noticed Derek had refused to attend class the night before, or even cared.

Wishing there was a great big do-over button somewhere she could push to wipe out all of it and start fresh.

All of that extra noise in her head made concentrating on her job increasingly difficult. The last thing she could afford now with her promotion hanging in the balance were any stupid mistakes.

Her promotion!

A jolt of anticipation helped clear a little of the haze from her head. It had been three weeks since her interminable lunch interview. Maybe he'd finally made a decision. It would be nice if one thing suddenly went right in her upside-down life.

Done with his perusal, he met her gaze without a flicker of shame. "My office, please. Five minutes."

"Yes, sir."

As he walked away, she struggled not to get her hopes too high. He'd called her to his office several other times over the past few weeks. And each time, it was only to ask a few more questions that could have just as easily been handled by email or on the phone.

But Hollingsworth always enjoyed every drop of power his position as petty functionary gave him. The gratification of making her present herself at his office on command was probably the highlight of his day.

She shuddered at the thought of being the highlight of that man's anything.

Pulling on the sweater, she grabbed her purse and made a quick dash to the ladies room. While she was reapplying her lipstick, the door swung open and Belinda came in. Amber grinned into the mirror at her.

"Hollingsworth wants me in his office. Again. Wish me luck I come back with good news this time."

The expression on Belinda's face was impossible to decipher before she swung away and headed for one of the stalls. "Like you need luck."

She frowned at the absence of Belinda's usual enthusiasm. Maybe not all of her coworkers liked the idea of her getting the supervisor's position as much as she'd thought. Which sucked, because she was counting on people like Belinda who she considered her work friends to help make the transition to her new job easier.

If she ever got the job.

Reminded of her ticking clock, she put off talking to Belinda until later and took the elevator up. Surprisingly, Hollingsworth's assistant showed her right into his office rather than making her cool her heels as usual. Taking it as a good sign, Amber let a little more cautious optimism creep in.

"Thank you, Ilsa. That will be all. Oh, and hold my calls until we're done here, please. I don't want to be disturbed for any reason."

"Yes, sir." The professional courtesy in the woman's tone was undercut by the look of pity she flashed at Amber as she shut the door between them with a soft thump.

An impending sense of disaster swept away all that budding optimism. What did Ilsa know she didn't?

"Ms. Lovett, have a seat."

Swallowing against her suddenly dry mouth, Amber took the indicated seat in front of the desk. Her fingers twisted on her lap before she forced herself to link them together to halt the nervous movement.

She'd come up here expecting good news. But what if it wasn't? What if she was in some kind of trouble? She hadn't done anything wrong, though.

Unless...did she somehow let her work suffer the past few days despite her best efforts not to? Had she made mistakes?

Oh, God. Was she getting *fired*?

Rising from his chair, Hollingsworth came around the desk and leaned his ample rump against the front of it. The pose was so reminiscent of Richard doing the exact same thing she nearly laughed, although it would have been bitter if she did.

Men and their damn dominance games.

The position also had the unfortunate consequence of placing his crotch eye-level in front of her. Which probably wasn't an accident.

She concentrated on keeping her gaze focused upward at all costs.

"Ms. Lovett," he said again, crossing his arms. His expression softened. "Amber."

Here it comes.

"I know you've been with the hospital for some time now—"

This can't be happening.

"—and you've always done an outstanding job in a very exacting position—"

How will I take care of Derek with no job and no benefits?

"—which is why I'm so pleased to offer you the position of unit supervisor."

His words sank in, halting her panicked inner monologue. "I...what?"

"The promotion. It's yours. If you still want it," he added when she was silent for too long.

She laughed. "Yes! Yes, of course I do. Thank you! That's...a relief." More than he'd ever know.

Holy crap, I got the job!

"Wonderful. Let me be the first to congratulate you." He stuck out his hand with a broad smile.

Still grinning like an idiot, she took the offered hand and shook it a little more vigorously than normal, her nerves getting the best of her.

"Thank you, sir. I promise I won't disappoint you."

But when she tried to retrieve her hand, he didn't let go right away. She tugged harder. When he released his grip, his hand slid from hers in a sweaty caress. Disgusted, she pressed her damp hand against her leg, only just refraining from wiping it off.

"I know this has been a lengthy process, Amber, but I hope you understand I needed to be sure I picked the person who best fit the requirements of the job. Some people think filling a position is nothing more than who has the most seniority or the best reviews. But in reality, it's knowing how all the cogs and wheels best fit together, and choosing the right piece for the right spot, so they continue to grind together smoothly."

She could have done without the way he pushed a little on the word 'grind,' but she got his point. Some people might be qualified on paper but a total fail in real-life performance. Hopefully, she wouldn't be one of them.

"I understand, sir."

"Good. I had a feeling you would."

"When do I start?"

"First thing Monday morning."

That surprised her. She'd expected a week, or even two, to clear up any outstanding work in her queue and psych herself up for the change. And maybe hunt through the consignment store downtown for a few work-appropriate wardrobe pieces she could rework and alter. If she wanted to be taken seriously as a supervisor, she needed to look the part.

And if she was going to be around Hollingsworth every day, she needed to better camouflage her curves.

"Wow, that's...fast."

"I don't believe in waiting once I have what I want within reach." He gave her what was probably supposed to be a sheepish look, but it skewed a little more wolfish to her cynical eyes. "Meaning the right person for the job, of course."

She had her doubts. But this was Horny Hollingsworth, after all. Inappropriate innuendo was like breathing to him. Taking this promotion meant being able to ignore it without giving him the reaction he was looking for. Starting now.

She gave a bland smile. "Of course, sir."

"Good, good." He clapped his hands and rubbed them together. "You'll need to fill out the paperwork with human resources to make it official. Get new credentials, security codes. All of that will probably take up most of the afternoon, so let me take you to lunch first, to celebrate."

Panic skittered down her spine. "Oh, thank you, but—"

"I insist." He grinned. "Remember, I always get what I want."

Not always, buster.

But although several excuses leapt to mind, she had a sinking certainty Hollingsworth might suddenly find some reason to rescind the promotion offer if she used any of them.

Until that paperwork was signed, she was stuck playing his petty power games.

"Lunch would be nice. Thank you, sir."

"Oh, no need to be so formal when we're alone. Call me Horace."

Play nice, play nice, play nice...

"Of course." There was a long pause before she realized what he was waiting for. "Horace."

He gave her a broad smile. "That wasn't so hard now, was it?"

She did her best to return the smile but held her tongue, since he wouldn't like her answer. No matter her reasoning, it still felt as though she'd just made a deal with the devil.

And as she followed the devil out of his office and Ilsa shot her another of those pitying looks, she wondered if perhaps she wasn't the only one who knew it.

After the longest hour known to man, she finally escaped Hollingsworth's company back to the third floor. Feeling both elated and disgusted as she collapsed into her chair, she mentally scrubbed away the thin layer of ick that came from too many casual touches and more than a few not-so-casual visual feel-ups.

It sucked, but she'd had to put up with worse. But one day he was going to go one step too far, and when he did, she'd be the first one knocking on the door to human resources with the proof that would finally get his inappropriate ass fired.

A quick check of her internal email showed the request from HR officially offering her the promotion and requesting she come by to sign the necessary forms. A small part of her that had been afraid Hollingsworth was lying relaxed.

It was real. The offer was there in black and white, and no one, not even old Horny himself, could take it back.

With a tiny squee, she spun her chair around and popped to her feet. Needing to share, she leaned over the top of the cubicle wall she shared with Belinda and bounced on her toes. "I got it! I got the promotion!"

Belinda flicked a look over her shoulder, then went back to typing. "Like there was ever any doubt."

It took a second to register that the sarcastic tone made the words something other than a compliment. The bouncing stopped. "What's that supposed to mean?"

"Nothing."

"Bull." She stared at the back of Belinda's braid-covered head, wishing she could see inside and figure out why she was acting this way. "Are you mad at me for something? I thought you were as excited about me getting this job as I was."

"Yeah, if you'd gotten it fair and square. I never expected you to—" Her hand came up. "You know what, never mind."

"No, not never mind. Tell me. What do you think I did?"

Belinda spun her chair around, lips pressed into a grim line as she nailed Amber with an angry glare. "Like you don't know."

A sick sensation she hadn't felt since high school crept over her, chilling her skin. "I don't."

"Really?" Belinda gestured towards Amber's face. "Looks like you wore your lipstick off since the bathroom."

She raised a self-conscious hand to her mouth. "It must have come off when I ate lunch."

"Lunch, huh? Funny, I didn't see you down in the cafeteria."

"Hollingsworth took me out to eat. He insisted. How could I say no?"

She hated feeling like she had to justify herself. Especially to someone who knew exactly how their boss could be.

"Yeah, I guess saying no isn't something you're good at."

The fettuccini Alfredo that tasted so good a little while ago did a nauseating flip in her belly. "You're not...you can't possibly think I...Jesus, Belinda!" The shock that anyone, least of all someone she'd considered a friend, would believe she'd trade sex for favors made her head spin. She gripped the top of the cubicle wall to steady herself.

"Oh, come on. What about all those times you've gone up to his office these past few weeks?"

"I told you, he wanted to verify some information in my personnel file. Routine stuff."

Things he didn't need to see her in person for. Hadn't she just been thinking about that herself?

"And taking you out to lunch for your 'interview'? Was that routine?"

"He did the same thing with Felipe," she replied, scrambling for footing on what was beginning to feel like a slippery slope.

"Yeah, to the diner across the street. Where'd he take you?"

To one of the trendiest restaurants in the city. The same place he'd taken her today.

Son of a bitch.

Her non-answer made Belinda sneer. "That's what I thought."

"Look, I had no idea he took us to different places. But that's not my fault, either. You know how Hollingsworth is. He's always playing games."

"Yeah, I just never expected you to play them, too." With a look that said her mind wasn't going to be changed, she swiveled her chair around, giving Amber her back.

The fettuccini did another dangerous twist, threatening to make a reappearance as she struggled for an argument, any argument, that would prove she hadn't been servicing their boss. But as she'd learned in high school when several boys she'd refused to have sex with started bragging about how easy she'd been, it was impossible to prove a negative.

Two years of being "Amber Loves It" had driven that truth home with cruel finality.

Just like Belinda's rigid back did now.

One hand pressed to her roiling stomach, she fumbled through shutting down her computer and made it to the bathroom just in time. After rinsing her mouth and blotting cold paper towels over her face, she stared into the mirror and wondered what she'd ever done to deserve everything handed to her this past week.

It's the curse of the Lovett women, Amber Lee, her mother once told her. *Blessed with good looks, cursed with bad luck and bad men. It's just the way it is.*

It might be the way it was, but it still sucked.

On her way to the elevator to go to HR, she noticed for the first time how there were no casual greetings from her coworkers as she passed. Only chilly, disapproving silence and a lack of eye contact. That answered whether Belinda was the only one to think she'd gotten her promotion on her knees.

The people she'd thought her friends, who'd always been her safety net the way she'd been theirs when dealing with Hollingsworth and his pervy tendencies, had condemned her without proof. Without even asking her side of the story.

And that was what hurt the most.

Stepping onto the elevator alone, she considered all of Hollingsworth's actions, right from that first lunchtime interview. Every one had seemed innocent enough at the time. But looking back, they laid a straight line for anyone with a bit of gossip dripped in their ears to follow to the worst possible conclusion.

They might like you now, but trust me, nobody likes you once you're the boss.

Hollingsworth's words to her weeks ago came back with haunting clarity. And a new insight considering her sudden pariah status. No, nobody would like her now. No one would have her back. Be her safety net. She was completely isolated, alone, and vulnerable.

He'd made sure of it.

Chapter 11

RICHARD WASN'T SURE WHAT he expected when he knocked on Amber's door Saturday morning, but it definitely wasn't the defiant Valkyrie who yanked it open looking like she was prepared for battle. Then there was a subtle shift in her expression, first to surprise, then relief, and finally settling back on defiant again.

Oh yeah. She was still hot.

No. More like she'd cheerfully remove his testicles with a rusty battle axe.

But he'd gladly subject himself to her full wrath and whatever punishment she saw fit to mete out if it meant healing the jagged rift he'd created between them. It might have taken a while for Rafe's words to really sink in, but once they did, he knew to his bones they were one-hundred percent on the mark.

He'd done more than hurt her feelings. He'd attacked her integrity.

If she was a man, he'd expect a punch in the mouth for that.

Hell, with the way she was glaring at him, he half expected one now.

"What do you want?"

Forget the axe. She was going to deep freeze his balls into oblivion with the ice dripping from that question.

"To apologize. Among other things."

"Yeah, well, you can take your other things and—" She glanced over her shoulder into the apartment and lowered her voice. "I think I've heard everything you have to say. Unless there was something else you forgot to accuse me of? Did any office supplies go missing while I was there? Want to search my place for some boxes of hot paper clips?"

He accepted the sting of her sarcasm as well deserved.

"I'm not here to accuse you of anything. And I'm sorry for everything I *did* accuse you of. I was an idiot."

"You were an ass."

"I was. A big one. And I'm sorry for that. For everything."

Her eyes narrowed slightly, as though trying to determine if he was being serious or not. "Saying you're sorry doesn't fix things, Rick." She sucked in a sharp breath. "Richard."

It was his name, and yet it sounded wrong coming from her mouth.

"You can still call me Rick if you want to."

"Why, so you can go on pretending you're something you're not?"

He winced.

"No. No pretending. Not anymore." He spread his arms. "This is me. No matter what you call me, I'm just a guy who fucked up, trying to fix what he broke."

An expression of infinite sadness flitted across her face. "I don't think you can."

The possibility terrified him.

"Can I at least come in so we can talk about it? Please?"

But she was already shaking her head. "Not around Derek."

"No, of course not." But she hadn't said they couldn't discuss it at all. A tiny bud of hope bloomed. "Can I take you out for coffee or something? Or we could go sit in my car if you prefer. Or right out here on the stairs. Wherever you want, whatever will make you feel the most comfortable, I'll do it."

Except give up. That he didn't think he could do, even if she put a gun to his head and demanded it.

"I don't...I have to pick up Mitch and Jesus in half an hour. We're doing the zoo today."

Right. The weekend trade-offs where the three friends rotated sleep-overs, allowing a break for the parents twice a month. Except for Amber, who used her free Saturday nights to earn extra cash.

And he'd considered her a gold digger. What a moron.

"I could go with you." Not that the zoo was the greatest place to have this conversation. But she was talking to him. He didn't want to lose that connection, or risk her having time apart to remember all the reasons she might not want to continue.

She pressed her lips together as she considered it, but then shook her head. "I don't think that would be the best thing for Derek."

Damn.

"Okay, I understand." And he did, unfortunately. "I, uh, noticed he wasn't at class this week. Is he okay?"

Fury made her eyes snap with blue fire. "No, Richard, he's not okay. He's hurt. You lied to him, too. He looked up to you!"

A shaft of shame lanced through him. "Hurting him—hurting either of you—was the last thing I wanted to do."

"Yeah, well, news flash, you did." She hesitated. "I didn't tell him...he only knows you were lying about who you are, not...not what you thought about me. He doesn't need to know that part."

Thank God.

"Agreed. Can I, um..." He cleared his throat. "It seems I owe him an apology, too. If you'll let me?" He'd seen her in full-on momma bear mode. She'd rip him to bloody shreds if he tried to get close to her kid without permission, no matter how good his intentions.

She seemed to take forever to decide. But after a few of the longest moments in his life, Amber nodded and stepped back, opening the door wider. "He's in his room."

Thankful, and humbled by her act of trust toward a man who'd had none for her, he went in and moved through the tiny apartment to the bedroom tucked behind the galley kitchen. The door was open.

Inside, Derek sat cross-legged on his bed, back against the wall, game controller clutched in his hands as he focused on the small tv perched atop a scratched and battered dresser against the opposite wall.

A quick look at the screen showed he was *not* playing MZA2.

Not a good sign, considering how obsessively he'd been working his way up the levels since the day he got his hands on it.

Not sure how he should approach this, Richard leaned his shoulder against the open door, not invading the kid's space without invitation. "Hey."

The only answer he got was the sound of a star cruiser exploding and the trill of Derek's character leveling up.

"Look, I know you're probably a little confused about what your mom told you about me—"

"Why would I be confused? You're a liar. Seems pretty simple to me." Derek's eyes stayed on the game, his tone dull and apathetic. But at least he'd spoken.

He chose to take it as a positive sign.

"You're right. I did lie about a few things, like my name, and who my family is. But *why* I lied about it isn't simple at all." Nothing. "Look, I didn't mean to hurt you or your mom."

That finally earned him a reaction. Derek shot him a look hot enough to burn.

"Well, you did. You made her cry." A battle claxon sounded, but he didn't even glance at the screen. He kept Richard pinned with accusing blue eyes so like Amber's they hurt to look into. "She doesn't think I know, but, well..." He shrugged, looking uncomfortable. "The walls are pretty thin. I could hear her at night, after she thought I was asleep."

Guilt filled him at the thought of Amber laying alone in bed sobbing into her pillow. Damn, he'd really screwed up.

"I know, Derek, and I'm incredibly sorry I said...things that made her so sad. But I'm trying to make it right. I need you to believe that."

"How can you make it right? You can't change a lie."

"No, you're right, I can't. But maybe I can explain it." He made a questioning gesture to the room. "May I?" Taking Derek's shrug as a yes, he sat on the end of the bed. "So, your mom told you who I am, right?"

"Yeah. Richard Beaumont. Your family owns like half the city or something."

"Not quite." But close.

He sighed when Derek gave another of his "whatever" shrugs. "See, that right there is part of why I didn't tell anyone at the community center my real name."

Derek's eyes narrowed in suspicion. "What?"

"Because the second you heard Beaumont, the only thing you thought was useless rich guy."

"You *are* rich."

"Yes, but that's *what* I am, not *who* I am." He struggled to come up with an explanation that would make sense to a ten-year-old. "My whole life, people have always thought of me first as a Beaumont, and only second as Richard. Even my parents, sometimes." It was the first time he'd allowed himself that admission.

Being the Beaumont heir was a tough gig, especially when he had his father's massive shoes to step into. There were days when he envied Peter and Lillian more than a little for going rogue and breaking from the expected path. Not that he didn't love his job. It was just sometimes...he started to feel like the job was all he was.

Until a curvy blonde spitfire and her son had come into his life and shook his structured existence and beliefs about himself all to hell.

"Telling you I was Rick Bowman wasn't meant as a trick or a joke on anyone. It was just my way of trying to leave the Beaumont name and the preconceptions that come with it out of the equation for a little while." Derek didn't look convinced. "Okay, tell me this. If I'd shown up the first day I took over class and told you I was Richard Beaumont, what would every kid's reaction have been?"

"Probably that you were just another rich asshole do-gooder spending an hour slumming on the poor side of town to post on your social media what a great person you are, helping out the less fortunate." Reluctance weighted Derek's words. He gave Richard a considering look. "Why *did* you take over the class?"

"Honestly? At first, because my mother asked me to fill in for a few weeks until they could find a more permanent substitute for Sensei. Her foundation helps raise the center's funding, and she's always got her ear to the ground about what's going on there."

Because Mrs. Gandy was a direct conduit to his mother. Something he'd forgotten when asking her how she'd come to choose Amber as the replacement on her ball committee. Whatever Mrs. Gandy knew, his mother knew as well.

Like seeing him leave more than once after class with Amber and Derek for pizza.

He'd go back and examine that little nugget of insight later on. Right now, he needed to focus on what he'd come here to accomplish.

"So, you're bailing the first chance you get." The flat tone was back.

He'd just been lumped back in with the rich asshole do-gooders.

"I said at first. But the more I got to know the kids in the class, the more I wanted to stay. And I am, until Sensei comes back anyway. So, no, I'm not bailing on anyone."

Including you and your mother.

"Really?"

"Really."

Derek chewed on his lower lip as he thought, something he'd seen Amber do as well. A small pang of longing made his throat tighten.

"Then why did you lie about the other stuff?"

"What other stuff?"

"About liking to hang out and eat pizza, and play video games, and...and...do stupid stuff like mini golf with me and my mom? Rich people don't do those things."

"Says who?"

"But...you can afford to do anything you want."

"And what I wanted was to do those things, with you and your mom." God help him, that was nothing but the truth. "Every single thing we did together this past month I enjoyed, because I enjoyed the people I was with. It had nothing to do with money. Does that make sense?"

"I guess." He didn't sound convinced. "But if you liked us so much, why couldn't you tell us the truth?"

He sighed. The kid didn't ask easy questions.

"Have you ever had someone pretend to like you, but it turned out to only be because they wanted something?"

After staring down at the game controller still clutched in his hands for a moment, Derek nodded. "Last year there was this popular kid in my class who started being really nice to me. Letting me sit with him and his friends at the cool table at lunch, picking me for teams in gym, that kind of thing. Turned out he just wanted to cheat off of me on the math midterm."

"How'd that make you feel?"

"Mad. And a little sad, I guess."

"And maybe a little suspicious of the next person who suddenly started acting nice to you?"

"Yeah, I guess, maybe a little."

"That's kind of how it is with me, all the time. When I was in school, my family's money was like you being good in math. There were people who wanted to be my friend not because they liked me, but because they liked what they could get from me."

Like being chauffeured around in the family limo, pool parties at the estate, seemingly unlimited funds for whatever they wanted to buy—that *he* would buy—thanks to his hefty allowance.

He'd been their own personal golden goose.

"At the time I didn't mind, because to my way of thinking, I was popular, so what difference did it make why?"

"But it did, didn't it?"

It was an insightful question for a kid his age. Richard hadn't figured that out until he was much older.

"It did. It meant I didn't know who my true friends were, and who were the freeloaders hanging around to leech off of me. So, in college, I got smarter and a lot more careful about who I gave my friendship—and my trust—to."

"And you met Max."

The obvious hero worship made him grin. "And I met Max. We roomed together for an entire semester before he knew about my family's money, and by then he didn't give a sh—darn."

Max's indifference was one reason they were still tight all these years after college. While there wasn't a single 'friend' from high school he'd bothered to stay in touch with.

"I guess that could kind of suck, always having to wonder if someone was faking being your friend." He gave Richard a sideways look. "I guess you probably had the same problem with girls, huh? Not knowing if they liked you or your money?"

Richard stared at him. "Are you sure you're only ten?" He shook his head as Derek laughed. It was a wonderful sound. "You're right, I had to be careful about that, too. Finding out a friend was using you is bad enough. Finding out your girlfriend was only with you for the presents and expensive dinners..."

"Sucks."

He nodded. "Sucks. And unfortunately, it doesn't change as you get older." Or richer. "People just get better at hiding their true intentions. The circle of people you can really trust gets regrettably small."

"Is that why you're not married?"

That surprised a laugh out of him. "Um, I guess maybe it might have something to do with it."

Hell, it had just about everything to do with it. But wise beyond his years or not, no way was he getting into a discussion with the kid about prenuptial contracts and equitable net worth.

"What about my mom?"

At first, his brain interpreted that as a suggestion he marry his mother. Stranger than the idea was the fact it didn't freak him out the way he thought it should.

In fact, it almost...intrigued him.

Then he realized what Derek was really asking.

"I know she wasn't being nice to me because of my money."

"But you thought she was. That's why you broke up with her."

"Um..." How was he supposed to answer that?

Derek rolled his eyes. "Come on. I may be a kid, but I'm not dumb."

"No, you're not."

Something he'd have to keep in mind if he was lucky enough to continue his relationship with Amber. A pat on the head and a few quarters for the arcade weren't going to cut it as a distraction. The kid was sharp.

For some reason, he felt a hint of pride about that.

"I hate to admit it, but yes, I let my suspicious nature get the best of me, and something happened to make me think maybe I'd misjudged your mom and her intentions. But I know now I was wrong, and that's why I came here to apologize and try to make up for being such an as—jerk."

"She really liked you, you know."

He winced at the past tense. "I really like her, too."

"And you made her cry."

Like he needed the reminder.

"But," Derek continued before Richard could apologize again, "before that, you made her really happy."

"She made me happy, too." He hadn't realized how much until he'd spent the past week with her hating his guts.

After pinning him with a long, thoughtful stare, Derek gave a single sharp nod. "Okay."

"Okay?"

"I accept your apology."

Air whooshed out of his lungs.

"Thank you. That really means a lot to me."

And it did. More than he'd thought it would.

Derek gave another of those expressive shrugs. "Mom says everyone should get at least one do-over card for when they screw up because no one's perfect."

"Wise woman, your mother." And hopefully one who took her own advice.

"Besides, you kind of had a good reason. I mean, being poor stinks, but I guess being rich isn't always so great, either."

"Not always, no." Not when it made you see plots and enemies where there weren't any. "So, since we're good now, what about class? Think you'll be back?"

"Yeah, I guess so."

"Good. It wasn't the same without you."

Derek's chest puffed out a little at his words. "And don't worry, I won't say anything to anyone about you being rich. Not even Mitch and Jesus."

"I appreciate it, but I don't want you to lie to your friends for me. You don't have to volunteer the information, but if it comes up, go ahead and tell them the truth."

"But didn't you say it would make things weird for you at the center?"

This time, Richard was the one who shrugged. "I've handled worse."

Like the first joint family dinner at the Delgado house over the holidays. It had been like walking into an enemy camp, all bristling hostility and veiled barbs being thrown his way. His Spanish might be a little rusty, but it was good enough to understand that much.

If he'd survived that evening, he could handle anything the kids threw at him.

"Okay, I guess."

Richard gave him a firm pat on the shoulder. "I'm done with lies, Derek. Even harmless ones, because they're really not. They'll always come back and bite you in the butt."

With that truth firmly in mind, he left Derek to his game and exited the room, intending to plead his case one more time before Amber had to leave to pick up the other kids. Once that happened, he wouldn't have the opportunity of a moment alone with her again until tomorrow evening, after Mitch and Jesus were delivered back to their parents.

He didn't think he could wait that long.

The knot in his chest would likely choke him by then.

As he closed the door behind him and stepped into the tiny galley kitchen, he stopped short. Amber was waiting there, leaning back against the counter, arms crossed tight across her belly as she stared down at the faded linoleum floor by her feet. Waiting to throw him out?

Damn it to hell

Five minutes. That's all he needed.

He hooked a thumb over his shoulder. "I, um...he accepted my apology."

"I know. I heard." Her voice was husky, as though she'd been crying. She raised her gaze to meet his. "I heard everything."

Fuck me.

She *was* crying.

"Amber..."

"I'm sorry."

He tilted his head, confused. "You're...wait, isn't that my line?"

"Yeah, but I think it's mine now, too."

That made no sense at all. With an uncomfortable glance at Derek's door, remembering his 'walls are thin' comment, he gestured toward the living room. "Is it okay if we..."

When she nodded, he followed her and hesitantly took a seat beside her on the sofa. "Now. Why should you apologize to me? I'm the one who screwed up."

Amber's fingers twisted together on her lap. "I heard what you told Derek. About people using you all your life because of your money. I never thought...well, I guess I always assumed people with money had it made. I never bought into the whole 'money can't buy you happiness' thing. But I guess there are times it really can't, can it?"

The unexpected understanding sent a wave of hope through him.

"No, it can't. Not happiness. Not trust. Not love." Her eyes widen and he cursed himself for carelessly tossing around a word neither of them was ready for, least of all him. "But regardless of my reasons, I still lied to you, and for that, I'm so, so sorry."

She sniffled and nodded. "Okay."

Since she'd admitted to listening to his conversation with her son, he wasn't sure if she'd echoed Derek's words on purpose or not. Not that it mattered. She'd accepted his apology, and that was more than he'd expected to get so soon.

"About the rest of what I said to you..."

"I get it. I don't like it, but I understand now why you might think—" She blew out a breath when Derek yelled "Mom, are we going or what?" from his room. After checking her watch, she cursed under her breath and stood. "I'm sorry. I have to go get the kids."

He stood as well, tamping down his disappointment and frustration. "It's okay. This can wait until it's the right time." He hesitated before adding, "As long as I know there's going to be a right time." He left it more question than statement.

Looking adorably shy, she bit her lip and nodded. "There will be. You deserve to have your say."

"Good." He grinned when Derek yelled "Mom, kiss him and make up already, we're going to be late!", enjoying the way Amber blushed. "I think that's my cue to leave."

"Do you still want to come to the zoo with us?"

The offer stopped him in the act of turning toward the door. He looked at her with surprise. "Yeah?"

"Unless you have other plans?"

"I can't think of a way I'd rather spend the day."

Except maybe wrapped in her arms. But he was a smart enough businessman to know when not to push too hard. She was willing to spend the day in his company.

For now, it would have to be enough.

Chapter 12

The afternoon had been...illuminating.

It certainly wasn't the way she'd been expecting to spend the day. But as Amber pulled into the parking lot in front of her building, she was very glad she'd extended the impulsive invitation for Rick to join them.

Not that they'd resolved the major issue still laying between them. Or even brought it up. The way he'd attacked her with his suspicions at his office the other day, and the indecent proposal he'd made, was still a silent, festering topic they'd both, in unspoken agreement, left untouched for the time being.

But it was still there.

Waiting.

Throbbing, right below the surface. And not in a good way.

Somehow, she'd been able to ignore it and have a good time at the zoo. A fact she attributed to having overheard—okay, shamelessly eavesdropped on—the conversation Rick had with Derek. At least now she had a better understanding of *why* that ugly scene happened. The honest hurt in his tone when he'd talked about women only being with him for his wallet had lanced a little of the resentment from the wound he'd left.

It also made her question what was wrong with them all. Hell's bells, the man was sweet, and smart, and incredibly, deliciously yummy. What woman overlooked all of that in favor of a bank balance?

A stupid one, that's who.

Or a greedy one.

Trailer trash without a pot to piss in will always look for a payday using what's between their legs to bargain with.

The echo of Mrs. King's words to her husband as though Amber hadn't been standing right there in front of them, young, terrified, and pregnant, put a damper on her upbeat mood. She knew now that wasn't how Rick saw her. Not exactly. But it didn't stop the old insecurities from making her confidence shrivel a little.

How far was the stretch really between trailer trash and gold digger?

As three sweaty, over-sugared kids piled out of the backseat of her rattling old Ford—*please don't let the muffler fall off until after the holidays when I can afford a new one*—she glanced at the man sitting in her passenger seat.

Though he'd offered to drive, she'd wanted the small amount of control taking her own car gave her. She'd expected him to argue, but he didn't put up a peep of protest.

Of course, that hadn't stopped him from hitting the non-existent brake pedal on the passenger side floor a few times on the drive home from Denver. Clearly, he wasn't a man used to being driven around despite his wealth. She found that oddly comforting.

Then again, it might have just been commentary on her driving.

"What's the smile for?"

Like she'd cop to that.

"Just thinking I had a really nice time today."

"So did I." He reached over and took her hand lightly in his. "Thank you for inviting me along."

It was the first time he'd touched her all day, other than when he'd used his quick reflexes to twist them both out of the way of two teens barreling through the crowd outside the reptile house.

The rest of the time, he'd been at her side but seemed hesitant to cross the physical boundary that still separated them.

So had she.

Now, though, feeling his strong fingers slide over hers in a gentle caress was like the return of something lost being found again.

She wanted to stay angry with him. She had a right to be angry, damn it. But after hearing him admit to Derek that he liked her, something he'd had no reason to say unless it was the truth, she was finding it harder and harder to hang onto the hurt.

And then he'd cared enough to be sure his actions wouldn't cause her son to give up the karate class he loved so much. Again, something he had nothing to gain by doing.

Except her gratitude.

And maybe another slice of her forgiveness.

Rick ran his thumb over the back of her hand. "So, I know you have the boys tonight, but would it be okay if I came over tomorrow night?"

She knew what he was really asking. Could they finish having the talk they'd started that morning. The thought both calmed and terrified her. "Yes."

"I could bring dinner."

"I think I still owe you a meal." Probably not smart, bringing up the shadow of what caused their last dinner plans to be so abruptly discarded. But if they were ever going to get past it, they needed to tackle it head on, not dance around it.

Something warmed in his eyes. "Then how about I bring dessert?"

"Sounds good."

That would have been the perfect time for them both to get out of the car and go their separate ways. Instead, they both sat, unmoving except for Rick's thumb as it traced in steady sweeps over her skin. It was as though that one small section of nerves was suddenly connected to the rest of her body, making every inch of it tingle with each movement.

"I should probably go." Was that breathy whisper her voice?

"Yeah, me too."

And still neither of them moved.

Finally, with a small shudder that ran core-deep, she withdrew her hand. "Okay, really going now." The heat in Rick's gaze told her he'd felt the ripple of arousal that had rolled through her. To his credit, he didn't try to press his advantage.

Thank God, because she wasn't entirely sure she'd be able to resist.

Which was why when they got out of the car, she waved off his attempt to walk her inside. For a moment she thought he'd argue, since he'd insisted on the courteous gesture every other time he'd brought her home, no matter how many times she said it wasn't necessary.

To her relief, he nodded and gave a tight smile. "Okay. Goodnight."

"Goodnight." There was another of those awkward pauses where neither of them moved before Rick muttered something under his breath and swung away toward where his car was parked a few rows over.

She indulged in a moment of pure visual pleasure as he walked away. As her mother would have said, *Lordy, that man could fill out a pair of Levis like nobody's business.*

Reigning in her wayward hormones before she got caught gawking, she headed inside. Derek had a key, so she didn't have to worry about the kids being left waiting in the hall, but she still didn't like them out of her sight for more than a few minutes.

Derek alone she could trust to behave. Usually. Leaving the three of them hyper and unsupervised, however, was asking for trouble, and she didn't need any more of that in her life, thank you very much.

Speaking of trouble...

Hunter had been conspicuously absent since his unwelcome appearance at her door exactly one week ago, despite his threat to return in a few days. She didn't know whether to be relieved or concerned. It was too much to hope he'd decided to forget his ridiculous scheme of blackmailing her to squeeze money out of her supposed boyfriend, Max.

Without Rick to ask for advice after their falling out, and short of packing what little they owned into her car and making a run for it, the only solution she'd been able to see was to face him with her one and only weapon. The truth.

No matter what he wanted, no matter what he threatened her with, there was no way on God's green earth she was getting money from Max Woodward, because she barely knew the man.

Period. End of story.

She could only hope Hunter wouldn't see any benefit to following through with his threats to try and snatch Derek away from her once he knew there was no pot of gold at the end of this particular rainbow. His actions were motivated entirely by greed. There hadn't been a drop of paternal desire in evidence when he talked about his son. If there was, it wouldn't have taken him ten years to show up on her doorstep. If he had nothing left to gain, then hopefully he'd slither back to Texas and forget she and Derek existed.

Again.

If only she could convince him he was wrong about her and Max. Maybe now that things were getting better with Rick again, she could ask him what he thought she should—

She stopped short on the top tread of the staircase as the truth hit her with enough force to nearly knock her over backwards. Oh, damn. Damn, damn, damn. She might not have Max, but she *did* have Rick. Sort of. Maybe. Hopefully.

Rick, who was really Richard.

Who was as rich—or maybe even richer—than Max.

And if Hunter ever found that out...

There would be no surer way to convince Rick he'd been right about her all along than having Hunter shift his greedy attention in his direction.

"Son of a biscuit!"

Nauseated by the spectacular irony of it all, she let herself into the apartment. The boys were nowhere to be seen or heard, which meant they were already planted in front of the tv in Derek's room. Well, at least she'd forced them out into the fresh air and sunshine for an afternoon. Spending the rest of the evening holed up playing video games wouldn't kill them.

And it would give her some time to think.

How could she possibly ask Rick for his help now? Or even tell him about Hunter and his dirty scheme? Any way she put it, it would sound like she had her hand out, expecting him to take care of her problem for her. Either by paying Hunter off, or running him off.

She sank to the sofa with a groan.

No. She refused to be just another woman who used him. He might be rich, and he might be intimidating when he put on that business mogul face of his. But she was from Texas, damn it. She could kick ass and take names, and she didn't need any man to do it for her. She'd fix this mess herself.

Somehow.

"Boys! Lunch!"

Almost before the words were out, a herd of hungry wildebeest came galloping out of Derek's room to the tiny cubby laughingly called a dining room by the property manager. At least, that's what it sounded like.

In reality, it was just three recharged adolescents who were already about to get on her last nerve. After Sunday breakfast and a brief trip to the park to let them run off a little energy before the drizzling rain started, they were crammed back into her shoebox apartment and getting restless.

So was she.

Although, to be fair, her edginess had less to do with being cooped up and everything to do with waiting for the proverbial other shoe to smack her in the face. With Hunter's reappearance a constant possibility, and Rick coming over later, it seemed like the perfect storm was brewing for ultimate disaster.

Melodramatic much, Amber Lee?

"Uh-uh," she said when the boys each tried to grab a peanut butter and jelly sandwich from the piled platter and escape back into Derek's room. "Eat at the table, then wash your hands before going back to your games."

There was a little grumbling in the ranks, but they complied, slouching into their seats with heavy sighs. At least she still had control over one small corner of her life.

The knock at the door signaled the other part she didn't.

A quick peek through the peephole confirmed her suspicions. Much as she didn't want to have this confrontation with him, and especially not with Derek anywhere in the vicinity, it was almost a relief he'd finally shown up. At least now she could stop wondering and worrying every minute.

And bonus, now he wouldn't show up later when Rick was here.

Nerves twitching like a horse approaching a starting gate, she turned back and fought to keep her expression normal. "Boys, on second thought, go ahead and take your sandwiches with you and play your game. Just be sure not to make a mess, okay?"

Her bending of the rules was met with whoops of delight as Mitch and Jesus grabbed their glasses of milk and plates and disappeared.

Derek, however, looked first at her, then the door, suspicion written on his pinched face. "Mom?"

The concern in his young voice almost made her tear up. "It's okay, baby. I just have to talk to someone. Grownup stuff, nothing to worry about. Go back in your room and close the door." She hesitated. "And don't come out unless I tell you to, okay?"

Because the last thing she wanted was for him to meet his father like this. And she wouldn't put it past Hunter to hurt Derek on purpose if he knew it would hurt her, too.

Especially after she told him no.

She waited until Derek reluctantly complied before turning back to the door. On impulse, she grabbed her phone and shoved it in her back pocket before steeling herself and opening the door as Hunter was raising his fist to knock again.

"Took you long enough. I thought you were going to pretend you weren't home."

If she wasn't so anxious to get this over with, she might have been tempted to do just that. "Well, here I am."

Hunter looked at her expectantly. "Aren't you going to invite me in so we can...*talk*?"

"No."

He blinked at the flat refusal. "No? Have you forgotten what it was we needed to discuss, darlin'? How *sensitive* some of that information is to certain ears?"

"I haven't forgotten a thing." And sensitive ears were exactly why she wasn't letting the bastard in. "We can talk right here, or not at all."

A scowl pulled at Hunter's mouth, highlighting the lines that ridged it and the puffy bags under his bloodshot eyes. After growing up one trailer over from the heavy-drinking Parker family, it was easy to spot the lingering effects of a night of overindulgence.

Good. I hope his head aches so bad it pops right off his neck.

"Fine, then. I guess that means you have good news for me."

"Then you'd guess wrong."

The scowl pulled deeper. "I don't think you appreciate the gravity of the situation you find yourself in, Amber Lee. Or have you forgotten exactly what it is you have to lose here?"

A punch of panic threatened to destroy the calm front she was presenting, but she fought it down.

Kick ass and take names, kick ass and take names…

She squared her shoulders.

"The thing is, *darlin'*, you're working under a faulty assumption. Yes, I attended a party. Yes, I had my picture taken with Max Woodward, and yes, I was even introduced to him. But I am not, nor have I ever been, in a romantic relationship with the man."

"Who said anything about romance?"

Ignoring the scoffing jab, she soldiered on.

"So, no matter what you want, no matter what you threaten, it won't make any difference. I can't give you any money, because I can't *get* any money."

"Bullshit," he snapped. "Don't try to jerk me around, you stupid bitch."

From darlin' to bitch in less than two minutes. How had she ever thought this man was charming?

"I'm not jerking anything. I'm telling you the God's honest truth. I met the man exactly one time. He has no reason to give me a dime, much less the amount you want."

The scowl shifted to a sneaky smirk. "I guess since you won't be able to do your part in this, I'll just be going inside to say hello to *my son*. In fact, I think it would be a real good idea to take him back home to Perrytown so he can get to know his grandparents for a spell. You know, the ones who haven't seen him since he was born?"

She whipped her phone out and dialed 911 without hitting send. "Try it, and I'll have your ass in jail for kidnapping before you get to the end of the block." She showed him the screen to prove she wasn't bluffing.

"You can't kidnap your own blood."

"Uh, yeah, you can, actually. You never claimed paternity, so legally you don't have any custodial rights." Not until a DNA test proved his claim, anyway. With luck, she'd be able to bluff her way through this before Hunter figured that out.

"Well, then, I'll just tell them how you stole my son from me, and how I finally tracked you here all the way from Texas. Who do you think they'll arrest as a kidnapper then?"

"Still you. Did you forget it's my name on his birth certificate, not yours?"

It was clear from the fury burning in his eyes that he had, and that he wasn't expecting her to push back against his threats like this. And why should he? They'd worked on her the last time around when his parents made them.

It was just too bad for him she wasn't the same scared, naïve girl she'd been ten years ago.

Not that she wasn't as terrified now as she'd been then. Hunter still had his family name and money to back him up. All she had was the hope the courts here in Colorado wouldn't be influenced by either. But unlike her seventeen-year-old self, she knew better than to let her fear show.

"You're making a huge mistake."

No, she'd done that a long time ago.

"Go back to Texas, Hunter." She couldn't keep the edge of weariness out of her voice. "There's nothing for you here." She tensed when she saw his eyes dart past her shoulder into the apartment, as though contemplating pushing past her and making good on his threat to grab Derek.

But instead, he gave a smile that made the hairs on her neck rise.

"Sure thing, darlin'. I'll go if that's what you really want. Just be sure to tell my boy I came by to see him. Again." He lowered his voice to add, "You'll be sorry you fucked with me on this, Amber Lee. And that's a promise you can take to the bank."

She didn't have to wonder long why Hunter suddenly turned on the wronged-party expression and said what he did before stomping down the hall. With the hairs still twitching on her neck, she turned. Derek was standing by the kitchen opening, staring at her.

No, staring at the empty space in the open doorway where Hunter had been.

"Derek." She didn't know what else to say.

His throat worked as he swallowed hard. "Was that...was that my dad?"

Shit, shit, shit.

She was going to kill Hunter for this. "Yes, baby, it was. But whatever you heard, it wasn't what it sounded like."

"It sounded like he was threatening you."

Okay, it was what it sounded like.

Her eyes narrowed. "Just how long were you standing there listening?"

"Long enough to know he's not anything like you told me he was." The disappointment was clear in his expression, but his tone held a note of disgust.

"Baby, he's...it's complicated."

"That's what grownups always say when they don't want to explain stuff." He shook his head when she started to protest. "You know what? Whatever. I don't care."

The slam of the door to his room said otherwise.

Emotions churning, Amber carefully closed the apartment door when all she wanted was to give it a good slam of her own. She might have solved one of her problems, but Hunter, the bastard, had left her a parting gift of an even bigger one. One with the potential to forever damage the relationship she had with her son.

She'd never lied to Derek about who his father was. But she might have painted a slightly nicer picture of him and the events surrounding Derek's conception and birth than were entirely accurate. And she certainly hadn't told him how they were all but run out of town by his own grandparents.

Lies and omissions. Hadn't Rick just been telling Derek about how even the most harmless ones could come back to bite you in the butt? Well, hers had just had a chunk the size of Denver taken out of it.

Rick.

Oh, lordy. He was due over in about—she checked her watch in a panic—four hours. How could she get through a dinner with him when she needed to deal with the Derek/Hunter disaster first?

And she couldn't even start on that until the boys went home at three. Which meant she'd have two whole hours to clean up the collateral damage Hunter's parting shot had caused with Derek before moving onto the *next* damaged relationship in her life.

Lord, give me strength.

She should cancel. It was too much to deal with all at once. But even as she raised her phone to dial, she hesitated. What message would that send to Rick? It could very well set their tenuous reconciliation back to the beginning again.

Or worse.

Especially since she couldn't exactly tell him *why* she was cancelling. Not without spilling the rest of the beans about Hunter and his stupid blackmail scheme. Which could *also* send their relationship back off course.

The weight of it all sat on her chest, making it hard to breathe. All she wanted to do was curl up on the floor and cry, kick, and scream out her frustration at the unfairness of it all. Couldn't something good happen in her life, just once, without there being an equally awful something to suck all the joy out of it for her?

Life ain't fair, Amber Lee. Never has been, never will be. All you can do sometimes is learn to smile through the pain.

"Not helpful, Momma," she muttered as she forced one foot in front of the other toward the kitchen. She'd start putting the lasagna together for dinner. Then, after the boys left, she'd see if Derek was in any mood to listen to what she had to say.

He wasn't.

After closing the apartment door behind Mitch and his mother, Amber went and knocked on Derek's door. When he didn't answer, she tried again. "Derek? Can I come in, please?" Still nothing. She knocked a little harder. "Derek?"

"Whatever."

Not exactly a warm invitation, but she'd take it.

Pushing the door open, she studied her son's downturned head for a moment as he pretended to be engrossed in the latest gamer magazine she'd brought home for him. Thanks to seeing Hunter again, there were so many similarities between him and her son she'd never realized before that she could see now, from the slope of his nose to the way his hair slipped over his left eye when he was reading.

And the petulance.

The longer he ignored her, the better she remembered that about Hunter, too. Most of the time, he was everyone's buddy. But if he ever felt slighted, best watch out. It was like you'd turned into the invisible man. And not just with him. When you were the class president and captain of the football team, people emulated you. If you liked someone, everyone liked them. If you snubbed someone, it was like they'd suddenly come down with the plague.

And she would know. Her last months of junior year had been pure hell.

Well, that was one similarity she could nip in the bud. Walking in, she sat on the end of the bed. "I want to talk to you about what you overheard earlier, between me and your father."

She nearly choked on those words, but they were nicer than sperm donor, which was all he'd ever really been.

"You don't have to."

"Yes, I do." After another moment of staring at the top of his head, she gave an annoyed growl and plucked the magazine from his fingers. "I don't appreciate being ignored, young man. I taught you better manners than that." She waited until he gave her his full attention. "Now, you probably have questions about who your dad is, so go ahead and ask."

He shrugged. "Not really. I already knew who he was."

"You..." Her mouth hung open as words deserted her.

"Mom, come on. It wasn't all that hard to figure out."

"How?"

"You slipped once and used his first name, like, a year ago. And I know where I was born. So, I used the computer at the library to Google him."

God save her from having a smart kid.

"You could have just asked me if you really wanted to know about him."

"I did, but all you ever said were things like he was just too young to handle being a dad, and he loved me even if he couldn't be around." His expression hardened. "None of that was true, was it?"

"It's—"

"Complicated," he said with her, disgust twisting his lips. "Right. Whatever."

She was really starting to hate that word.

"Fine. You're right. I probably should have told you more about him. But honestly, he wasn't ever going to be a part of our lives, so I didn't want to say bad things about him and make you hate him."

"Why shouldn't I hate him? He didn't want me."

"Yes. But try to remember, he was only eighteen."

"Well, you were only seventeen, so that shouldn't matter."

As soon as he'd started being able to do math, she'd known it would be impossible to keep the truth of her age when he was born a secret. Instead, she'd been very matter-of-fact about it, and he'd never acted like it made any difference.

But it was clear he was old enough now to understand the implications.

"No, it shouldn't." Because he was right. Hunter *had* been old enough to take responsibility for his actions. Leaving her to deal with the consequences on her own was a shitty, cowardly thing to do.

She just hadn't realized how much his abandonment had affected Derek.

"But *I* wanted you. And your Grandma Ruby wanted you. We loved you from the second the nurse put you all red-faced and crying in my arms, and I've never stopped once."

"Even though I ruined your life?"

Reaching out, she cupped his face to ensure he looked at her. "Listen to me. You did not ruin my life, understand? You're the very best part of it. I thank God every day that you're mine. I'd be lost without you."

She let out a soft *oof* when Derek launched himself into her arms, hugging her tight, face buried in her shoulder. Probably to hide the tears she'd seen glistening in his eyes.

"Love you." His words were muffled and a little rough.

"I love you, too, baby." She dropped a kiss on his head and squeezed him tight. "Your father made a huge mistake when he gave you up, and he's too stupid to even realize it. He'll never know what he's missing."

And with any luck at all, Derek would never know the full truth of what a rat bastard his father really was.

She'd make sure of it.

Chapter 13

"This has to be some of the best apple pie I've ever had."

"Glad you liked it." Richard watched as Amber scraped the tines of her fork against the plate to capture the last stray pieces of gooey fruit before licking it clean. He swallowed and looked away. It was totally not cool to pop wood with her kid sitting across the table, but Jesus, what that mouth did to his self-control.

Shifting in his chair, he concentrated on the last few bites of his own dessert, doing his best to get the image out of his brain.

For once, his best just wasn't good enough.

Derek held out his empty plate. "Can I have another piece?"

Richard bit back a laugh. The kid had practically inhaled the first slice, along with a huge scoop of the vanilla ice cream he'd brought to go with it. On top of a gigantic piece of the lasagna Amber served for dinner.

And after all that, he still managed to give the impression of a starving urchin begging for food in some Dickensian play.

A look his mother must have seen a million times, because it had no effect.

"It's may I, and no. Not unless you want to be up all night with a stomachache."

The kid heaved a sigh worthy of the stage. "Then *may I* be excused?"

Amber nodded and added as he popped up from his chair, "Put your dishes in the sink."

"'kay." He grabbed his dirty plate and glass and started for the kitchen before pausing to look back at Richard. "Thanks for the dessert."

"You're welcome. Thanks for sharing your dinner with me."

Derek looked from him to his mother and back. "I'll say goodnight now, since I won't be coming out of my room again. For anything," he added with extra emphasis, in case Richard missed his point. "And I'll be using my headphones to watch a movie, so the noise doesn't bother you."

Christ. All that was missing was a thumb's up and a wink.

Not sure how he felt about being given the green light by a ten-year-old, he tipped his head in a half-nod. "Goodnight." He looked at Amber, whose napkin was pressed to her mouth to hold back whatever reaction her son's pronouncement caused.

When her eyes caught his, he saw it was mirth.

"I'm so sorry," she said after Derek's door closed with a little more emphasis than normal. "I don't know what got into him." Though even as she said it, something flickered across her expression, draining the laughter from it.

"What?"

She shook her head. "Nothing. Let me get these dishes into the sink."

It wasn't nothing. There'd been a strange vibe in the air all evening. He'd thought it had to do with him, but now he wasn't so sure.

He stood, picking up his own plate and coffee cup before she could. "I've got it." He took the few steps to the kitchen. "How about I wash and you dry?"

"Oh, I was just going to do them later."

"You already went to the trouble of cooking. The least I can do is help clean up." Especially since he'd noticed she didn't have a dishwasher in that closet-sized kitchen of hers. He put his dishes in the sink with the ones from dinner, then took hers from her hands and added them as well.

Then, because she looked so adorably flustered, he couldn't help teasing her by picking up the sponge from the lip of the sink and screwing on a puzzled expression. "Now, how do I work one of these again?"

After a second of shocked silence, she smacked his shoulder and laughed. "You jerk."

He soaked up the sound of her laughter like a man dying of thirst. Without giving her another chance to protest, he made good on his offer and got started on the dishes.

When he was rinsing the last plate, he frowned over a good-sized chip on the edge.

"Damn, did I do that?"

"No, it came chipped." She snatched the plate from him and gave it a brisk rub with the dish towel. "Most of my stuff comes from either thrift stores, yard sales, or consignment shops. You'd be surprised what great things you can find there." She put the plate in the cupboard and turned to give him a defiant glare, begging him to comment.

"There's nothing wrong with giving things a second life. The world's become much too disposable these days. Use it once, throw it out, buy something newer and better to replace it." He paused. "But you've still made sure all of Derek's stuff is new, though."

That much he'd noticed. Clothes, sneakers, school backpack...not pricey name brands, but good quality and store-bought all the same.

Amber hesitated. That obviously wasn't what she'd expected him to say.

"Yeah, well, I know how it feels to be the kid with the hand-me-down clothes at school. There's nothing more humiliating than having one of your classmates notice you're wearing one of her old outfits that went to Goodwill. I didn't want that for him."

She glanced at the door to his bedroom, all the love and worry she felt for him clearly etched on her face. "I know he said he'd be wearing his headset, but..." She tipped her head toward the living room.

As soon as they settled on the sofa, much too far apart for his liking, he asked, "Is everything okay? I kind of got the feeling there was something wrong. Something besides our something."

"Um..." Blinking like Bambi on a four-lane highway, she straightened the hem of the flowy black and red wraparound dress she wore. "It's nothing, really. Derek and I just had a, well, not an argument, but a discussion earlier. About his father."

There was no good reason for it, but that news rubbed him on the raw. "I thought he wasn't a part of Derek's life."

"He wasn't. He isn't. He just...it wasn't a very pleasant conversation, and I'd really rather not talk about it, or him, if you don't mind."

"Okay. I'd rather talk about us, anyway."

But a part of him wanted to know why this up-till-now absent dad suddenly came up in conversation, today of all days. Was it because of Richard being—hopefully—in their lives again? Perhaps on a more permanent basis? Was Derek wondering if that might make Richard start thinking and acting in a more paternal role? Was Amber?

Was *he*?

The thought didn't totally terrify him. Which in itself should have scared the crap out of him. But no, the only thing that did that was the possibility of not earning this woman's trust back.

Without it, he'd never get a second chance with her.

"I know I already apologized, but I don't think I can say it enough times to make up for what an ass I was. I should have told you who I was before our first date, and I certainly shouldn't have suggested what I did about continuing our acquaintance for the sex."

That bit of idiocy still ate at him.

"My only defense is that I panicked and said the first stupid thing that popped into my head when I thought of you walking out of my life for good. You deserved so much better from me, and I'm so damn sorry I hurt you."

No mere words could convey just how sorry he was, but he had to start somewhere. If he had to, he'd even do some of the groveling Rafe suggested.

Whatever it took, he'd do it.

"I know you are. And I even understand why you might have thought I'd be happy to trade on my body to get what I want." Her expression soured. "It seems to be the popular opinion lately." Amber shook her head before he could ask what she meant. "Never mind. Different stuff. We need to concentrate on this stuff. Our stuff."

He didn't like it, but she was right. They needed to clear up the issues between them first.

Then he could find out who or what put that bleak look on her face and hand them their ass for it.

"Whoever thinks that is wrong," he said, reaching out to take her hand. "Including me. *Especially* me. You're one of the strongest, most independent women I know. It's true," he said when she scoffed. "You actually remind me a lot of my mother and sister that way."

"I don't feel strong and independent right now, but thank you." She squeezed his hand. "And since I've met your mother, I'll take that as a huge compliment."

"You should. Mom can be pretty kick-ass when she needs to be."

She quirked a brow. "Kick-ass? Mrs. Beaumont?"

"In a pearls-and-high-heels kind of way, but yeah." His mother might be refined, but she didn't take shit from anyone. Most especially her kids. "So…I know I haven't earned the right to ask yet, but I'm going to anyway because it's making me crazy. Do you forgive me? *Can* you forgive me?"

The wait for her answer felt like the frames in an action movie, wondering if the bomb would either explode or be defused. Every second ticked by with painful slowness as the tension ratcheted higher and higher.

Her face, for once, gave nothing away. He'd gotten so used to reading her always open expressions, it was like having a blindfold suddenly put on.

He didn't like it one little bit.

Her honest reactions were something he'd treasured without even realizing it. If he'd caused her to lose that refreshing openness with his cynicism and derision, he'd add his own ass to the top of the 'needs to be kicked' list.

"You hurt me a lot," she said finally, her voice a little wavery, "but yes, I think I can."

Relief swept through him, though his elation was tempered by the fact she'd said "can" and not "have." But he could work with that. Now that she'd opened the door to the possibility, he'd do whatever it took to earn her complete forgiveness.

Even if it took a lifetime.

"Thank you." He wanted nothing more than to grab her up in his arms and kiss her until they were both totally breathless, but settled for raising her hand to his mouth for a lingering kiss on her knuckles. He was rewarded by a tiny shudder that ended with her breath catching. "I won't give you any reason to regret it." He dropped another kiss on her hand before releasing it. "I promise."

"I, um, good. That's good." She gave a shaky laugh as she cradled her hand to her chest. "Has anyone ever told you how potent that sex appeal of yours is?"

"Really? You think so?"

"I know so. You're a dangerous man, Richard Beaumont." She bit her lip.

It was the first time she'd used his full name, and it looked like it stunned her for a second.

Not about to let her get too far inside her own head thinking about it and set back the progress they'd made, he gave her a lazy grin. "Actually, I don't think it's so much either you or me, but us."

"Us?"

"We wouldn't both be feeling like this if there wasn't something special between us. You're sexy as hell, sweetheart, but no other woman has made me feel this way just by being in the same room with her."

"Oh?" Her pink tongue darted out to moisten her lips. "And how do you feel?"

"You sure you want to know?"

His groin tightened when she gave a tiny nod.

Locking his gaze on hers, he said, "Achy. Needy. Like there's a thousand fire ants marching all over my skin. Hard as a rock." He groaned when her gaze flicked down to his lap and back, her cheeks pinkening. "It's wrong, I know. You're mad as hell at me, and all I've touched tonight is your damn hand, but it wouldn't take much more than a stiff breeze to finish me off. *That's* how much you affect me."

"Me too," she whispered. "You do that to me, too. It's...almost too much."

"And still not enough."

"No. It's not." Without warning, Amber closed the distance between them and kissed him. Unlike the increasingly hot and heavy embraces they'd shared in the past, this one was soft and gentle. Passionate, yet restrained.

A new promise.

A new beginning.

He groaned softly against her mouth. She tasted sweet and spicy, like the apple pie they'd had for dessert. But under that was just Amber. Her taste, her smell, her feel...they were so ingrained in him now, even in a pitch-dark room he'd know it was her.

When she finally broke off the kiss, her forehead pressed to his as they both fought to steady their breathing. He asked, "Too much?"

To his everlasting gratitude, she shook her head. "Not nearly enough."

In one lithe move, she slid her leg over his, straddling his lap as she faced him. She cupped his face in gentle hands, but the kiss that followed was anything but.

Her sharp little teeth nipping at his lower lip to demand entrance nearly sent him over the edge. His erection pulsed in response. Still wary of moving too fast, he let her set the pace, even though the heat of her radiating through the thin barrier of her panties was like an unbearable erotic tease.

Every touch she gave, he gave her back. For every kiss, every lick, every sound, he made sure she knew he was right there with her, willing to follow wherever she would lead.

If they'd been alone in the apartment, that might have been to bed.

But they weren't.

Which was why the moment he felt himself approaching a point of no return as she slowly ground herself against him, mouth hot and wet on his neck as he caressed her through the soft cotton of her dress, he forced his hands to her hips to still her undulating movements. It took a moment for her to comply, as lost in the tidal pool of sensations as he'd been.

"Amber. Sweetheart." He pressed a soft kiss to her temple, waiting for the glaze of arousal to fade from her eyes. "Even though I'd love to do this all night long, I'm afraid I'm about to embarrass myself here. And as much as I might enjoy it, it wouldn't make for a very comfortable ride home afterward."

She looked at him for a second as his words processed. Then the little witch smiled slowly and gave her lower body a small shimmy.

"You could always go home commando."

It was so tempting, and he was so damn close. But he sucked in a wild breath and grabbed hold of the last threads of self-control he had left. Hands still on her hips, he used his upper body strength to slide her back on his thighs a few inches. The loss of her heat on his groin made him want to growl.

Still, it was the right thing to do.

Damn it.

Caressing her pouting lower lip with his thumb, he said, "When I get to come with you, it's going to be long, loud, and dirty. I promise it will be worth the wait." From the way her eyes dilated, she liked that idea. "I can give you some relief before I go, though, if you want."

Slowly, she shook her head. "I want to be loud and dirty, too." She curled her tongue around his thumb for a sensuous lick. "I'll wait."

"*Jesus*!" He pulled her toward him, devouring her mouth, eating the little kitten sounds purring from her throat as he kneaded her swollen breasts, thumbing the hard tips he was desperate to uncover and taste but which would, for now, still have to remain a mystery yet to be savored.

With a curse, he wrenched back and threw his head against the cushion, chest heaving. "If I don't leave now, all my good intentions are going right out the window." Along with his sanity.

She sighed, but slid off his lap, collapsing on the sofa beside him as though her bones had gone to jelly. "Too much?"

There was a thin thread of uncertainty in her voice, surprising him. He swiveled his head to look at her.

"Never enough."

———◦———

Hot. Damn.

The man knew how to give good eye contact. The heat and promise she saw in that dreamy brown gaze was enough to send her lady bits into overdrive. Not that they weren't already fully revved. Holy hell, when was the last time a man almost made her orgasm with all her clothes still on?

That would be never.

She smiled and ran a caress down his arm, ending at his hand where she twined her fingers with his. "Thank you."

"For?"

"Understanding why I can't...*we* can't...do this here, now. And for being the one to know when to put on the brakes." That part was a little embarrassing. At the same time, it meant a hell of a lot more to her than any promises or apologies he could make.

For a man to be in enough control to pull back the way he did, for the sake of her kid, especially when she was egging him on? It showed while he wanted her—and lordy, she'd felt just how *much* of him wanted her—it really wasn't all about the sex for him.

The thought made her a little giddy.

So did the memory of his rock-hard erection doing delicious things to her clit. And that was through several layers of clothing. Imagining how much better it would be skin-to-skin made her entire body flush with heat.

Rick let out a soft groan. "Don't look at me like that." He rose jerkily to his feet, pulling her up along with him. "I should go."

No, you should come.

Shushing her inner hussy, she allowed him to tug her to the door. A hundred different things to say ran through her head like rabid rabbits, but not a single one of them seemed right. Because things still weren't a hundred percent settled between them. She was still mad at him.

At least, she should be.

But somehow the man had snuck beneath her defenses and salved the wound he'd sliced into her heart and soul. It wasn't healed yet, but it was on its way. Her pride, though, might take a little longer to scab over.

Her hormones were clearly over it entirely.

Rick turned to her at the door. "Thanks again for inviting me."

She knew he wasn't just thanking her for the meal. "I'm glad I did." The smile she got from those words sent another hot flash through her, making her breasts ache.

"Can I take you out this weekend? Just the two of us?"

"Um..." It took a second to unscramble her brain enough to remember her schedule. She'd been planning to pick up a shift at the restaurant, since Derek would be at Jesus's. His birthday was less than six weeks away, and Christmas a little over a month after that. Even if she didn't need to buy the new MZA2 game anymore, she should still be socking away every extra dollar she could make.

But maybe...maybe it was time to be a tiny bit selfish and claim one weekend for herself. To see where things could go. To see if this could be something real.

Before her practical side had time to talk her out of it, she smiled. "I'd love that." Her heart gave a little thump. There. She was committed.

She just hoped she wasn't making a mistake.

After a goodnight kiss that threatened to destroy both their good intentions, she closed the door behind him, leaning against it with a sigh as she struggled to bring her body under control. This was stupid. It was crazy. She knew what happened when a woman like her tried to fit with a man like him. And yet...

Rick was nothing like Hunter.

Maybe it was time she stopped using her bad experience with him as a measuring stick. Hunter was, and always had been, a selfish prick. She'd just been too blinded by his looks and charm to realize it until it was too late.

Rick, on the other hand, had already proven that while he wasn't perfect, he was normally kind, considerate, and willing to delay his own gratification until circumstances were more private.

Like they'd be this weekend.

She pressed a hand to her belly, where nerves started doing a little do-si-do at the thought of finally getting naked with him. It had been a long time for her. Too long. What if she couldn't satisfy him? What if he was turned off by her body? She stayed fit, but there were effects from pregnancy and birth no amount of working out could erase.

Stretch marks were forever.

Before she could work herself into a panic over things she couldn't control, she pushed all thoughts of next weekend and whatever might or might not occur to the back of her mind. She had an entire week to get through before then. If she spent all of it obsessing about everything that could go wrong, she'd be a nervous wreck long before Saturday ever arrived.

After putting the kitchen to rights, she gave a tentative knock on Derek's door. When he didn't answer, she opened it a few inches to peek in. True to his word, he was sprawled across the bed on his belly, headphones on, watching one of the Transformers movies for probably the hundredth time.

She stood there for a moment and just looked.

No matter what else happened, Derek was the one shining prize that made going through all the crappy stuff worth it. He was the light of her life. Her best thing ever. And despite the threat of Hunter doing something underhanded and nasty still hanging over their heads, she wouldn't change a single thing about what had happened between them, because it had given her Derek.

Okay, maybe she'd change him coming back into their lives at the very worst time possible.

And that he'd hurt Derek on purpose.

And that he was such a douchebag.

She moved into the room to catch Derek's attention to say goodnight, only to realize he was sound asleep. Shaking her head at how he could zonk out anywhere, anytime, she turned off the tv and slid the headset off him.

He half woke up while she was maneuvering his limp body under the covers, squirming into place with a grunted "g'nite" before passing out cold again even before she pressed a kiss to his forehead.

After gathering her clothes for work the next morning, her first in her new position, she turned off the light and shut the door, but not before giving him one last long look. He was growing up so quickly. It was like every time she looked, there was something different about him.

One day soon, she was going to look and her little boy would be gone entirely, transformed into a teenager who probably wouldn't want anything to do with being tucked into bed with a goodnight kiss. But until that happened, she'd hoard every special moment she could get.

Just like she'd take every giddy, exciting minute she could with Rick.

Instead of focusing on what might go wrong, she was going to only think about all the things that could go right. Hopefully very right. Many, many times.

A little shiver of anticipation rippled through her.

It was going to be a very long week.

Chapter 14

"Oh, THAT FEELS SO good."

"Told you it would."

Amber wanted to toss something at Rick's smug face, but the cool water running over her naked toes was too delicious for her to muster up the effort. Instead, she leaned back on her elbows and tilted her face up to the sky, absorbing the rays of the autumn sun as a gift. The smooth rock beneath her still held the heat of the above normal temperature mid-October day, warming her while the chill of Boulder Creek's rushing water soothed her tired feet.

Hiking in Eldorado Canyon Park wouldn't have been her first guess for what Rick had planned for their day, but it turned out to be the perfect choice. The scenery was gorgeous, and despite it being Saturday, they'd practically had the place to themselves. All that tranquility and solitude had made it easier for them to talk.

About everything.

Rick told her about his family and all their little quirks. How his father had his roots in New Orleans, working shrimping boats as a teen to make enough money to pay for college. A struggle which had been the impetus for creating a financial empire to pass on to his own children so they'd never have to know a hungry day.

His youngest brother, Peter, who'd chosen a career as a police officer over a position in that empire, preferring to serve and protect the community rather than crunch numbers.

Peter's twin sister Lillian, recently featured in one of the big art magazines as one of the up-and-coming talents to watch.

His brother Theo, who was all Armani and Hugo Boss by day, and North Face and Black Diamond on the weekends as he skied and climbed the numerous mountains Colorado was famous for.

There had been a bit of envy in Rick's eyes when he talked about Theo's extreme recreational choices, but thankfully he'd admitted hiking was as adventurous as he ever got in the mountains. The crazy stuff he'd leave to his equally crazy brother.

It was said with love, but, she thought, a bit of worry, too.

Understandable. If someone she loved was climbing up sheer rock cliffs on a regular basis, she'd be a little freaked, too.

In turn, she'd told him about the double-wide trailer that had become her Grandma Pearl's home with her only daughter, Ruby, after her husband left her for a woman barely out of high school.

It had become Amber's home when she was about three, when Ruby moved back in after Amber's father, who'd thankfully not married her mother, was sent to the Texas state penitentiary for armed robbery. As far as she knew, he was still there.

And it had been Derek's home for a short time after he was born, until her momma passed away unexpectedly after a short battle with breast cancer.

If she'd been sitting in her apartment, or in a restaurant, or pretty much anyplace else in the world, she didn't think she would have been able to say any of that to Rick. But being out in the open, walking among the trees and waterfalls, it felt like being in the lord's own confessional. The embarrassing secrets spilling from her lips seemed to wash away in the cool breeze, leaving her feeling drained but more at peace with herself and her roots than she'd been in years.

Or maybe that had been because of the quiet acceptance from the man walking at her side. His only reaction to learning about her somewhat questionable gene pool was to reach over and take her hand. With one gentle squeeze, he'd let her know it didn't matter.

None of it mattered.

It had been such an immense weight off her shoulders, she'd almost confessed the rest. About Hunter, and her stupid, naïve belief he'd cared for her, when all he'd cared about was scoring with the girl with the biggest rack in school. Him turning his back on her after she got pregnant. His parents' threats, and her subsequently being all but run out of town on a rail when the trailer that'd been home all her life was yanked out from under her right after her mother's death.

She'd wanted to. Oh, how she did.

But when she opened her mouth to say the words, they wouldn't come. Not yet. She could only open herself to so much risk at a time.

Instead, she'd glossed over that section of her story with a simple "I got pregnant my junior year by a boy who dumped me, and had to leave school and get my GED after Derek was born."

He'd known there was more. The man wasn't stupid. But he hadn't pressed. He'd taken what she'd given him and left the rest alone, to be told in her own time, at her own pace. For that alone, she'd wanted to kiss him.

So she did.

The kisses would have turned to more if there wasn't the risk of them being stumbled upon by other hikers, although she knew she wasn't the only one who'd briefly considered throwing caution to the wind in favor of getting naked and crazy. In the end, though, they'd come back to town instead, where he'd surprised her a second time and taken her to the Dushanbe Teahouse for afternoon tea.

Which, honestly, was more about the three-tiered tower of sweet and savory goodies that came with the service than the delicious variety of teas they were famous for.

After stuffing themselves on scones and sweet cakes, Rick suggested a walk along Boulder Creek Path, almost directly across from the teahouse's entrance, to help things digest. A little way down the path, he'd led her through a few trees to the secluded spot on the water's edge where they both now sat, dangling their bare feet in the rushing water.

Best. Day. Ever.

Well, so far, anyway.

There was still the possibility of an even better ending, depending on whether the evening went the way she hoped it might. And after that kiss in the canyon, she had very high hopes indeed.

In fact...

Shifting on her elbows, she looked over at Rick. Flat on his back, arms stacked beneath his head, he looked as comfortable as if he were laying on a feather mattress rather than a rocky embankment.

He always did, she realized with a start. No matter where he was—hiking a trail, leading his karate class, standing in the middle of his palatial office. Rick always looked like he belonged.

Probably because he felt like he did.

What she wouldn't give to know that feeling, just once.

As if he knew she was staring, he opened his eyes and smiled at her. "See anything you like?"

She matched the smile with one of her own. "Yeah. Very much." And while he was deliciously gorgeous with his dark weekend scruff and lazy grin, it wasn't his looks alone she meant.

Something flashed in his eyes when he realized it. His smile faltered for a second before being replaced with something that looked almost like determination.

Before she knew what he was doing, Rick had grabbed a hand towel from his daypack and tossed it to her, using a second one to dry his feet. "Come on. I want to show you something."

"Okay."

Curious, and just a bit wary, she quickly dried her feet and shoved them back into her socks and sneakers. After accepting Rick's hand to help her up, she was surprised when he didn't let her go. In fact, his grip tightened until it was almost painful.

Her tummy did a nervous little flip. "Rick?"

"Trust me?"

Those words again.

Caught in his dark gaze, she nodded. A hint of a satisfied smile twitched his lips before he started tugging her back through the trees to the path. She followed, swallowing her questions. Whatever they were doing, wherever they were going, it was important to him. That was all she needed to know.

For now.

Instead of heading back toward where they'd left the car, Rick cut across the wide swath of grass separating the walking path from the street in this section of the park. After emerging onto the sidewalk, they walked a short distance to the corner and waited to cross over to the other side of Boulder Canyon Drive. And still, he didn't say anything.

She glanced up at him, unease growing. "Is everything okay?"

"We'll know in about five minutes."

The muttered reply wasn't comforting, but the light changed and they were walking again before she could question his meaning. After a few minutes of walking past apartment buildings with discrete entrances which barely hinted at the swanky price tag of the spaces inside, the unease had settled into a hard knot.

She knew even before he angled them toward one of those doors where they were going.

Rick greeted the doorman—of course, because places like this wouldn't be without one—and led her to an elevator. Seconds after the door closed, it opened again, the ride so smooth it hadn't even felt like they'd moved.

She blinked a few times as she stepped out into what felt like a spread in Architectural Digest. She knew the real estate in this part of downtown was spendy, but this...this wasn't an apartment. This was an honest-to-God penthouse.

Amber Lee, you're damn sure not in Texas anymore.

"Wow."

It seemed that was as articulate as she could be at the moment.

"Want the nickel tour?"

All she could do was nod. Her hand still firmly in his, he led her through the living room to the kitchen, the office, the game room, then past several bedrooms—how many did one person need?—and back around to the main room and its magnificent view of the Flat Irons through a wall that was nothing but glass panels.

She must have made some noise of appreciation, because he opened one of the accordion-style panels. He led her out onto the terrace, which could comfortably hold a few dozen people without them ever bumping elbows.

"So, that's my place," he said, finally allowing her hand to slip from his as she stepped to the railing. "What do you think?"

"Hell of a view," she murmured.

"It is." He moved beside her but gave her some space. "But that's not what I meant."

No, it wasn't. But she was still processing the enormity of Rick's—Richard's—oh-so obvious wealth.

Before, it had been a vague idea, how rich he was. But seeing his condo, the elegant furnishings and artwork and the overall size and grandeur of the place...it was a tangible reminder the world he inhabited didn't even come close to the reality she lived in. They weren't just worlds apart.

They lived in different solar systems.

"Don't," he said, his voice rough with emotion.

She looked at him in surprise. "Don't what?"

"I didn't judge you by your apartment. Do me the same courtesy and don't judge me by mine."

His words stung, but he was right. She had been. But it was damned hard not to, not when she was standing there looking at his million—probably multi-million—dollar view.

"I'm sorry. It's just..." She gestured around herself. "This is pretty hard not to be impressed by. And a little intimidated, to be honest."

"I didn't mean for you to be either." He dragged his hand through his hair, looking adorably frustrated. "I just wanted to show you the rest of me. No more lies, no more omissions, wasn't that the deal? Well, this is me. Where I live. How I live. But it's just a place. It doesn't define me."

"No, you're right. It doesn't." Ashamed for having gone all judgy when he hadn't blinked twice at the shoebox she called home, she reached out and laid her hand over his on the warm metal railing.

"Thank you for bringing me here. For trusting me with the truth." She twined her fingers with his and stepped closer until their heat mingled in the cooling late afternoon breeze. "And it really is one hell of a view."

Only this time she wasn't looking at the mountains when she said it.

With a soft growl, he captured her mouth. The low noise vibrated through her, teasing nerve endings that sparked with instant arousal. She met his kiss with equal fierceness, the taste of honey and sugar sweet on her tongue from his. Her entire body went up in flames as his hand settled on her ass, pulling her tight against him.

With a groan, she dragged his shirt from his khakis and ran her hands along the strong line of his back. Muscles flexed at her touch. She dug her nails in lightly before reversing the direction of her wandering touch, curving her fingers over the very biteable ass she'd drooled over since the day she met him.

She squeezed.

Rick groaned into her mouth, flexing his hips forward in a grinding motion that made her want to strip him naked right then and there so he could stop teasing her and get on to the real deal.

The only thing that stopped her was the wolf whistle from the street below.

"Oh my God." Hiding her face against Rick's chest, she let out a mortified laugh. "You're turning me into an exhibitionist."

It was the second time today she'd almost thrown caution to the wind in public. Having spent most of her life trying to avoid being noticed, that said a lot about how badly this man scrambled her brain every time he touched her.

"He's just jealous. Ignore him."

With an ease that showed the strength he hid beneath his trim build, he slid his hands under her thighs and lifted, urging her legs around his waist. Once she'd locked her ankles behind him, he walked them back inside, the friction where their bodies pressed together restoking the fires momentarily cooled by the unexpected interruption.

She thought he'd stop at the nearest sofa, but they kept moving deeper into the condo, his long legs eating up the distance while his hands and mouth stayed busy distracting her, until he finally came to a stop. Expecting to be in his bedroom, she broke the kiss, only to discover they were still standing in the hallway.

Heart thundering, body aching, she had to bite back a whimper. "What's wrong?"

"Nothing." But even as he said it, he tugged her legs from around his body, setting her gently on her feet.

The sudden halt made her head spin and her tummy tighten with all-too familiar embarrassment. Was he seriously going to stop? *Now*? "Then why?"

He had the nerve to grin at her aggrieved tone. The bastard.

"Because I need to know you really want this before we go any further."

She huffed out a half-laugh. "Like there's any doubt?"

"I just want to be sure there isn't, on either of our parts." He caught her chin between his fingers, his gaze solid and serious. "I will not be another guy who takes advantage of you. If we move past this point, it's entirely your decision. Your choice."

Something hit her, hard, right in the heart as she took in his softly spoken words. Had any man, ever, given her that kind of control? That much consideration?

It left her feeling a little shaken, but also stronger and more sure of herself than she'd ever felt before.

Gently, she stepped back from his touch. Rick let his hand fall to his side, a slight flash of disappointment in his eyes, but he didn't try to stop her. Wanting to take that unintended pain away, she smiled and took another step back.

Over the threshold into his bedroom.

"How should I prove to you I'm sure?" She kicked off her sneakers and took another backward step. "That I'm totally"—she unbuttoned her jeans and slid the zipper down—"one-hundred percent"—she yanked her top off over her head—"absolutely positive?"

She sent the jeans down her legs with a shimmy to pool around her ankles, leaving her standing there in her bra and panties. Putting her hands on her hips, she cocked her head and smiled at him.

Ball's in your court, buster.

He didn't waste any time. With the swiftness of a panther, he rushed her, lifting her from her feet on a surprised squeal that turned into a laugh as he dropped her onto what had to be the biggest bed she'd ever seen in her life. The way he stood between her legs as they dangled off the edge, staring down at her like she was something on the teahouse's sweets tray, melted away the last threads of her self-consciousness.

She bit her lower lip as she looked at him through her lashes. "How do I know *you're* sure?" It was probably foolish to poke an already aroused bear, but she was feeling reckless and a little wild at the moment. Not at all like herself.

And she liked it.

She liked not having to always keep herself reigned in, tied down, buttoned up. Worried people would see her natural sexuality as proof positive of her "slutty trailer trash ways."

There was a piece of herself coming out now she'd never let anyone see before, and it felt *so good* to let it loose.

Without a word, Rick took a single step back and copied her movements, stripping himself of his hiking boots, shirt, and pants until he stood there in his knit boxer briefs, his erection barely contained by the stretchy gray fabric.

Good lord, but the man was *fine*. The smattering of hair on his chest emphasized the lean muscles honed by years of martial arts study rather than pumping iron at a gym. The dip in at his hip bones brought her gaze directly to the hard evidence that he was holding onto his self-control by the barest of threads.

Her fingers twitched. "I want to touch you."

"Yes." The word was a groan that turned into a hiss as her hand curled around his erection through the damp fabric. He pressed into the touch, hips jerking forward with what was likely an involuntary thrust because he stilled and muttered, "Sorry."

"Don't apologize for enjoying yourself. In fact..." Fingers dipping under the waistband, she slid off the bed and dropped to her knees as she shucked the briefs down his long legs. His thick penis bobbed against his belly as though to thank her for freeing it, right before she closed her mouth over the flushed top and gave it a firm suck.

This time she was prepared for the reflexive thrust, allowing him to glide almost to the back of her throat without hurting either of them.

"*Fuuuck!*"

Rick gripped her shoulders, although she wasn't sure if it was to stop her or to steady himself. When she gave another suck and he gave another slow thrust, she had her answer. Smiling inside, she wrapped one hand around the extra length that didn't fit in her mouth and found a rhythm between the two that had Rick groaning and shaking in just a few quick minutes.

One of his hands moved to her head, tangling gently with her hair. "Sweetheart, enough. Please."

The desperate edge to his voice told her he was close to the limit of his control. She considered ignoring it, but as much as she wanted to give him pleasure, she also didn't want to take away his choice.

Or miss out on everything yet to come.

With a last lick, she reluctantly let him slide from between her swollen lips. "I intend to finish what I started at some point tonight." She barely recognized the sultry voice as her own as she looked up at him.

His eyes glittered as he helped her to her feet. "And I intend to let you. But first, I think it's my turn."

She expected him to go for the bra first, because with guys it was always all about the boobs. But he surprised her by kneeling in front of her and slowly easing her panties down off her hips and along her thighs, sowing kisses along the path all the way to her knees. Urging her back onto the bed, he slipped them off her and flipped them somewhere behind him.

He never once took his gaze from hers. Not on the way down, and not now, as he kissed his way back up again.

By the time he reached his destination between her legs, they willingly fell open with no input from her at all.

"*God*."

The word fell from her lips as his tongue found all the right spots, licking and nibbling along tender flesh that throbbed and pulsed under his ministrations, skyrocketing her up into the stratosphere and over into ecstasy faster and hotter than she'd ever gotten there before.

Lord have mercy, the man had a magic mouth.

Which was grinning at her from between her legs with a smug wickedness that would have annoyed her if she wasn't still floating on a cloud of euphoria. Watching as he wiped her wetness from his lips, she tried to think of something to say.

Nothing came to mind.

"Watching you come was the hottest thing I've ever seen." Pressing a last kiss to her thighs, he stood, fisting himself as he looked down at her, hunger etched into his face.

Seeing him touch himself like that was pretty damn hot, too, but her brain was still too muddled to form the words to tell him. The best she could do was extend her arms, urging him to her.

With a guttural groan, he practically tore the nightstand drawer open and came out with a condom. Covering himself with shaky hands, he came down on top of her. The kiss was fierce and demanding, and she met it with equal force.

And still he didn't make a move for her breasts.

Rick pulled back, using his knees to spread her legs wider. Slowly, he eased himself inside her, thrusting in gentle motions. Every inch she took inside touched nerve endings sensitized by her orgasm, making him feel even bigger than he already was. When he finally gave one last thrust, fully seating himself, they both groaned.

"You feel so damn good, I don't think I'm going to be able to last long."

"Well, I guess we'll have to work on improving your stamina." *Poke, poke.* She was totally playing with fire, and she knew it.

So did Rick, who gave her a wicked grin. "I'm going to hold you to that." He flexed his hips back, almost withdrawing from her body, then reversed his path and pressed in again, slow enough to make her crazy.

Head thrashing on the bed as he repeated the torturous process all over again, she begged, "Please, faster!"

"What happened to improving my stamina?"

"Stamina later. Fuck me now!"

It was like the command uncorked the genie's bottle. With a growl, he took firm hold of her hips, holding on tight as he proved those muscles she'd admired weren't just for show. His hips moved with fluid grace, filling her with himself over and over as the sensations threatened to drown her in a sea of ecstasy.

She let out a cry as her orgasm overwhelmed her, but she still knew the second he followed her over, his perfect rhythm stuttering to a sudden standstill.

She couldn't take her eyes off him. With his head thrown back, neck muscles corded as he groaned out his pleasure like some great lion on the tundra, he was magnificent.

And she knew she was lost.

There was no turning back now. Whatever happened between them going forward, her heart would never be wholly hers again.

This man would own a small piece of it forever.

Chapter 15

WHAT THE HELL JUST happened?

Lying beside her, Richard studied Amber's face, so peaceful and relaxed in sleep. And, if it wasn't too conceited to think so, extremely satisfied. That last made him grin. He *knew* she was satisfied. She'd been all but boneless as he'd stripped off her bra and maneuvered her beneath the sheets after taking care of the condom. Hell, he'd barely had the strength in his own legs to get to the bathroom and back.

It wasn't his most impressive showing with a woman, but damned if it didn't feel like the most important. Something passed between them during their little give-and-take. Something more than just good sex.

Okay, it was great sex. Superlative. Sex so good his brain was still trying to reboot after the short-circuit it suffered as he'd lost control and pounded into her, finishing with an orgasm that felt like it came from somewhere much deeper than just his balls.

And that was what had him freaking the fuck out.

Carefully, he slipped from the bed and dragged on a pair of cotton sleep pants before escaping to the kitchen. He'd had mind-blowing orgasms before, but this...this was something way outside his experience. The feelings swirling inside him were foreign, but at the same time, they felt good. Like he'd finally gotten something right.

But what?

Dragging a hand through his hair, he laughed at himself. He had the most gorgeous, sexy woman in the world tucked into his bed, and he was standing here worrying about his *feelings*. How ridiculous was that?

Richard Beaumont didn't *do* feelings. He did assessments of social and financial suitability, with a small nod toward chemistry and cohabitation compatibility. Feelings never entered into things before.

And maybe that was the problem.

He groaned, then swore. Rafe was right, damn him. All of his previous failures had stemmed from basing his matches on things more suited to a business merger than a healthy personal relationship. Only with Amber had he somehow managed to get out of his own way and let his feelings take the lead.

Which was all well and good, but what the hell was he supposed to do now?

"Getting back into bed with her so she doesn't wake up alone would probably be a good start, dumbass," he muttered to himself. With a shake of his head, he grabbed two bottles of water from the fridge, downing one in several long gulps. The other he brought back with him to the bedroom.

It didn't look like she'd even stirred while he was gone. But as soon as he slipped between the soft zillion thread count sheets, she curled into his side with a sleepy sigh. "Missed you."

He felt a sappy grin turn up his lips. "I got some water, in case you were thirsty." As he said it, though, he wondered if he should have brought back a bottle of wine instead. Or champagne. Something special. It's what he would have brought any other woman he'd just had sex with for the first time. Offering Amber water suddenly seemed like an insult.

If she thought so, though, it didn't show.

She gave him a full body hug before sitting up, accepting the bottle he offered and taking several long swallows before handing it back. As soon as he turned from putting it on the nightstand, she kissed him, long and soft and with enough intensity to make his body stir with interest again.

Ending the kiss, she smiled almost shyly at him. "Hi."

"Hi, yourself." He reached over and brushed her hair from where it was curling wildly into her face. "Is everything good? I didn't hurt you, did I?"

"Everything is marvelous, and not in the least. That was...wow."

Good. At least she seemed as befuddled by the whole thing as he felt.

He grinned. "Marvelous, huh?"

"Fishing for compliments again?"

"Just making notes on what I got right, so I remember for next time."

"Next time, huh?" She ran a finger down his arm, the light touch leaving goosebumps in its wake. "And when do you think that might be?"

He would have said *now* if her stomach hadn't chosen that moment to give a loud rumble.

"How about after I feed you?" He captured her wandering finger as it slipped below the sheet and gave it a nip for being naughty. "We need to keep our strength up for later."

Her eyes dilated slightly. "Later?"

"Mm-hmm." He turned her hand in his and pressed a kiss to the palm before folding it closed, like it was a promise for her to hold onto. "Later."

A tiny shudder ran through her body as she stared down at her hand.

Not waiting to see if he'd just made an ass of himself or not with the sentimental gesture, he got out of bed and headed for the walk-in closet. "Let me get you a robe or something."

"I can just put my clothes back on," she protested, following him.

He threw a wicked grin over his shoulder at her. "Why bother when I'm just going to take them off you again?"

"Isn't unwrapping your presents half the...holy crap on a cracker."

At the shocked words, he turned back from where he was reaching for the exquisitely embroidered Daniel Hanson cashmere-silk robe his sister had given him for his last birthday. Amber stood in the doorway to the closet, gloriously naked and tousled, looking absolutely gobsmacked. He took a quick look around to see why.

Okay, so maybe he was a bit of a clotheshorse when it came to his bespoke suits. But that shouldn't elicit the wide-eyed reaction which seemed to have frozen her in place, jaw officially dropped. "What?"

"Jesus, Rick." She took a tentative step past the threshold, eyes darting everywhere. "This is practically bigger than my whole apartment."

An exaggeration, yes. But when he thought about it, only a slight one. "Should I apologize?" He couldn't keep the touch of trepidation from his tone.

"No, of course not. I'm just having a tiny moment of closet envy, that's all." She smiled, but he could tell the humor was forced.

Damn.

Changing his mind about the expensive silk robe, he grabbed one of his white dress shirts instead and offered it to her. "How's this?"

"Perfect."

She slipped it on and buttoned it closed with nimble fingers before he helped her roll back the sleeves to her elbows so they wouldn't hang past her fingertips. The tails reached well below her butt, concealing all of her lower glory, which was good for his sanity.

Not so for the top half of her body.

The buttons over her breasts strained when she tried to do them up, so she left them open, allowing tantalizing peeks of cleavage to show whenever she moved. Watching her walk out of the bedroom in front of him was like an erotic peep show, her ass twitching beneath the white fabric with every step.

It took everything he had not to drag her back to bed and change his promised 'later' to 'right now.'

But he'd also promised to feed her. That took precedence, so he gritted his teeth and stuck to the plan.

There wasn't much in the way of food in the kitchen, but they scrounged together the ingredients for soup and grilled cheese sandwiches. They took their improvised meal to the living room and tossed throw pillows on the floor to sit on as they ate at the coffee table, enjoying the last of the sunset happening past the glass wall as though it were a giant television screen.

"That was incredible," she said as the last colors filtered from the sky and faded to the dark purple of twilight.

"It was just cheese and bread, but you're welcome." He laughed and dodged her half-hearted swat.

"I meant the sunset, but yes, the sandwich was good, too. Thank you for feeding me. I needed that." She leaned against him with a contented sigh. "And thank you for the rest of today. I needed that, too."

Something eased in his chest at her words.

Taking her hiking in Eldorado Canyon had been a gamble. But she'd seemed to enjoy their picnic so much he'd decided to try and recreate that day without being obvious and going back to the same spot.

It was an old gamer technique. When you screwed up and didn't know how to move forward, you reset to the last point you were on firm ground.

Thank God it seemed to work for real life, too.

He wrapped an arm around her. Pulling her closer into the curve of his body, he pressed a kiss to her head, inhaling the faint scent of fresh air and sunshine that still clung to her despite their more recent activities. "Anytime, sweetheart."

"You really mean that, don't you?" she asked after a lengthy silence.

"I really do." Amber wasn't the only one who'd found the day an enjoyable respite. Outdoor activities might be more Theo's thing, but it hadn't been the setting so much as the peaceful alone time with her that had given him a new sense of balance.

It was as though his world, slightly off-kilter for the last two weeks, was slowly righting itself more every day he spent with her.

Today, that realignment became complete.

But something about the way Amber made her off-handed comment about needing today nagged at him. He knew he risked fracturing the cozy mood cocooning them, but he had to ask.

"How are things going with the new job?"

She tensed a bit at his words, but didn't pull away. Instead, she sighed and sank deeper into his embrace as though needing the comfort.

Or the shelter.

"Still a little rocky. But it was only the first week. Things will straighten themselves out. It'll just take a little time for everyone to get comfortable with the new power structure. Including me."

It sounded so much like she was trying to convince herself of that, it made his heart ache.

The subject of her recent promotion had come up Tuesday night during what was becoming their regular after-class pizza stop. She'd been a lot more subdued in her excitement than he would have expected for such a momentous announcement, but with all the little ears around the table, he didn't have a chance to ask many questions. All she'd say was the transition from coworker to boss wasn't as easy as she'd thought it would be.

He had a feeling it was a lot more than that.

Rubbing a comforting hand along her arm, he asked, "Is there anything I can do to help?"

She snuggled closer. "You're doing it."

"Anything else?"

"No. I can handle my own problems. But thank you," she added, sounding contrite but firm.

"There's no doubt in my mind you can handle anything that comes your way, sweetheart. But part of being in a relationship means you don't always have to do it all yourself."

They both stilled.

"Is that what this is?"

He barely heard the whispered question over the thunder of his own heart. Was it? Was he sure he wanted to cross the line from casual whatever-this-was to something more defined and real? More public? Had he actually chosen feelings over checklists?

It seemed he had.

"It's exactly what this is. If that's what you want."

It nearly killed him to give her the out after laying himself on the emotional chopping block, but he had to do it. Just like at his bedroom door, he needed to know every step they took forward was her choice. He didn't know much about her past, but it wasn't hard to fit the pieces he'd learned together into a not-so-pretty picture.

Life had stolen so many choices from her. He aimed to give them back where he could.

Except now that he had, her silence was damned unnerving.

He cleared his throat. "Is it?"

Turning her head toward him, Amber's expression of nervous joy matched the feelings clawing at his belly. "Yes. It kind of scares the hell out of me, but yes, it is."

"Thank God." He gathered her up into his lap and kissed her. When he tried to shift them both to a more comfortable position, though, his knee banged against the coffee table with a painful crack.

Without care for the expensive hardwood flooring, he used his foot to shove the table away with an ear-jarring screech of wood-on-wood, allowing him to tumble a giggling Amber onto the pile of pillows around them. He followed her down, balanced over her on all fours like a predator claiming its prey.

Or its mate.

She grinned up at him. "Does this mean it's later?"

"Oh, yeah."

"Good."

With that green light, he lowered his mouth to hers again, taking his time to properly explore before moving his kisses down her cheek to her neck. She squirmed as he nibbled along the tender cord that ran to her collarbone before laving the sting away with his tongue. When he ran into the barrier of the shirt as he moved even lower, he growled with displeasure. "You're wearing too many clothes."

"Well, it was your idea to put it on. Why don't you do something about it?"

He loved the way she tossed challenges his way so fearlessly. Most of the women he'd taken to bed were content to let him take the lead, almost without exception. Sometimes without even much participation. Honestly, after a while it got a little monotonous.

But not this woman.

He had a feeling his life would never be boring again as long as Amber was in it.

Her eyes glittered in the dim twilight as she nudged her chin out a bit further. "Well?"

Challenge accepted, sweetheart.

Letting the smile that terrified grown men in the boardroom slowly pull at his lips, he watched her expression go from bold, to wary, to nervous, and finally to hot and aroused as he reached down and yanked the gaping shirt apart in one swift motion.

Buttons pinged everywhere around them.

Fuck the two-hundred-dollar shirt. All that mattered was getting Amber naked in the least amount of time possible.

He took more care, though, when he sat her up and slid the shirt off her shoulders, flinging it toward the sofa once it was free of her arms. Laying her back down, he studied the bounty before him. God, she was incredible. And she was all his.

Could a man get any luckier?

His long scrutiny must have unnerved her, because her hands fluttered up to cover her body, one over her stomach, the other her chest. As though that would be enough to divert his gaze.

"Flat on your back isn't the most flattering position for someone with big girls." She brought her arms closer to her body, forcing her breasts back up front-and-center with a wry grin. "Gravity's got a mean sense of humor."

"It just proves they're all you." Because silicone didn't move like that. He should know. One woman he'd dated had breasts so firm and perky they'd nearly given him a black eye.

He'd take soft and real any day.

Gently, he brushed her hand aside and placed his own over the silken globes. Her hard nipples raked at his palms as he learned the size and feel of them, her skin warming at his touch. Oh yeah, they were definitely all her.

When he leaned down to take one of the stiff strawberry tips into his mouth, they both groaned. Switching the kiss to its twin, he gently licked and sucked until she was squirming with need.

"Took you long enough to find them," she gasped between whimpers.

"I knew where they were. They just aren't the most important thing about you."

Her breath caught. "How do you always know exactly the right thing to say?"

Because he wasn't always an idiot. Although it seemed most of the men in her past had been.

Which was why he moved his attention to the second spot she'd instinctively tried to cover. The pale line across her lower belly was so faint it was almost invisible. "You had a c-section?"

Amber bit her lip before nodding. "It wasn't planned. Derek's heart rate dropped suddenly during labor, so they didn't have a choice."

He couldn't imagine the terror she must have felt. Bad enough being a single, pregnant teenager, but then to undergo emergency surgery to save your baby's life? No wonder this woman was so tough. She'd been through more trials by fire before she turned twenty than he'd encountered in his entire privileged life.

It was a humbling moment.

And an eye-opening one.

With tender reverence, he touched a finger to the scar. When she tried to push it away, he grasped her hand and placed both of their hands on the pale line. "Stop that. You're beautiful. All of you."

"Not that."

"Especially that."

She made a scoffing noise and tried to pull her hand away.

He wouldn't let her. "You brought a life into the world through this scar. Never try to hide it from me." Removing their joined hands, he bent down and pressed a kiss to it before she could act to stop him.

She let out a strangled noise that ended in a small, hitching gasp when his mouth slid lower, unerringly finding the hidden jewel in the soft thatch of blonde hair between her legs. With deliberate slowness, he stoked her desire with his lips and tongue until she was panting like a racehorse nearing the finish line.

Then she shocked the hell out of him by pushing at his shoulders to stop him before she got there.

"Not without you this time." The words were almost a growl. With frantic fingers, she tore at the waistband of his sleep pants to free him.

He had to sit back to strip the cotton pants from his legs, then stopped as reality came crashing back with rude clarity. "Condoms. Be right back."

Before he could get up and make the sprint to his bedroom, she put a hand on his arm to stop him. The smile she gave was what he expected his earlier one had looked like, full of steely will and determined intent. "No."

His penis gave an unhappy throb. "No?"

The smile turned seductive as her gaze went to the erection he was fisting. "I get to finish what I started before. You promised, remember?

Fuuuck yeah, he remembered.

He remembered the hot, wet feel of her mouth, and how close he'd come to spilling himself in it while she stared up at him with those expressive eyes glazed with lust and a glimmer of feminine power.

And he remembered how difficult it had been to make himself stop her before he got to come, wishing he didn't have to.

Looked like his wish was about to come true.

It took no effort at all on Amber's part to topple him onto his back. She hovered over him, looking her fill before running her hands over his chest to his abs, then down to his hips. She seemed overly fascinated by the slight indent of muscles that dipped inward there before focusing on the part of his body waiting with growing impatience for her undivided attention.

With the same reverence he'd used to touch her, she wrapped her hand around his erection and lowered her head to swipe her tongue over the tip.

A long groan escaped as his head dropped back onto one of the scattered pillows. Through slitted eyes, he watched as she adjusted herself to get a better angle before taking him into her mouth, nearly blowing the top of his head off when she deep throated him.

Holy. Fuck.

Hard as it was, he forced himself to lie still and let her take the lead, not wanting to thrust despite the incredible need to do so, afraid like before he might hurt her.

Then her hands joined the party. One on his penis, the other sneaking down to cup his balls, rolling and squeezing them like they were some new toy she was figuring out.

All of his good intentions went out the window as, against his will, his hips started to buck and grind.

As the first tingles started at the base of his spine, his hands reached out, fingers grasping, seeking something to anchor himself with. One found the edge of the sofa. The other tangled in her hair, brushing it away from her face so he could watch.

The sight of his shiny erection gliding between her lips was the end of him.

He tried to warn her, tried to use her hair to tug her away, but she stayed stubbornly attached. Trusting her to know her own mind, he gave up trying and let the orgasm sweep through him with a guttural shout.

The pleasure went on and on, his hips mindlessly moving as she milked every last drop of gratification from his body until he was wrung dry in every way possible.

When she crawled along his lax body and nestled against him, he barely had the strength left to wrap his arms around her. "That was…"

"I believe the word you're looking for is 'wow.'"

He chuckled at her smug tone. "I think you're right. Wow." Pressing a kiss to her temple, he was content to lay there and bask in the afterglow for a while. But eventually the euphoria burned off enough to remind him they were laying on a hard floor when there was a luxurious California king beckoning right down the hall.

"I'm not sure I can walk yet, but what do you say we take this back to the bedroom?"

Where the condoms were. Because he'd be damned if he didn't have her again tonight. Not even a spectacular blowjob like that one was as good as sinking balls-deep into her tight, hot body.

Of course, he might need a few hours to recover before he could make good on those intentions.

They stumbled back to his bedroom, holding onto each other like a couple of drunks after last call. After crawling under the covers, he pulled her close to his side and let out a sigh of pure contentment.

A soft bed, a soft woman, and the entire night still in front of them. It didn't get any better than this. And to think, he'd almost thrown this away because of a stupid misunderstanding.

Which reminded him...

"Are you doing anything next Saturday night?"

"Um, no, nothing special. It's the off weekend when all the kids stay home, so I'll only have Derek. Why?"

"Would you go to the ball with me?"

"*What*?" She pulled away and sat up, staring down at him with a shocked expression. "The ball? You mean, your mother's ball?" Her voice got a little shriller. "The ball I was supposed to be helping her with and walked out on my first day? *That* ball?"

He winced, but was quick to set her straight. "I found two other people to help my mother the next day, so don't worry about that part."

"Found, or paid?"

"Found." The fact they were already on the Beaumont payroll was incidental.

"Hmph." She didn't look like she believed him. "Even so, I'm not sure I can face your mother after what I did, taking off without a word. It was so unprofessional. Not to mention just plain rude."

Hating how embarrassed she seemed, he sat up as well and took her hand. "Don't worry. She knows why you left. The basics," he added when her eyes widened in horror, "not the details. Believe me, she doesn't blame you. At all."

He was the one still on her shit list.

Amber still didn't look convinced, furrows lining her forehead. "I don't know…"

"Sweetheart, please. I'll beg if I have to. If I go by myself, I'll be bored out of my mind within an hour. If you're there, I won't need to gnaw my own arm off to escape before it's over." He grinned when she laughed.

Unfortunately, he was only half joking.

"Please? Go with me and keep me sane?"

"What will people think when you show up with me?"

And they finally got to the crux of the problem.

"That I'm one lucky son of a bitch." Cupping her face in his hands, he kissed her gently on the lips. "This is a part of my life, like the penthouse, and the Ferrari, and—"

"Ferrari? What Ferrari?"

Damn.

"We'll save that for tomorrow. What I'm trying to say is, being in a relationship with me means stepping out of your comfort zone sometimes. Being around people who might think they're better than you because of their money. But trust me, they'll only have the chance to think it once." Before he crushed their narrow-minded little lives to dust. "What do you think? Is that something you can handle?"

Making it a challenge had the desired effect.

Her forehead smoothed and her lips firmed, the glint of the fighter he knew her to be shining from her eyes. "Any day."

He was careful to hide his satisfaction. "Good. Now, let me ask this again. Amber, would you go to the masquerade ball with me next Saturday?"

Chin tilted up, her smile was all teeth. "I'd love to."

Chapter 16

"Can I look yet?"

"No. And don't frown, you'll end up lopsided."

Amber smoothed the expression from her face and kept her eyes closed despite the burning impatience raging inside. She had no idea what Elena's friend was doing to her. Lin had been working on her makeup for what felt like hours now, and with every layer she added, the deeper Amber's worry grew of what the finished product was going to look like.

"Have a little faith," Elena said from somewhere behind her.

Easy for her to say. She could actually see what was going on.

Still, she knew her friend wouldn't let her go off to the ball looking like a fool. So, she grabbed hold of her nerves and sat quietly under Lin's ministrations.

The reality was, short of looking like a rodeo clown, anything the enthusiastic young woman with the bright pink hair did would be better than she could have managed on her own. Everyday makeup she could handle. But the look she needed to achieve tonight required a much more talented hand.

That was where Elena's friend and roommate came in. Lin Hu currently made her living doing makeup services for weddings and proms, but her passion was the theater. Which was why Elena had dragged her into the craziness of the past week when Amber called her in a frenzy of doubt that she'd ever be able to pull off the costume she'd committed herself to.

To her credit, Lin had jumped in to help with one-hundred percent enthusiasm.

Now Amber just had to hope she had the abilities to match it.

"Okay." There was one last dab of a brush on her forehead. "I think that's it. You can look now."

Moment of truth.

Amid a flurry of butterflies bouncing around in her stomach, she opened her eyes and looked into the tri-fold makeup mirror in front of her. It took a second for her brain to realize the image blinking back at her was her own.

"Oh!" With a shaking hand, she grabbed her phone and brought up the picture she'd shown Lin as a reference to work from.

The shimmering arc of silver-white wings around her eyes made their own mask, meaning she wouldn't have to wear a real one, while the rest of her face was highlighted with a subtle golden glow that seemed to come from the inside. The line of rhinestones along her forehead was the crowning touch. With her unruly hair subdued into a tight coronet threaded with gold and silver cord, she looked almost...regal.

She couldn't have asked for a better match.

"It's perfect." She leaned closer to the mirror in awe. "Lin, you're a genius."

"Told ya."

She was so thrilled with her makeup, she totally forgave Elena's smugness. It was worth every "I-told-you-so" she'd hear for the rest of her life.

Lin was looking pretty pleased with herself, too. "Can I take a few pictures to add to my portfolio?"

"Sure, of course."

After taking a dozen headshots from all angles with her phone, Lin asked, "Can I take some of the costume, too?"

"Oh, um, sure, I guess. If you want to."

"Are you kidding? Of course I want to! It's gorgeous. My makeup is just the icing on the cake. The people in my theater group are going to flip over that dress!"

The praise helped ease some of the nervousness she'd been suffering through about her decision to hand-make her costume for the ball.

After firmly refusing Rick's offer to rent a professional costume for her, it had mortified her to discover she couldn't afford the obscene rental fee on her own. Not without wiping out her entire bank account. Worse, nothing at the local party stores even came close to being suitable for such a high-brow affair.

Out of desperation, she'd scoured her usual haunts of consignment shops and thrift stores for ideas. And there, in the last store, crammed on a rack in a dark corner behind a molting faux fox jacket, she'd found her inspiration.

The two heavily beaded floor-length gowns were a few decades out of style and three sizes too big, but they started her imagination galloping, and an idea was born.

She'd snapped them both up for a song.

After a quick stop at the fabric store, she'd taken everything home and gotten to work picking seams and cutting silk. She'd spent every free second for the rest of the week bent over her sewing machine to create the ivory and gold masterpiece she now wore.

Standing, she ran a nervous hand over the finished product. Liking it in the privacy of her apartment was way different from walking into a room filled with a few hundred strangers who, between them, probably possessed the net worth of several small nations. Hearing that Lin thought it was theater-quality good helped quiet the panic in her brain.

A little, anyway.

"Wait, don't forget the wings."

Amber turned so Elena could hook the small, gossamer fairy wings to the hidden hook sewn onto the back of the dress. She'd made them smaller than the ones in the movie she'd taken her inspiration from to allow for easier maneuverability.

Feeling the tug of their weight now, she was glad. Anything larger would have given her a backache by the end of the night.

"Oh, my God." Elena clasped her hands together, looking a little teary-eyed as Lin snapped away with her phone. "You look *amazing*."

As she was posing, there was a knock at the door. Amber froze. It couldn't be time for Rick to pick her up already.

It was.

"You're going to be fine," Elena assured her as she and Lin hustled her out of Lin's bedroom toward the door.

No, she was going to puke. Or faint. Or—

All of her fears went out the window when Lin opened the door and she saw Rick standing in the hallway wearing an exquisitely tailored black tux, complete with tails. She'd thought he looked amazing in a suit. The tux made her want to strip it off him and eat him up right where he was standing.

Holy crap on a cracker, the man was gorgeous.

Lucky for her, Rick didn't seem to notice her greedy stare, since he was busy doing some gawking of his own. He raked her from head to toe with his hot gaze, then went back for seconds.

They both started when Elena cleared her throat.

"You look…" Rick shook his head.

"So do you."

When Elena cleared her throat again, a little louder this time, Amber rolled her eyes at her friend, who grinned. "Rick, this is my best friend, Elena, and her roommate, Lin, who was nice enough to help me with my hair and makeup tonight."

"Ladies, a pleasure." He swept them a bow worthy of a prince, making them both giggle. "And thank you for being Amber's fairy godmothers. You did an exquisite job."

"We can't take all the credit," Elena said. "Amber made the entire outfit herself."

Rick's eyes widened and did another sweep. "You did? Okay, now I'm really impressed. I thought it was a rental."

Her cheeks warmed at the sincere compliment. "We should get going."

With air kisses for Elena and Lin to preserve her makeup, Amber took Rick's offered arm, careful to turn as they went through the doorway to avoid bumping her wings, and again as they entered the elevator.

"I can see these things are going to be more of a pain than I planned on. Maybe I should leave them off."

"No, don't. I like them. My Lady Danielle." Rick ran a finger over the upper curve of the wing closest to him, and Amber could swear she felt the caress shiver straight to her core.

"You *do* know who I am," she said with a pleased smile. "I thought you might, with the fairy godmother comment, but I wasn't sure."

She'd figured most people would take the fairy costume at face value. And that was fine. The fact she was actually going as the character who wore the costume to a masquerade ball in the movie was more of a private joke.

If ever a woman had the right to feel like Cinderella tonight, it was her.

"Please," he scoffed, leading her through the small lobby and out to where a black stretch limo sat double-parked at the curb, attracting attention. "After you mentioned *Ever After* was your favorite movie, did you think I wouldn't watch it?"

"But...it's a chick flick." At least according to Derek, who'd bailed on watching it with her inside of twenty minutes.

"Yeah, but with a Cinderella who kicks ass and saves herself rather than waiting around for her prince to show up and do it."

"And she saves the prince, too, don't forget. From the gypsies." That was her second favorite part of the movie. Danielle de Barbarac had been one tough lady. Fictional character or not, she admired the heck out of her.

"Right." He shot her a wry look as the black-suited driver opened the rear door for them. "It was actually a pretty good movie."

"I'm glad you liked it. Wait, can you unclip my wings? I don't want to crush them." After she was free, she carefully gathered the fabric of her beaded skirt and slid gingerly into the limo with a smile and a thank you to the driver, who smiled and nodded in return.

The rear of the limo was *huge*. She did her best not to stare like a country rube, but it was tough. There were even two televisions, for Pete's sake. Not to mention enough room for about eight more people. For just the two of them, it seemed a little too much.

Rick followed her in. After the driver retook his seat up front, the glass panel between the two spaces quietly slid into place, leaving them in dimly lit privacy. Rick took her hand in his and kissed it.

"I neglected to do that upstairs. Forgive me?"

"O-of course."

Being enclosed in the back of the limo with him, the light aroma of warm sandalwood and spice wrapped around her senses, making her think things she shouldn't be thinking. Not if they were going to get to the ball with both their costumes still intact.

Desperate for a distraction, she blurted, "I can't figure out who you're supposed to be."

Grinning, probably because he knew exactly how much he was affecting her, he reached on top of the mound of black fabric on the curved seat she hadn't noticed when he'd put down her wings. He picked up a distinctive white half-mask and held it to the right side of his face.

"Oh! Phantom of the Opera!"

Rick tossed the mask back. "Not that I'll be wearing it long. Damn thing makes my face sweat." He placed his index finger under her chin and studied her for a moment. "Is there any way I can kiss you without messing up your makeup?"

"You can try." She held her breath as he lowered his lips to hers. It was the softest, gentlest kiss in the world, and then it was done. She opened eyes she didn't remember closing and blinked up at him.

Something passed between them. She didn't know what, but she felt something shift inside her, something that went way beyond lust and attraction.

Before she could ask if he'd felt it, too, the driver's voice piped in over the intercom. "We're here, sir."

Rick held her gaze for a few more seconds. "Thank you, Les."

The spell, or whatever had just happened, was broken.

Rick gathered up their costume pieces and got out when Les opened the rear door, handing everything to the driver so he could reach back and help her from the limo.

Getting out with the gathered mound of heavy material was a lot harder than getting in. Careful not to catch her heel in the back hem that fell in a tiny train behind her, she looked around the underground parking garage in surprise. "Oh! Is this right?"

"I know you weren't exactly comfortable with the media blitz at Max's party," Rick said as he helped her clip her wings in place. "The ball attracts the whole red carpet paparazzi element, which is a lot worse, so I thought a stealth entrance might be more to your liking."

"Oh! Yes, thank you."

Especially when the last set of pictures had brought Hunter out of the woodwork. Showing up on Rick's arm would only give him a new target for his dirty schemes.

But as they rode the elevator up to the ballroom level of the hotel, a tiny niggle of doubt wormed its way into her head.

Had he really thought about avoiding the photographers for her? Or for himself? Was he worried what being publicly linked to her would mean despite his talk of wanting a relationship with her?

Then the elevator doors opened and there wasn't any time left to pick at the problem. There were several people in costume roaming the marble-floored hallway between them and the oversized doors to the ballroom. Each of them nodded in greeting at Rick as they passed, which he returned, but none stopped to engage in conversation. That struck her as odd until she realized why.

They weren't guests. They were security.

And one more unnerving reminder of the rarified air she was about to breathe.

Lord, please let me get through this evening without making a fool of myself.

When they got to the closed doors, Rick sighed in resignation and slipped the mask on. "Ready?"

Oh, how she wanted to say no.

But she gave him her best smile instead. "You bet."

He nodded. The man dressed in old-fashioned livery at the side of the door pulled it open, and they stepped...

...into a magical realm.

At least, that's what the decorations made the enormous ballroom feel like. Round tables with crisp white linen circled the room, decorated with fresh wildflowers and glowing centerpieces of frosted glass. Fairy lights were strung everywhere, looking like thousands of fireflies filling the night.

The lights projected on the slightly domed ceiling looked like stars against a dark twilight sky. Despite the crush of people milling about talking, the faint sound of music filled the air, soft and ethereal, as though it came from everywhere and nowhere all at once.

Since she'd seen the plans during her one truncated day at the Foundation, she knew the orchestra was hidden away in a musician's gallery up above the ballroom floor. Just like she knew all the other little theatrical tricks used to achieve the desired effects.

But knowing didn't stop it all from really feeling as though they'd somehow been transported to a meadow out under the night sky.

"Your mom sure knows how to put on a shindig," she said softly as she soaked it all in.

"You know, she really does. Sometimes I don't give her enough credit for how much effort she puts into these things. Probably because I'm always too busy trying to figure out a way to avoid attending them." The chagrined tone seemed aimed at himself.

"You don't like parties?" That was a surprise, considering how many pictures of him attending them over the years she'd found online.

Not that she'd Googled him or anything.

Okay, she totally had.

"Going to them, yes. But not the ones where I have to play host, working the crowd for donations."

"It can't be that bad. It's clearly billed as a charity ball. People have to know they're going to be asked for money when they come. Isn't that why they're all here?"

"You'd think so. But you'd be wrong. Most people are here to see and be seen. Make deals. Get their name and picture in the news. For them, being philanthropic is only fashionable when there's some profit on the back end."

"That's really sad."

Rick shrugged. "That's life. Ah, here." He lifted two champagne flutes from a passing waiter and handed her one. "Forget about all of that for now. Let's concentrate on us. To a magical evening."

Since the only two times she'd ever drank champagne before—once at a retirement party at work and once on New Year's Eve—it tasted like fizzy vinegar, she gamely took a small sip to seal the toast. The lovely flavor that exploded over her tongue was a pleasant surprise.

Evidently, she'd been drinking the wrong champagne.

Of course, she'd probably have to sell a kidney to afford a bottle of whatever this was, so she hummed her appreciation and took another sip. No sense getting used to it, but she could enjoy it while it lasted.

"Richard, you made it. Finally."

The sudden sound of Mrs. Beaumont's voice behind them almost made her snort the bubbly liquid out through her nose. Without missing a beat, Rick handed her a handkerchief before turning to greet his mother, dutifully kissing her offered cheek.

"I told you I'd be here."

"I know, but no one told me you'd arrived."

"By no one, you mean whatever spy you have watching the front door of the hotel."

Mrs. Beaumont smoothed the sleeve of her gorgeous gown. "I don't have spies. I have very capable employees."

"Who report everything they see to you. Something I'll be discussing with you at a later date, by the way, about your collusion with the inestimable Mrs. Gandy to meddle." He was grinning as he said it, though. He slipped his arm around Amber's waist below the wings and drew her closer to his side. "Mom, I believe you remember Amber Lovett?"

That was when she realized his little moment of banter had been on purpose, to give her a few extra seconds to recover. It was almost enough to make her smile despite her mild case of stage fright.

"Of course, I do. How lovely to see you again, dear."

"And you, too. Mrs. Beaumont, I just wanted to apologize again for—"

"No need for apologies. I would never expect you to stay someplace you felt uncomfortable. And I know exactly who's to blame for *that*." Mrs. Beaumont shot Rick a glare which had him rolling his eyes.

"Well, I'm still sorry I didn't help out. This"—she spread her hands to encompass the room—"is incredible."

"Thank you. I'm rather pleased with the way it came out myself."

"You truly outdid yourself this time, Mom. It's amazing."

His mother sent him a startled look before turning a blinding smile on Amber. "I don't know what you've done to him, dear, but please, keep right on doing it!"

Cheeks bursting into flame beneath the makeup, she stuttered something unintelligible before burying her face in her champagne glass. If the woman only *knew* what she'd been doing to her son!

Not to mention what he'd been doing to her in return.

Rick, bless him, came to the rescue again. "So, Mom, why aren't you wearing a costume? I thought it was mandatory."

"Oh, but I am." She flipped up the hood of the red cape Amber hadn't noticed she was wearing over her burgundy gown before letting it fall again.

"Let me guess. Dad's the Big Bad Wolf."

"What else?" She gave him a critical look. "And where is the rest of your costume? I know that tuxedo isn't part of what I had sent over."

"I'm wearing the mask and cape, aren't I? Everyone knows who I'm supposed to be."

She fussed at his bow tie. "But it looked so much better with the period clothing."

"Mom, men stopped wearing frilly shirts and cravats for a reason."

With a *hmph* as reply, Mrs. Beaumont shifted her attention to Amber. "You, on the other hand, look absolutely exquisite."

"Thank you, Mrs. Beaumont."

"Oh, please, call me Patricia."

The offer felt like she'd passed some kind of test. A lingering sense of guilt nagged at her, though. "If there's anything I can do to help tonight, please let me know."

Mrs. Beaumont patted her arm with a smile. "Thank you, dear. You're already doing it." She glanced around with the look of a general surveying a battlefield. "Well, time to mingle. I'll see you both later." With a wave, she was gone.

Amber let out a *whoosh* of air. Okay, that hadn't been as bad as she'd imagined. Mrs. Beaumont—Patricia—didn't seem at all annoyed with her for being there as her son's guest.

In fact, she'd almost seemed...pleased.

Not the reaction she'd been expecting. But it gave her hope the night might end up being less stressful than she'd worried it would be.

"Well, I think we've just been given our marching orders." The smile Rick gave her looked odd under the half mask. More like a grimace.

Or maybe that's because it really was one. She couldn't tell.

He offered his arm again, placing his hand over hers possessively when she took it. "Now, we mingle."

Chapter 17

THEY SPENT THE NEXT twenty minutes slowly working the room. She tried, but it was impossible to remember all the people Rick introduced her to. Thankfully, she didn't think she was expected to. She just needed to smile and make small talk, which always came around to the charity portion of the charity ball. Once Rick had secured a promise of a donation, they talked a little more before moving on to start the process over again.

He was right. It wasn't very much fun. But the fact the money raised would go to keep the community center running for another year made the discomfort bearable.

It might have been the champagne's doing, but as the minutes ticked by and no one ignored her or, worse, questioned her being with Rick, the rest of the tension that had been riding her slipped away.

Rick steered them towards a clump of people occupying a corner of the ballroom. One of them, a tall man who looked so much like Rick they could almost be twins, grinned as they approached. He stuck his hand out, palm up, to the man beside him.

"Told ya he'd still be wearing it." The other man, who also had the Beaumont stamp on his features despite his much broader build, scowled as he slapped a bill into it. The petite woman with a pixie haircut just rolled her eyes and shook her head, while the dark-haired man at her side kept his expression neutral and watchful, especially when it came to Amber.

Holy crap on a cracker.

The tension came roaring back as realization hit. This was his *family*!

Something Rick confirmed when he glared at the two men. "Seriously? You fu—freaking bet on me? And where the hell are *your* costumes? No way Mom let you in here without one." When the first man corked a thumb over his shoulder to the nearby table, Rick muttered something under his breath and stripped off the mask and cape, adding them to the assorted pile of discarded costume pieces.

Seeing all of his gorgeous face again stunned her enough that she almost missed his introductions.

"Amber, this is my brother, Theo"—he indicated the man who'd won the bet—"my youngest brother, Peter"—the brawny one—"my sister, Lillian"—the little kewpie doll—"and her fiancé, Rafael Delgado." The last was drop-dead gorgeous, and clearly in love with the woman he was hovering somewhat protectively over. It was weird—they didn't look like they matched, and yet, they matched perfectly. "Everyone, this is Amber Lovett. My girlfriend."

Girlfriend.

Hearing the word fall from his lips with such satisfaction stunned her for a second.

It seemed to have the same effect on everyone else as well. There was a brief silence, followed by an explosion of greetings and smiles that almost knocked her back a step with their enthusiasm.

"So, you're the one!" Lillian's exclamation as she grasped Amber's hand in both of hers sounded both amazed and intrigued, making her immediately wary.

"What one?"

"That Richard borrowed the picnic hamper for. I hope he took you someplace nice. Did you have fun? I know when Rafe and I go on picnics, it's always so relaxing to get away from the rest of the crazy world and just be on our own for a little while. Where did you go? We found the most adorable spot. I'd share, but I kind of want to keep it private, you know? There's nothing less romantic than having a brother show up when you're trying to have sexy time with your guy. Am I right?"

"Um…" She blinked. "Sure."

Rafe pressed a kiss to Lillian's temple. "*Querida*, remember how we talked about letting people actually answer a question before asking them five more?" The look on his face was exasperated yet indulgent. Clearly, this wasn't a new struggle for them, because Lillian just grinned at Amber, unrepentant.

"*You* went on a picnic?" That was Theo, who eyed Rick with something akin to a scientist discovering a new species. "Mister I Hate Dirt and the Outdoors?"

"I don't hate the outdoors. I just don't feel the need to throw myself at every cliff and rockface out there like some deranged Spiderman, unlike some other people."

"Deranged Spiderman?" Theo sounded caught between amused and insulted.

"Hey, if the rock-climbing shoe fits, bro." Dimples popped on both sides of Peter's mouth when he grinned, making him more boyishly good-looking than his more classically handsome brothers.

Talk about hitting the gene pool jackpot. No family should produce this many good-looking people in one generation.

"Oh, and pumping weights at the gym is a better use of recreational time?" Theo asked with a scoff.

"It's a hell of a lot less dangerous than hanging off a mountain by a rope and a prayer."

"A hell of a lot less fun, too."

"How is it fun to risk life and limb every time you go up?" Lillian asked, crossing her arms, toe tapping. "You've already broken a leg and an arm. What's next? Your stupid head?"

"Don't exaggerate. It was only a fractured ankle and a dislocated shoulder."

Lillian made a noise that sounded like a hiss. "*Only.*"

"Plus, it wasn't my fault. Accidents happen. Baby bro here could pop a nut when he's lifting—"

"Oh, nice language."

"—or Richard could wrap one of those sexy speed machines he drives around a tree, so stop making it sound like I'm some crazy danger junkie, because I'm not."

Feeling more than a little uncomfortable at the argument that ignited seemingly from nowhere, Amber eased herself a few steps back as the four siblings continued to snap and snarl at each other. She started when Rafe appeared at her elbow. It seemed he, too, was distancing himself from the fray.

"Did I cause that somehow?" she asked in a low voice.

"Nah. Needling each other is a time-honored tradition among the Beaumont brood. It's how they show they love each other."

"I see." No, she didn't. But she didn't have any brothers or sisters, either, so who was she to judge?

The argument shifted with no rhyme or reason from dangerous hobbies to costume choices, with Peter getting the brunt of the ragging over his Sherlock Holmes getup. Evidently because he was studying to take the police detectives exam in real life.

She turned to Rafe to ask how long these "loving" discussions usually lasted, only to catch him giving her another of those intense, dissecting looks. Her hackles went up. "What?"

"Nothing. I'm just glad Richard finally came to his senses, is all."

"I'm sorry?"

"About his, ah, misunderstanding with you."

She froze.

Rick had told his family?

"What? You...you know?" Where was a convenient hole when you needed one?

"About him being an ass? I've known that for over a year." As though sensing her distress, he placed a light hand on her arm. "Don't worry, I'm the only one who knows anything about it. Richard came to me for advice. It's the only reason he said anything at all."

Part of her cringed at even one other person knowing the humiliating details of what happened between them. Another part was curious why he would have gone to Rafe for advice rather than one of his own brothers.

Although, judging by the ongoing bickering, maybe that part was self-explanatory.

Hoping she sounded calmer than she felt, she asked, "And what was your advice?"

"To be sure he brought kneepads."

The reply was so not what she was expecting, she just stared at him a moment, then let out a laugh that had all of the Beaumont siblings turning to look. When Rick raised a questioning eyebrow, she looked at Rafe, and both of them burst into laughter again.

"Why does it sound like you all are having a wonderful time without me?"

Still grinning, Amber turned toward the newcomer with the boisterous tone who sauntered into the circle of Beaumonts like he owned it. A little shorter than the other men, who all topped six feet and then some, it was immediately clear the size of his personality more than made up for what he lacked in inches. His dark skin and eyes, which hinted at a Mediterranean heritage, perfectly offset the rich jewel-toned wide-legged pants, tunic, and robe he wore like he was born to them.

"Des!" Lillian gave him a huge hug and did the double-cheek-kiss thing Amber had only ever seen before in the movies, but it was clear there was nothing phony about it. "You look awesome!"

"Thank you, kitten. I'd return the compliment, but..." He *tsked* as he swept his disapproving gaze over the group. "Look at you all. Your darling mother slaves for months to put on a *masquerade ball*, and all she asks is that you show up in costume to do your part. And what do you do? Take them off as soon as she isn't looking and hide out in a corner while she does all the work of keeping the guests, whom you all are supposed to be schmoozing with, happy." He gave a dramatic sigh and clutched a hand to his chest. "That poor woman is a saint. You don't deserve her."

Amber stared, not sure if she should be impressed or horrified.

Lillian snorted, clearly not upset in the least. "What did she promise you for that little set down?"

With the nimbleness of an actor, Des shed the look of disappointment like a coat and grinned. "Too much?"

"With you, Des, too much is a relative term," Rafe said with a shake of his head. He clasped the other man's hand in greeting. "Who are you supposed to be, anyway? Valentino in *The Sheik*?"

"No, that would have entailed a lot more eyeliner than I thought this crowd could handle. Good guess, though." He threw his arms out wide, turquoise and gold silk shimmering under the fairy lights. "I'm the Genie."

"Then that must make Michael Aladdin?" Rafe glanced around, presumably for the man in question.

"It took some convincing, but yes." Des made a face. "He wanted to come as a doctor."

"What's wrong with that?" The question popped out before she could think better of it. She fought not to cringe when Des turned a sharply quizzical look on her.

"Because he *is* a doctor, so it would just be wearing work clothes to a party and oh, my God, where did you get that absolutely *scrumptious* costume?"

"Um…" She seemed to be saying that a lot tonight.

"Amber made it," Rick said, slipping one arm lightly around her waist as he shook Des's hand with the other.

"Shut your mouth, she did not!"

"Not from scratch," she was quick to say. "I used pieces from two dresses I found at the thrift store and some material from the remnants place to put it all together."

Still studying her with a critical eye, Des asked, "No pattern? You did all of this freestyle?"

"I based it on a dress from a movie." She wasn't about to take credit for something that wasn't hers.

A smile softened his expression. "You did an amazing job, *Mademoiselle* de Barbarac." He said the name of Drew Barrymore's character with an impeccable French accent. "Color me *trés* impressed."

More pleased he knew the movie than with his praise of her efforts, she sketched an awkward curtsy. "*Merci, Monsieur* Genie."

"May I?" Even as he was asking permission, Des started walking a slow circle around her, crowding Rick a few steps away with a shooing motion. She shot Rick a wide-eyed look, but he just shook his head and grinned, which she took to mean this wasn't out of character for the man.

All well and good, but it didn't stop her from feeling like a prize filly being looked over at auction.

If he asked to see her teeth, she was out.

Once he was done with his examination, Des crossed his arms and tapped a finger against his lips. "How many weeks did this take you to do?"

"Um, about five days."

His eyebrows shot up. "*Days?*"

"Well, I only found out I needed a costume over the weekend, so…"

"You did all this in a week, without a pattern. Incredible." Des shot Rick a cagey look. "Not too many socialites have this kind of mad design skill."

"I'm no socialite." It might be a masquerade ball, but she wouldn't pretend to be something she wasn't. Not even for Rick's family and friends.

That never went well for Cinderella of any incarnation.

"I remake a lot of my clothes for work from consignment stores, so it's not like I've never done it before."

There. The God's honest truth. Let them do what they wanted with it.

To her surprise, Des's smile only widened. "Oh, I *knew* I was going to like you."

"Um. Thank you?"

He laughed. "Call me, kitten. I think we have a lot to talk about." He gave her a double-cheek air-kiss before turning back to Lillian. "I need to go find Michael before he crawls onto the dessert table and inhales an entire angel food cake. We've been doing Paleo all month, and he's teetering on the brink of rebellion." He gave a fond but exasperated sigh. "The man loves his sweets."

"Poor Michael," Lillian said with a laugh. "Why didn't you bring him over here with you, then?"

"He didn't want any part of my mission. I think your brothers and the oh-so yummy Rafael still intimidate him a wee bit when taken *en masse*. Which reminds me." He held up an imperious finger and bent a stern eye on everyone. "Costumes, people. Mingle. Make your mother proud." He clapped his hands twice. "Make it so."

Then, with a swish of silk, he was gone.

Amber stared after him, feeling a little like she'd been sucked up and spit out by a brightly colored tornado. "Who the heck *was* that?"

"A force of nature," Rafe said with a chuckle.

Lillian clapped her hands over her mouth. "Oh, I'm so sorry, I didn't even introduce you! Please don't take it personally. It's just, it seems like Des knows everyone in the world, and I sometimes forget not everyone knows him back."

"Des is a good friend of Lillian's," Rick said, reclaiming his place at her side. "And besides having his fingers in a half-dozen different entrepreneurial pies, he also happens to have his own line of clothing."

"And he wants to talk to *you*!" Lillian bounced a little with an excitement Amber didn't understand.

"But, why?"

"Because he loved your costume, because seriously, what's not to love, it's abso-freaking-lutely gorgeous and to die for, and that means he must think you're incredibly talented, which duh, you obviously are, and he probably wants to offer you a job before someone else snaps you up before he can!"

Amber's head spun a little trying to follow Lillian's whirlwind explanation. "All I did was copy a dress from a movie."

"Trust me, Des wouldn't have said anything if he didn't think you had talent above and beyond being able to use a sewing machine," Lillian replied. "He's got an uncanny knack for seeing beneath the surface to someone's true potential."

Rick's thumb was rubbing small, soothing circles on her hip. "It couldn't hurt to see what he has to say. But if you don't want to, that's fine, too. It's entirely up to you."

Did she want to?

She considered the question as she once again took Rick's arm and they started another round of mingling. She couldn't deny it felt good to have a professional like Des think she had talent. It soothed an ego pretty bruised and tattered from the silent treatment she'd been getting at work.

But what if, on closer inspection, he decided she wasn't really all that great? It might be one blow too many for her to recover from right now.

A familiar face in the crowd dragged her away from her maudlin thoughts, making her smile. "I didn't know Max was going to be here."

"Should I be concerned you seem so happy to see him?" Rick asked in a low murmur against her ear as Max bore down on them.

"You can ask that after last night?" she teased back.

"Just checking." His lips brushed a kiss to her neck. "God, I can't wait until I don't have to worry about ruining your makeup anymore. I want to kiss every inch of you until you come apart in my arms."

Warmth spread from her belly in all directions at his low words. Only the knowledge they were surrounded by people kept her from groaning out loud. "You're a horrible man. And I'm holding you to that promise."

He laughed. Then Max was there, and he released her briefly to do the handshake/one-armed hug thing guys did. "I didn't think you were actually going to show."

"I could say the same about you." Max slapped Rick's shoulder before turning to look at Amber. Was it her imagination, or did his smile dim a little? "It's nice to see you again. You look amazing."

"Thanks. So do you." And he did. He wore the Han Solo look really, really well. If she wasn't already head-over-heels for Rick, he'd definitely be worth a second look.

Max hesitated, just enough to make her uneasy.

"So, um, would you mind if I stole this guy away for a few minutes? There's something we need to discuss." The look he gave Rick as he said it only increased her disquiet.

"Can't it wait until tomorrow?" Rick asked.

"No, it's okay." She smiled as though she didn't have a flock of seagulls swooping through her stomach. "You go ahead and talk.

I'm going to go, um, freshen up." Wasn't that what rich people said when they needed to use the bathroom?

As if they didn't have to pee like everyone else.

"Are you sure?"

"Absolutely. How about I meet you by the dessert table Des mentioned?"

"Okay." He took her hand and kissed it, making her shiver as the tip of his tongue traced between her knuckles. "Ten minutes."

"Ten minutes." She cranked up the wattage of her smile for them both and headed off in the direction Rick pointed. By the time she located the ladies room, which was more of a suite of rooms rather than a simple bathroom, with several small clusters of chairs and sofas in a separate room from the stalls and sinks, her cheeks ached.

The little sitting room was empty for the moment. Letting the smile die, she grasped the back of one of the chairs and sighed, not wanting to sit and risk damaging her wings. She stood there for a few long seconds, eyes closed, absorbing the blessed quiet.

There was no reason for her to feel like Max had snubbed her. He just needed to talk to Rick about something private, that's all. Maybe about his donation. Or maybe it had something to do with the game.

Rick had confided he was Max's silent partner in the company, the "bow" half of Woodbow Entertainment, using his alias's spelling to help obscure his identity. Maybe there were issues he needed to talk over with him that were proprietary and not for her ears.

She let out a relieved laugh at her own paranoia, stifling it as she heard the outer door open, letting in the noise from the ballroom before cutting it off again as it swung shut. She needed to stop being so sensitive and overreacting all the time. Max needed to talk to Rick, period.

Everything wasn't always about her.

"Well, well, well, what do we have here? If it isn't Richard's little rebound lay."

Except, of course, when it was.

RICHARD'S GAZE FOLLOWED AMBER'S retreating figure until the crowd swallowed her before turning his attention to a troubled-looking Max. "This better be important."

"Oh, it is."

"Well?"

"Not here. Where can we go that's private?"

He almost snapped at Max to just cut the bullshit and talk, but he could tell from the uncharacteristic tension in his friend's demeanor that whatever he had to say, it wasn't good. Silently cursing, he led Max to the edge of the room and pushed open a panel which was really the door leading up to the musicians' gallery.

Max stopped to examine it, his inner nerd clearly intrigued. "A hidden door. Cool. How'd you know it was there?"

"My mother throws a lot of parties here." During which he'd dragged more than one willing woman into the shadowy seclusion of the stairwell for a hot, fast fuck. Not his finest moments. "Max, focus. What's going on?"

"How well do you really know Amber Lovett?"

A wave of furious protectiveness swept through him. "I'd be very careful about what you say next, my friend."

Max stared at him. "Shit. You love her, don't you?"

There was no way in hell he was going to confirm or deny that. Especially when he wasn't really sure himself. What he felt for Amber was like nothing he'd ever felt with any other woman before.

"None of your business. Now, talk."

"Okay, fine." But he didn't.

Richard's patience shredded. "Max!"

"Derek's father came to see me," he blurted.

"Derek's...father?" Richard felt the word like a punch in the chest. "How is that even possible? He's not in the picture. And what the hell would he go see *you* for?"

"Money."

The punch became a vise on his lungs, making it hard to breathe. "What?"

"He wanted money."

He lowered himself onto a step with a hard thump. "I think you need to start at the beginning."

"Right. Okay, so this guy, Hunter something, he shows up at my door this morning with this wild story about how Amber stole his son away from him, that she moved to Boulder to hide him away all these years."

"That's bullshit. Amber would never do that." But even as he said it, he remembered her bitter expression when she'd mentioned the "discussion" she'd had with her son about his father just last week. He'd never revisited the question of why the man had been a topic of conversation after all this time.

Maybe he should have.

Max spread his hands in a don't-shoot-the-messenger gesture. "I'm just telling you what the guy said."

"What else did he say?"

"That he could have Amber arrested and charged with parental kidnapping and a bunch of other things, but he didn't want to put his kid through the trauma of watching his mother dragged off to jail."

"Let me guess. He'd be willing to consider not pressing charges if offered the right financial incentive."

"You got it."

Disgust filled him. What kind of man used his own child as a bargaining chip to make a profit? "That still doesn't explain why the hell he'd go to you about this little offer. It would make more sense if he came to see—"

Me.

The old feeling of being nothing but a bank account for people to tap into in exchange for their friendship threatened to crest over him like a breaking wave. But then it receded, leaving him calm and untouched. If Amber was somehow involved in this scheme, she'd have directed her partner in crime to the right man.

Still, he had to ask. "Why you?"

"It seems he saw those pictures from the launch party and was under the mistaken impression Amber and I were involved."

Which only made Richard calmer. Whatever plot was afoot, Amber wasn't a party to it. He was a little ashamed he'd even considered the possibility. But at least this time he'd kept his old fears from overwhelming his common sense.

He'd already made that mistake once with her. He didn't plan on making it again.

"Did you tell him the truth?"

"Well, I tried. But once he started throwing around threats about calling the police and filing charges, I just shut up and let him talk. When he finally got down to what he was asking for, I told him it was a lot of money, and I wanted a day to think things through. He was pissed, but he agreed."

"How much?"

"A hundred grand."

It *was* a lot of money. For most people. For Richard, it was less than he'd dropped on his beloved Spider. But it was nothing compared to what he'd willingly pay to keep Amber—and Derek—safe.

"How are you supposed to contact him?"

"He gave me his phone number."

Richard was already nodding, sorting through the things he needed to do before tomorrow. One of them was getting the full story about this Hunter asshole from Amber. He needed all the facts if he was going to protect her.

Something he knew she was going to hate.

She was too damned independent for her own good sometimes. But that was just too fucking bad. No way would he allow the slightest chance the bastard could make good on his threats.

"So?" Max looked at him expectantly. "What are we gonna do about this douchecanoe?"

With a grim grin, he stood and clapped a grateful hand on his friend's shoulder. "We're going to destroy him."

"Good."

They parted ways after reentering the ballroom. Richard headed straight to the dessert table, hoping Amber wasn't too annoyed with him for being a few minutes later than promised. But it appeared he'd actually beaten her to their meeting spot.

He breathed a sigh of relief.

Accepting a miniature éclair on a tiny plate from a white-gloved server, he wondered if perhaps she was having a problem with her costume. Those wings could be tricky. Remembering his reaction when the door to her friend's apartment opened, he couldn't help but smile.

She'd had him gobsmacked with his first look. And it wasn't the costume. It was her. The whole package. The gorgeous woman, the single mom, the enthusiastic lover.

She was it for him.

"Richard, there you are. Thank goodness."

He stifled a groan. "Mom, I'm mingling, I swear. I just stopped for something to eat so I don't pass out from all the hard work you're making me do." He popped the last of the éclair into his mouth, wiping his fingers on a napkin.

"What? Oh, never mind that. Richard, I'm so, so sorry. I had no idea."

His mother's concerned tone wiped the playful smirk from his face. "No idea about what?"

"Damien Carlisle, the dirty sneak. I was only just informed that he didn't bring his wife with him this evening, as he RSVPed. He brought his daughter instead."

Son of a bitch.

Katherine Carlisle. Exactly what the evening didn't need.

"I don't know why he would do such a thing, considering the two of you...you know. Split up."

"That's exactly why," he said grimly. "Either she wants a second chance, or she wants to cause trouble. You know what she's like. Which do *you* think it is?"

"I will not have that bitch ruin this evening." The fact the word passed his mother's lips in public shocked him almost as much as her icy tone.

"Don't worry, Mom. She enjoys her reputation too much to cause that kind of public scene. The only person she'd want to screw with is me."

Or Amber.

Who'd gone to the ladies room alone.

Who was late coming back.

Who had absolutely no idea who Katherine was, or how sharp her claws could be when unsheathed.

With a curse, he ripped the mask from his face and headed for the restrooms. If Kitty had gone after Amber to get back at him for their breakup, she'd be sorry. He didn't care if he lost Damien Carlisle as a client. He didn't even care if he ruined his mother's party.

All he cared about in that moment was protecting the woman he suddenly and irrevocably knew that he loved.

Chapter 18

ALTHOUGH SHE LOOKED VAGUELY familiar, Amber didn't recognize the woman who had spoken. But she did recognize the type.

She'd been dealing with mean girls all her life.

That experience gave her the armor to let the nasty words bounce right off as she started for the door. There could only be a fight if both people participated, and she'd learned a long time ago walking away was a lot easier than trying to defend herself against vicious lies and rumors.

Except the woman stepped into her path, blocking her escape.

"Where do you think you're going?"

"Back to the party. Excuse me." She tried again to step around, but the woman was quick, aggressively moving into her path once more.

"Back to *darling Richard*?" The sneer in her voice was bitter and very, very personal.

"Yes." Another step, another block. Amber sighed. "Go ahead."

The woman blinked. "What do you mean?"

"You're obviously not going to let me leave until you've said whatever it is you came in here to say, so let's have it."

"Do you have any idea who I am?"

Amber studied her for a moment.

She was gorgeous, or she would be if the stick-up-her-butt expression didn't make her look constipated. Tall—she had to top six feet with the heels she was wearing—model thin, her hair dressed up in one of those sexy, just-tumbled-out-of-bed styles that probably took hours to achieve. The royal blue gown wasn't a costume, just something that looked expensive enough to match the jewels at her neck and the diamond tiara sitting on her head.

Which she had a feeling *also* weren't costume.

She shrugged. "I don't know. Princess Anorexia?"

The woman puffed up like a peahen. "I'm Katherine Carlisle." When Amber didn't react, she added, "Richard's fiancée."

It was meant to shock and wound, and it worked.

For a second.

"Funny, I don't see a ring."

"We had a fight. I gave it back."

Possible. And yet, she wasn't buying it.

"Really? When was that?"

"At the beginning of last month."

Which was right around the time Amber first met him. And it was the second week of September they'd started their strange little dance, after she'd invited him out for pizza.

Her confidence faltered. Only for a split-second, but the other woman pounced like a shark smelling blood in the water.

"I'll bet he jumped right from my bed to yours," she said with a disdainful sniff. "Richard doesn't deal well with rejection. Or being alone. He would have needed to find someone to soothe his fragile ego with and make him feel important again. Someone he could impress with his money."

"Then you'd bet wrong." Amber gave her a sardonic smile. "And if you think Rick—Richard has a fragile ego, then you don't really know him as well as you seem to think."

"Are you saying you haven't slept with him?" Katherine raked her with a dissecting look that felt all too familiar. "Please. Why else would he be with you?"

Not about to confirm or deny her and Rick's sexual status—or admit the question hit a little too close to home not to hurt—she said, "If you gave the ring back, then who he is or isn't sleeping with is none of your concern."

To her surprise, Katherine smiled.

She didn't trust it for a second.

"You're right. I can deal with Richard having his little revenge fuck."

Ouch.

"After all, I did break his heart when I called things off. And it's not like he's going to keep you around after I tell him I've forgiven him. Which I plan to do tonight." She held out her expensively manicured left hand and smiled dreamily at it. "By midnight, I'll be the future Mrs. Richard Beaumont again."

Pain stabbed Amber straight through the heart. She didn't want to believe a single thing from this woman's mouth, but it all sounded so plausible, so almost-true.

It was the almost part that kept her sane.

That, and knowing how well mean girls could thrust the knife when they found an opening.

"Oh, don't look so disappointed, dear," Katherine purred. "I'm sure Richard will give you a nice parting gift to remember him by. Some jewelry, or maybe a nice, big check. You know, for services rendered." She tittered at Amber's reflexive flinch. "Oh! Oh, my. Don't tell me you thought he might actually *marry* you?"

Enough.

Gritting her teeth, she made one more attempt to leave. This time Katherine let her by, but stopped her in her tracks with her next words.

"I know who you are, you know. More importantly, I know who you're not. And if you're honest with yourself for just a second, you know it, too. You can't possibly imagine you'd ever fit into our world. You'd make him a laughingstock if you even tried."

She turned back, fists clenched at hearing her own greatest fear voiced by this spiteful bitch. "Rick didn't seem to think so. He brought me here, didn't he?"

But was she simply a substitute for the woman he'd originally planned to have on his arm? The question of being spirited secretly up the elevator from the parking garage flashed through her mind again. For her privacy? Or his?

"Of course he did. Because he knew I'd be here, and he wanted to make me jealous."

Lies!

But was it? Had he known Katherine was going to be at the ball? How could he not?

"Don't feel too badly." Katherine's tone was so sugary it made Amber's teeth ache. "You'll probably get more from him now than if you somehow managed to marry him, anyway. Richard's lawyers would never let him walk down the aisle without an iron-clad prenup in place."

"Is that why you broke up with him?"

Fury flashed briefly through the other woman's eyes. "Why would it matter to me? I have my own money."

Which wasn't an answer, but still was.

"You know what? It doesn't matter, because I don't care about Rick's money, and he knows it. Just stay away from us both for the rest of the night." This time when she turned to leave, she ignored the other woman's parting shot, although it caught her straight through the heart.

"You'll never be good enough for him. You'll see. And so will everyone else."

Furious at herself for letting the spiteful bitch get under her skin, she stuck to the edges of the ballroom, blindly trying to put as much distance between them as possible. Tears burned her eyes, but she refused to let them fall and ruin all of Lin's hard work. Besides, what did she have to cry about? Rick had chosen *her*.

After Katherine had broken off their engagement.

An engagement he'd never mentioned.

Like a burr under a saddle, that fact nagged at her with every step. They were in a relationship, damn it. Something as important as an ex-fiancée, a very recent one if Katherine was to be believed, was something that probably should have come up.

Amber stopped in her tracks. If Katherine was to be believed?

She wanted to smack herself for being so gullible. The woman obviously cornered her intending to cause trouble. Why was she taking *anything* she said at face value?

Maybe because deep down was still the certainty this thing with Rick was too good to be true. That it wouldn't—couldn't—last. That everything the other woman said about her not being good enough, about being an embarrassment to him, was right.

Loser.

Trash.

Gold digger.

For once, the old voices in her head didn't make her cringe. She wasn't any of those things. She'd proven it to Rick. Or maybe she'd finally proven it to herself. Either way, the words had lost their power over her.

The only opinions that mattered going forward were hers and Rick's. Everyone else could go hang.

Confidence still a little shaky but mostly restored, she looked around and realized in her rush to escape she'd gone in the opposite direction of the dessert table she was supposed to meet Rick at. With a sigh, she started to work her way back. As she neared the alcove that led to the restroom area, she gave it a wide berth, not wanting to risk running into Katherine again, especially not before she'd talked to Rick first.

Speak of the devil.

Even without the cape billowing behind him as he stalked through the crowd, she would have recognized him. There was something about him she just knew, something that called to her. Like an electric spark arcing between them despite the distance.

Shaking her head at that flight of fancy, she started after him. In avoiding bumping into other guests, she lost sight of him a few times, before finally spying him again standing near the restrooms. She smiled to herself. He must have decided to come and get her rather than wait by the desserts.

Several people passed in front of her, halting her progress and blocking her view for a few seconds. Once they were gone, though, she couldn't seem to get her feet moving again.

Rick wasn't alone any longer. Standing with him was Katherine, and they seemed to be having a very intense, very intimate discussion, judging by the way his head was bent toward hers.

The way she looked up at him, face tipped as though waiting for a kiss, was enough to make Amber's breath catch. When Katherine threw her arms around Rick's neck and the kiss became reality, it was stolen away completely.

"Kitten, there you are! I was hoping to run into you again. Michael, sweetie, this is who I was telling you about. Isn't her costume positively *divine*? I mean, just look how perfectly she..." Des's voice changed from delighted to concerned. "Amber, is everything okay?"

It took a lot to tear her eyes from the damning sight of her boyfriend—*ha!*—locking lips with another woman. She swallowed hard, afraid she just might throw up.

"No. I...no." She couldn't stop herself. She darted another look back at Rick. The kiss had ended, thank God, but his hands were now cupping her arms as he once again talked to her with serious intent.

Begging her to come back? Asking her to wear his ring again?

"What has you so...oh." Des stared, his expression startled by what he was seeing.

Join the club.

Unable to keep torturing herself, she looked away, only to find herself looking into the kind, blue gaze of a stranger dressed in colorful silks that matched Des's.

And my mortification is complete.

"Excuse me, I need to go."

"Oh, no." Des took a surprisingly firm hold of her arm. "You are not going to pull a Cinderella and disappear as the clock strikes twelve."

"Why not? I'll even leave Rick one of my shoes. You can tell him to stick it up his two-timing behind."

A smile flickered over his face. "Oh yes, I definitely like you." He glanced in Rick's direction again. "Seriously, though. Are you going to concede the field that easily? Without even putting up a fight?"

"Of course not." But she was planning on licking her wounds first. "I can't do anything about it here, though. Not without making a scene and ruining Mrs. Beaumont's party."

"Hmm. True." He tapped a long finger to his lips. "Ah! I know. Michael, darling, take her up to our room. That should give you all the privacy you need to have things out with each other."

"Oh, I..." She'd hoped for a little longer to get her emotions back under control, but maybe this way was better. If things were going to end between them, she'd rather know now than spend the night in an agony of wondering.

"Thank you. You're very kind." She managed a weak smile. "Both of you. I mean, you don't even know me."

"Des can never pass up an opportunity to interfere in other people's love lives." Michael smiled fondly at the other man, who preened as though it were a compliment.

"What can I say? Love is precious and life is short. If I see someone who needs a little nudge, well, then I give it to them. I haven't been wrong yet." The two shared an intimate look before Des turned his attention back to Amber. "Now kitten, you be a good little cinder girl and go with Michael. I'll send Richard along shortly." His lips pinched. "After I have a few words with him first."

"Des…" Michael gave him a look that had Des flapping his hands impatiently.

"I know, I know, no scenes. I'll be the soul of discretion."

"Lord help us," Michael muttered.

With a little nudge, Des said to Amber, "Go on, now. And don't be too quick to judge, kitten. Things aren't always the way they seem."

No, she acknowledged as she let Michael lead her from the ballroom.

Sometimes they were much worse.

⸺◆○◆⸺

AFTER RUSHING THROUGH THE milling crowd, Richard pulled up short in front of the door to the restroom, his hand inches from the ornate filigreed handle, stopped by the deeply ingrained taboo of intruding on that totally feminine domain.

Which was ridiculous, of course. It wasn't like he'd be peeking under any stall doors. He was just going to poke his head in, grab Amber if she was there, and go. His feet might never even have to cross the threshold.

And yet, he hesitated.

"I believe the little boy's room is the other door, darling."

The hairs on the back of his neck stirred at the sound of the familiar purr. Turning his head slowly, the way you would in a horror movie, he saw Kitty standing a few feet away. She looked lovely and expensive, just as she always did.

And she left him completely cold.

"Katherine. What a surprise."

She smiled. "Exactly what I was going for."

"You shouldn't have bothered."

His flat pronouncement wiped the smile from her face, replacing it with a pout he recognized all too well. "Really, Richard, are you still carrying a grudge?"

"A grudge? Not at all. Ending things was the best thing you've ever done for me. For both of us. In fact, I should be thanking you." He could tell by the angry flash in her eyes she didn't like hearing that. Too bad. It was the God's honest truth. Life with her would have been hell. "Why are you here?"

"Because of you, of course. Because of us."

"Us? There is no us."

"Oh, but darling, there can be." Without warning, she flung her arms around his neck and pressed her mouth to his.

Just as quickly, he wrenched her away. The kiss had tasted of desperation and deceit, and he wasn't playing that game with her. "Don't do that again." He kept a grip on her arms as he felt her tense for another lunge. "I mean it, Katherine."

"Oh, Richard, how can you be so cold after everything we've shared?"

Aware a few of the people milling just feet away were giving the two of them speculative glances, he bent his head closer and kept his voice low as he replied.

"Anything we shared is in the past. You shouldn't have come here tonight. Go home, Katherine."

"But I had to see you. I've missed you. Haven't you missed me, just a little?"

There was a time when he might have let her down gently. Told her what she wanted to hear while still making it clear things between them were finished. But now there was Amber, and he wanted no misunderstandings to come back and bite him in the ass.

"No, Katherine. I'm sorry, but no. I've moved on, and you should, too. Please, just go home."

Disbelief slackened her features before rage took over. Flags of red colored her pale cheeks like a declaration of war. "How can you honestly prefer that little tart to me?"

His eyes narrowed. "What did you call her?"

"Oh, please. It's painfully obvious you went out and found someone you'd be able to impress right into bed with all your precious millions. But she won't make you happy, Richard. She's nothing like me."

It was tough, but he hung onto his temper by the barest of threads. "You're right. She's nothing like you. Which is just one of the many reasons I love her."

"You..." She uttered a nervous laugh. "You can't be serious."

"As a heart attack."

"Richard!" She sounded honestly aghast. "It's one thing for people like us to sleep with someone like that. But we don't fall in love with them."

The way she said "someone like that" snapped the last thread.

Or maybe it was the echo of himself thinking the exact same thing not too long ago.

"I don't want to hear another word about her pass your lips. You know nothing about her."

"Oh, really?" With a toss of her head, she glared at him with enough venom to make his balls shrink. "I know she's planning to get your ring on her finger."

"And how would you know that?"

"She was bragging about it to me a few minutes ago when she cornered me in the restroom. Just like she bragged she'd screw your brains out until you agreed to forget all about making her sign any prenup."

Something cold shot up his spine. Then common sense retook control. He gave her a grim smile. "Nice try. Now, for the last time, go home. If you don't leave on your own, I'll be more than happy to have security escort you out."

She sucked in an indignant breath. "You wouldn't dare!"

Leaning closer so they were almost nose-to-nose, he said, "Try me." He released his hold on her arms and took a step back.

"How dare you threaten me. When my father finds out—"

"Your father is more than welcome to take his business elsewhere. In fact, I think it might be in everyone's best interest if he did just that. You can tell him to call me Monday morning to set up the transfer."

A call he knew would never come. Damien Carlisle loved his only daughter to the point of spoiling her rotten, but he loved making money even more. Any threat to that would be dealt with swiftly, even if the threat happened to be Kitty herself.

Which she knew, judging by the hate-filled look she gave him.

"You're a bastard, Richard Beaumont. I hope your little piece of ass takes you for every penny you have." With a swish of Swarovski crystal-encrusted skirts, she turned and made a regal retreat through the crowd.

He wondered briefly if he should follow her to make sure she didn't cause any more trouble before she left, then discarded the idea in favor of finding Amber. While he didn't believe a word Kitty said about her, he was more concerned about what poison she might have dripped in Amber's ear.

He needed to find her.

Fast.

He turned and nearly walked into Lillian's friend Des who, for some reason, was waiting right behind him like a big, brightly colored shadow. He made to step around him.

"Excuse me. I need to go find—"

"The woman who saw you locking lips with the catty Miss Kitty?"

He froze, his heart actually missing a beat. "Please tell me you're joking." But he could tell from the other man's rare expression of total seriousness he wasn't. "Son of a bitch."

"Yes, almost exactly what I was thinking when I saw the little tableau the two of you were making over here in the corner."

"I didn't kiss her. She kissed me."

"Normally I would call bullshit on a statement like that, but after hearing the end of your conversation just now, I'm inclined to believe you."

"Gee, thanks."

"I'm not so sure everyone else will, though."

Everyone else being Amber.

Fucking hell.

This was a nightmare. Just as Kitty intended, if not the way she'd planned. So much for not having misunderstandings bite him in the ass.

"I need to find her and explain."

"Yes, you do. But she's not here anymore."

"What?" His heart didn't just skip a beat, it went into a staccato of full-blown panic. "Where the hell is she?"

"Don't worry. She's tucked away safe and sound in my room upstairs. Fourteen ten. Michael is keeping her company to make sure she doesn't bolt before you get there." He held out a plastic keycard, holding tight when Richard tried to snatch it from his hand. "Don't screw this up, my friend."

"I don't plan to." He yanked again, and this time Des let go. Every instinct in him screamed to hurry, but he paused long enough to give him a grateful nod. "Thank you."

"For butting in?" Des gave a wide smile and spread his hands. "It's what I do, darling. Now, go and get your fairy princess."

It only took a minute to grab an elevator and be standing in front of the room. But then he froze, the hand clutching the keycard suddenly damp and clammy. What if he screwed this up? What if she didn't listen, didn't believe him when he told her he'd been an ambush victim of the kiss she'd witnessed?

Nut up, Beaumont.

Tapping the card to the lock pad, he took a deep breath and opened the door. His eyes went immediately to Amber. Standing in front of the floor-to-ceiling windows, her stiff back aimed in his direction, she didn't even glance over as the door latched behind him. Her wings had been removed and were laying on the end of the bed next to where Des's partner, Michael, sat.

With a look of combined relief and worry, Michael rose and walked toward him.

"Good luck." A sympathetic pat on the shoulder accompanied the soft words as he passed by.

Once the door closed behind him, Richard waited for Amber to say something. Anything. Then he realized that was the coward's way out. He needed to be the one to start, to apologize, even if he hadn't done anything wrong.

"Des told me you saw Katherine kiss me in the ballroom. I know you probably won't believe me, but I wasn't a willing participant. She kissed me, and I pushed her away."

"I believe you."

He wasn't sure he believed the low words. Especially since she still wouldn't turn to look at him. "You do?"

"Please. I met the woman. I wouldn't put that move past her for a second." There was the soft clatter of ice against glass as her right arm raised and lowered. Michael must have gotten her something from the room's minibar.

Hopefully, it was to steady her nerves, not drown her sorrows.

Tired of talking to her back, he walked to where she was standing at the window. "Then why did you leave?"

"Because it hurt to see the two of you together like that, all intimate and gooey-eyed for each other."

"Gooey-eyed? I'm not even sure I know what that means."

"It means you should have told me you were engaged until practically the day we met."

It took a second for the words to process, they were so foreign to his brain.

"Engaged? To *Katherine*?"

"Unless there's another ex-almost Mrs. Richard Beaumont out there I don't know about." She raised the glass again, draining it this time.

"There aren't any ex-almost anythings. I wasn't engaged to Katherine, or to anyone else for that matter, at any time in my life. Ever."

Finally, she looked at him, and the bruised shadows in her eyes nearly gutted him.

"Is that really true?"

"I swear." He hesitated, but knew he needed to be completely honest. "I'll admit, the subject of marriage did come up, but only because I showed her the prenup papers my lawyer keeps on file. I was nowhere near ready to actually pop the question."

"Then why show her the papers?"

Suddenly, the collar of his tux felt about two sizes too small. "Because that's the only way I'd know. It's the only way I ever know."

"Know?"

"If it's worth taking the relationship any further. If they bail, then I'm not wasting my time. Or theirs."

And they'd all bailed. Every one of them.

Understanding dawned in her expression. "Oh, Rick. That's..."

"Cold blooded?" One of the nicer accusations hurled by Katherine on realizing what he was handing her.

"No. Sad." She placed her free hand on his arm. "I hate there's been no one in your life you could trust with all your heart."

"It's okay. Because there is now." He took the glass from her and set it aside. Clasping both of her hands in his, he did the complete opposite of what he'd done his entire life. Instead of speaking words prepared with deliberate care, he spoke from the heart.

"You've shown me I can be a much better man than the one I've been all these years. That by always expecting the worst of everyone, I've kept myself from seeing there are people who are exactly who and what they say they are. Who can accept me for who I am, not what I'm worth, or what I can do for them."

"You had your reasons for being cautious," she said, squeezing his hands.

"The reasons of a seventeen-year-old with his heart and ego bruised." He gave a rough laugh. "Damn it, Theo's right. I've let what Maryanne Alcott did all those years ago color the way I see all women."

"And what did she do?"

Much as he'd rather not pick at that particular scab, he'd been the one to bring it up. And she had a right to know where his ghosts came from.

"You remember I had asthma as a kid, right?" She nodded. "Well, that meant I wasn't exactly Joe Jock when I got to high school. I was more the chess club, debate club, student council kind of guy. President of each, actually, which only made it worse. I was the ultimate trifecta of nerds. All but invisible to the girls in the school. But then junior year, I started tutoring this senior in math."

"Maryanne."

He kind of liked the way she made the name sound like it tasted bad.

"Yes."

"Let me guess. She was a blonde, busty, cheerleader."

Nailed it.

"Pep squad, but yeah. And desperate enough to pass her calculus final to ask nerdy me for help. But after a few weeks, she started to hang out after our tutoring sessions were over. Just...talking.

Like she wanted to spend time with me. Like she actually saw me as more than a means to an end. Then, before I knew it, she was asking if I wanted to go to the senior prom with her."

"And you said…"

"Yes, of course. I was a nerd, not an idiot." They shared a small laugh before he continued. "Although I guess I was an idiot, too, because I footed the bill for everything. The tickets. Her hair, makeup, spray tan, and spa treatment the day of. Not to mention the very expensive couture dress she just *had* to have to look perfect for me but, sadly, couldn't afford, and a pair of sparkly Louboutins to match. I was a teenage boy," he said in his own defense when Amber made a choking noise. "What did I know about that kind of thing? Shoes were shoes."

"Which was probably what she counted on."

Yeah, it was.

"Honestly, I didn't even care about how much it all cost. I was happy because she was happy. And because I was at the prom with a pretty girl on my arm, rubbing it in the faces of all the jocks she passed over to ask *me*."

There might have been a tiny chip on his shoulder about jocks back then.

Okay, maybe a boulder.

Which only made how that evening ended all the more humiliating.

"The prom was a little awkward, since I didn't have any friends there, and her friends were, well, a bunch of teenage girls. But it wasn't horrible. Until I came back from the bathroom and overheard her bragging to her girlfriends how she was going to get me to buy her a car next. They told her she was crazy, and she bet them she'd have a Mercedes parked in her driveway by the end of the summer, and that she wouldn't even have to put out for it."

Amber's eyes widened.

"Wow. That's a whole different level of greed right there."

"Oh, it gets worse. After I took a long walk around the parking lot to cool off after hearing that, I went back inside to confront her. One of her girlfriends very helpfully pointed out the direction she'd seen her go."

"Uh-oh."

"Yeah, I was so clueless." And that 'friend' had really wanted Maryanne to lose the car bet. "At least until I saw her in the corner with one of the football player's hands shoved down the dress I bought for her."

"That bitch." She rubbed his arm. "I'm so sorry she did that to you. Especially if you really liked her."

It was strange, but her touch and her words were like a balm, calming and soothing the decades-old festering wound.

"I loved her. Or, at least, I thought I did. The only upside to the entire night was that I hadn't actually spilled my guts and said it to her yet. I had this whole speech planned for the ride to the after-party. About how I felt. That I'd like to keep seeing her over the summer and do the long-distance thing when she left for college. Followed, in my mind, by hopefully making it to second base for the first time in the back of the limo."

Needless to say, none of those things happened.

"So, that's the Maryanne saga, for what it's worth."

"It's worth a lot. You have legitimate reasons for being so cautious about women after how she treated you."

"Maybe. But I could have been cautious without closing my feelings off the way I did. And the really sad part is, I didn't know how much I was missing. Not until you showed me." He leaned in, slow enough to give her the chance to pull away if she wanted to.

She didn't.

His lips met hers, the kiss so gentle and sweet it nearly wrecked him. He pulled away enough to see her face. "I love you."

Her eyes widened almost comically large before she shook her head. "You don't have to say that."

"Yeah, I do. I promised you, no more lies, no more omissions, remember?"

"But…"

"I. Love. You." Words which had always terrified him, that seemed like a trap, and now he couldn't get enough of saying them. Every time he did, he felt stronger. Freer.

But the more seconds that ticked by without hearing them said back, the more he wondered if he'd made some kind of strategical error.

Damn.

This was why he always planned things out rather than acting off the cuff.

"I'm sorry. I shouldn't have blurted it out like that. You deserve something romantic. Something special. Not standing in a borrowed hotel room after dealing with the wicked bitch of the east."

She gave a tiny, ladylike snort. "Isn't that the west?"

"Well, she's from New York, so…"

"Ah." Freeing her hands from his, Amber laid them on his face, her thumbs caressing his cheeks as she stared at him with those fathomless blue eyes. "I don't need a romantic dinner or fancy party or anything else. Just hearing you say that you love me is as special as I need. And in case you were wondering, I happen to love you, too."

"Thank Christ." With a groan, he pulled her into his arms, his mouth devouring hers as he let the last bonds of uncertainty slip away. She tasted like the rum and ginger ale she'd drank, sweet and fizzy and something he wanted more of.

As he angled his head to deepen the kiss, he realized dimly he was probably destroying her carefully applied makeup, but didn't care.

All that mattered was getting her naked and showing her without words how much she meant to him.

As his fingers sought the closure for the dress, he walked her backwards toward the bed, never once taking his mouth from hers. But when her legs bumped the mattress—finally!—she wrenched her lips free with a gasp.

"We can't. This isn't our room."

He wanted to argue that Des wouldn't care, but the uncomfortable look in her eyes told him she did.

With an impatient growl, he grabbed her by the hand and started for the door. They were in a hotel, for fuck's sake. He'd find them a room if he had to buy the whole damn place to get one. There was no way they were leaving until he finished branding himself as deeply into her body—and heart—as he possibly could.

Chapter 19

She should have known he'd get them a suite.

Not that she cared. As long as it had a door that locked and a bed that didn't belong to two very nice almost-strangers, she was good to go. Des probably wouldn't have cared, considering he'd all but forced her and Rick together to work things out. But she didn't think she'd be able to face either man again without blushing, knowing they knew what had been going on in their bed.

Rick didn't even have to go down to the front desk to get the room. He'd just called, told them what he wanted, and by the time they rode the elevator to the top floor, there was a hotel employee waiting outside the double doors at the end of the hall to let them in.

That's how she knew how close to the end of his control Rick really was. If he'd flaunt the power his wealth gave him like that in front of her, he really did have to love and trust her.

Love.

Oh, her giddy Aunt Fanny. She'd thought she'd fall over when that word passed his lips. Good thing he'd been holding onto her at the time. She'd hoped he felt that way. But she'd never dreamed he'd be the one to say it first.

Hell, she wasn't even sure he'd be the *second* one to say it.

After all of his issues with women in the past, she'd accepted it might take a long while before he got comfortable enough with the idea to actually use the words.

And then he'd gone and said it when she totally wasn't prepared. Not to hear it, and not to say it back. Not yet. At least, that's what she'd thought. But looking into his eyes, seeing the absolute truth to what he was saying, freed something in her that had been keeping her as tied up in old fears and doubts as Rick had been.

After that, the words had been easy.

She watched with controlled amusement as he tipped the dark-suited man, who was very carefully not reacting to the silver glitter smeared across Rick's cheek like stripper blush. Which meant her beautiful winged mask was ruined.

And she couldn't have cared less.

All she wanted was both of them naked and in a bed before her entire body went up in flames.

As soon as the door thumped shut, she exploded into action. She wrapped her arms around Rick's neck, her mouth finding his with desperate need. The heat that had been temporarily banked came roaring back to life, searing away any doubts.

This man touched a part of her she'd forgotten even existed. Hadn't dreamed could ever exist again. With him, and only him, she could be the woman she'd always been meant to be.

Free. Uninhibited.

Sexy.

Clothes were shed with shaking hands, strewn like a trail of breadcrumbs leading to the enormous bedroom. By the time they reached the bed, the only thing she wore were her lacy white panties and crystal-encrusted heels. Rick took a long moment to stare at her, top to bottom. Not once did she feel the urge to cover any part of her body.

He did that for her.

"Lord have mercy, woman," he groaned. "You're killing me. No!" He held up a hand like a cop when she went to kick off the shoes. "Leave them on for now."

She grinned. "Having a little Cinderella fantasy, are we?"

"No. Having a *you* fantasy." Dropping to his knees in front of her, he pressed a kiss to her belly right above her navel before hooking his fingers in the scrap of underwear and slowly teasing it off her. Then he pressed another kiss to what he'd just uncovered.

This time, she was the one who groaned.

And sighed.

And begged when he left her hovering on the edge for long, torturous minutes.

Then she screamed as he pushed her headlong into an orgasm that radiated out in waves of pleasure which engulfed her entire body like a tsunami.

He caught her as her legs buckled and laid her gently on the bed.

Before she had time to catch her breath, the shoes were gone, Rick stripped off his boxer briefs and he was between her legs, the hard tip of his erection pressing unerringly into the part of her that wanted him most.

Then he froze. She wanted to scream again, only not in a good way.

Then she realized why he'd stopped.

"I'm protected," she gasped between ragged pants. The very first thing she'd done once she'd gotten health insurance was go on the pill. Something she'd never mentioned before. He'd always worn a condom, and she'd let him.

She saw the question in his eyes, followed by understanding.

Derek had been conceived despite the use of a condom. Much as she loved him, couldn't picture her life without him, she'd done everything in her power to ensure the next time she got pregnant it would be by choice, not chance. Double the birth control meant half the risk.

"Are you sure?" The words sounded like they were torn from somewhere deep inside him.

"Yes." Her head fell back as he pushed inside. The feel of him, hot and hard and bare, caressing already sensitized nerve endings, was indescribable.

His eyes never left hers, and she realized this wasn't just about her trust. This was about his, too. He had no proof she was using contraceptives. How many women might have made the claim, hoping they'd get pregnant and get, if not a ring on their finger, then at least a hefty child support check every month?

And here he was, entering her naked and vulnerable. Trusting her not to be one of those women who'd shaped him into the closed-off man she'd met a mere six weeks ago. Loving her enough to believe she'd never hurt him that way.

"I love you," she gasped as he moved inside her.

The words made him thrust harder, so she said them again, and again, until she couldn't form words anymore and just hung on for dear life until the pleasure overwhelmed her. When he came his neck arched, the strong tendons standing out, his face clenched in an agony of ecstasy as his body strained to find every last bit of sensation.

Then he collapsed on top of her, his nose pressed into the curve of her neck, and whispered his reply. "I love you, too."

She lay there, absorbing the warmth of the large, firm body blanketing her. How had her life turned around this much, this fast?

There'd been a time, not so long ago, when she believed nothing good came without a price. She still did. Only now, she knew she was willing to pay whatever cost it took to keep the happiness she'd found.

When Rick finally shifted off her to the side with a reluctant grunt, she snuggled into him and ran a finger along the firm contours of his lightly haired chest. "I could get used to this."

"You'd better. I plan on ending all our days like this from now on."

Her body tingled at the promise.

Her finger dipped down along his chiseled abdomen, running slow circles around his bellybutton and its delightful swirl of dark brown hair. "You know, I can take speech lessons if you want me to."

"Hmm?"

"Or, what are they called? Etiquette lessons." She'd hate every minute of them, but she do it. For him.

"Wait, what?" He seemed to rouse from the post-sex stupor he'd fallen into and gave her a confused look. "What are you talking about?"

"You know. Where you learn which fork to use, how to sit, what to wear—"

"I know what they're for," he interrupted impatiently. "What I don't know is why you'd think you need them."

"So I don't embarrass you."

"Embarrass me? Where is that coming from? You've never—" He stopped and snarled a word she would have washed Derek's mouth out for using. "Katherine. She said something, didn't she?"

She nodded.

"I thought we already established she's a lying bitch out to cause trouble between us?"

"We did, but..."

"But?"

"But she's not wrong."

"The hell she's not!"

While she loved his vehement defense, she still shook her head. "Rick, I have a twang, especially when I'm tired."

He grinned, the bastard.

"I love your twang. Especially when you're screaming out 'oh, God, Rick, yes, do it harder!'" He broke off in laughter as she swatted his arm.

"I'm serious."

He waggled his eyebrows. "So am I."

Men.

With a sigh, she forged ahead. "I need to know how to fit into your world. I don't want to be the clueless woman on the sophisticated guy's arm who doesn't know how to eat snails."

"What the fuck? Snails?"

"Haven't you ever seen *Pretty Woman*?"

Understanding dawned in his expression. "Okay, gotcha. In the restaurant where she doesn't know what silverware goes with what course. Sweetheart, I can show you that kind of stuff if you really want to know. It's not hard. And besides, it's not like there are a lot of occasions when we'd be dining that formally."

"But there would be some."

"Yes, probably. But it's not something you need to worry about, I swear. There's nothing about you that could possibly embarrass me. Ever." His brow wrinkled. "Well, unless you fart in church. Then I don't know you."

The ridiculous statement surprised a laugh out of her. Tension broken, as he'd no doubt intended, she smiled and pressed a kiss to the warm curve of his shoulder, inhaling the musky aroma of heated skin and sex.

"Okay, if you're sure. I just don't want anything from my less-than-ideal past doing anything to screw up our very nice present." And, hopefully, future. She didn't say it out loud so she wouldn't jinx it, but she felt the way Rick tensed as though she had.

When she looked at him, there was a tension line down the middle of his forehead that yanked her right out of her happy place. "Rick? Is something wrong?"

"Now's not really the time to talk about it."

That sounded ominous.

And like something she was a little too naked to deal with.

She scooted up into a sitting position against the headboard, grabbed the sheet from where they'd kicked it aside and tucked it tight against her breasts. Her heart tripped a little faster. "No omissions, remember?"

With a sigh, Rick mirrored her position against the headboard but ignored the sheet, comfortable as ever with his nudity. "I didn't want to kill the mood. But I guess that ship has sailed," he muttered when she flipped the sheet up to cover his lap.

"For Pete's sake, Rick, you're making me imagine one horrible thing after another. Just tell me!"

"Fine. Derek's father tried to shake down Max for a hundred grand in exchange for not having you arrested."

Okay. It was way worse than any of the horrible things she'd imagined.

"That's ridiculous." And terrifying. Because she wouldn't put it past the son of a bitch to try and use her own strategy against her. "I was the one who said I'd have *him* arrested."

"I thought you said you had no contact with this jackass."

Hell's bells, you've stepped in the cow patties now, Amber Lee.

"I haven't. Not until he showed up at my door a few weeks ago."

"Because he wanted his son." It was a flat, emotionless statement that sounded just like the old Richard.

She hated it.

"No, because he wanted money." She nodded at his incredulous expression. "I know, right? Talk about blood from a stone. But then he said I should be able to get it from my rich boyfriend." He'd actually said sugar daddy, but close enough.

"Which he thought was Max because of the pictures that were online of the two of you. At least, that's what he told Max."

She nodded. "He threatened to take Derek back to Texas if I didn't get him what he wanted."

"But you never asked Max for the money."

"Of course not! How could I? I barely know the man."

"You didn't ask me, either."

Did he sound a little hurt by that? Or just surprised?

"No, I didn't, because it wasn't your problem. And there was no way in hell I was going to treat you like my own personal piggybank." She emphasized the last three words with her finger into his chest, which he captured and held onto.

"Besides, the first time he showed up was right before we had our big blow-up. Over you thinking I was after you for your *money*," she added, in case he'd forgotten. Which, judging by his pained expression, he hadn't. "And for the record, I actually did plan to tell you about him before that happened, to see if you had any ideas on how to handle him. When I still thought you were plain old Rick Bowman."

"Then why didn't you? After things got straightened out between us, I mean."

"Because I'd already dealt with it. At least, I thought I had. When he came back for his money, he was pissed I didn't have it. I told him if he tried to snatch Derek and take him back to Texas like he threatened, I'd have him arrested, since he's not listed anywhere as Derek's father. So he has no parental rights and it would be kidnapping."

"Is that true?"

"No idea. I was kind of bluffing my ass off."

"I meant about him not being listed anywhere as Derek's father."

"Oh. Yeah, that part's true."

"But he is?"

Something about his voice gave her a sudden chill, deep inside. She tucked the sheet a little tighter around her body. "Unfortunately, yes. Why?"

"Because he told Max you took Derek and ran so he couldn't find you. He's accusing *you* of parental kidnapping."

"He..." A laugh of disbelief broke from her lips. "What a load of crap. He never wanted anything to do with Derek." Her eyes widened as the grim look on his handsome face sunk in.

"Oh, my God, you believe him!"

HE HAD. AT LEAST he'd entertained the possibility.

Having once been the focus of Amber's maternal fury, Richard didn't doubt for a second she'd do anything necessary to protect that boy. Even if it meant breaking the law.

He wasn't stupid enough to admit it, though.

"I'm not about to believe the word of an extortionist without proof. But there's obviously something more going on that I don't know about, so why don't you tell me so there won't be any more surprises? Your turn to meet the no omissions clause."

Amber got the mulish look that came when she was going to be stubborn. Then it disappeared, and she sighed. "You're right. You're a part of this now, so you should know everything."

She told him all about her experience with Hunter and his parents when she'd learned she was pregnant. How she'd been at first rebuffed, and then outright threatened if she said or did anything to sully Hunter's reputation by naming him the father.

"As if everyone in town didn't know he was a teenaged manwhore by then," she said with a small shake of her head. "But no one says boo to the Kings. Not when it's their ranch that helps keep the town alive. They have all the power. At least they did then. Enough that they got the bank to call the loan on the trailer after my momma died. She'd had to mortgage it when she got sick and the chemo made her too weak to stay on at her jobs."

Shock and fury flashed through him. But not enough that he missed the plural on jobs.

"They forced you out into the street with a baby? While you were still grieving your mother?"

"I would have lost it eventually, anyway." She sounded entirely too pragmatic for such a traumatic event. "There was no job I could've gotten with a GED that would've paid enough for me to keep making the monthly payments, much less pay for childcare so I could work in the first place. But at least I would have had a little time to make a plan. As it was, we ended up living in my car for a little while until I could figure things out."

With every word, his rage grew, until it was like a living flame inside, waiting to be released to devour the Kings right down to their malicious black hearts.

"Bastards," was all he managed to grind out.

He couldn't begin to process the hell she'd gone through. Where were all the adults who should've been looking out for her? The teachers, the school counselors, the social workers? Aside from her mother, it didn't sound like there had been a single other person on her side, and a whole hell of a lot who were aligned against one pregnant teenage girl.

No wonder she was so wary about people with power and money. The Kings had used theirs to all but destroy her life.

Needing her close, he slid his arm around her shoulders and tugged her against him, relieved when she came willingly. In fact, she snuggled against him as though trying to burrow inside. Which told him more than anything how hard recounting that part of her life had been for her.

"So, there you have it. The whole sordid truth about my past. Still love me now?"

"Sweetheart, the only thing that could make me stop loving you is...honestly, I can't even think of a reason. Everything you just told me only makes me prouder of what a strong, resourceful woman you are, and how lucky I am you're in my life."

"Oh."

The small word, so filled with surprise and relief, made his heart hurt. He held her tighter and dropped a kiss on her head, smoothing back the hair torn loose from the thousand little pins anchoring it. "I love you. Get it through that thick head of yours."

"I'm trying."

"Try harder."

She snorted with repressed laughter. Then she asked quietly, "What am I going to do about Hunter?"

"We." He thought she'd argue, but thankfully she just took a deep breath and nodded.

"What are *we* going to do?"

"Don't worry. I have an idea, but I want to talk to a few people first before I tell you what it is."

Like his lawyer. It was a risky plan, but given what he knew of Hunter King, it was the surest way to neutralize the threat he posed to the woman and child he was coming to think of as his.

"I'm just afraid he'll find a way to hurt Derek even more than he already has."

"I won't let him. I promise."

This time when he kissed her temple, she turned her head and her mouth found his. What started as something to seal a promise turned into a promise of its own, becoming hot and passionate as the sheet was once again kicked aside. By the time Amber straddled his legs, he was more than ready.

Recovery time seemed to be a non-issue when she was the one he was getting hard for.

"Oh, God, you go so deep like this," she moaned as she sank onto him.

"And you're so damn tight." He sucked in a sharp breath as she started to move. It was so good with her.

Every. Fucking. Time.

She leaned down to capture his mouth, sharpening the angle of entry even more, making them both moan. He took the golden opportunity she presented to caress and explore her magnificent breasts as they bobbed in time with her.

As her movements sped up, becoming needier and more intent on the finish line he could feel rushing up on them both, he cupped them more firmly to keep them from bouncing too hard and hurting her. Something she'd mentioned as one reason she usually preferred the bottom during sex.

Right now, he was damn glad she'd given this way another try, and would do whatever it took to make her want to try it again.

With a keening cry, she shuddered around him like a hot little volcano erupting. The feel of her inner muscles clenching on his penis, holding it tight as though never wanting to let go, rocketed him into his own climax.

It seemed to go on forever, both of them gasping and sweaty by the time the last residual tremors passed and they lay wrapped in each other's arms.

"Have I mentioned lately you're a sex goddess?"

She giggled against his neck. "I think you mean sex addict. You've totally ruined me for other men."

Something fierce and possessive inside him raised its head and snarled.

"Good."

After a quick shower to rinse off the glitter and makeup now smeared all over them both—the careful non-eye-contact the concierge had given him earlier suddenly made sense—they dressed and rode the elevator back down to the garage and the limo he'd texted Les to bring around. *After* he asked her if she wanted to leave through the front doors or not.

Never let it be said Richard Beaumont didn't learn from his mistakes.

Which was why he also asked if she still wanted to go back to his condo, as planned. Thank God she said yes. Not that there was likely to be any more sex tonight. But it didn't matter if all he did was hold her as they slept.

He just didn't want to let her go.

Chapter 20

RICHARD KNEW THE SECOND Hunter King walked into his office he was an arrogant ass. Between the cowboy swagger and the restless eyes darting around, taking in everything as though calculating its cash value, he was the kind of man Richard most loathed dealing with.

And most relished taking to his knees.

"Where's good old Max? We had us a little bit of business to take care of this afternoon. I hope he didn't decide to renege on what we talked about." The good ol' boy joviality in his tone sounded a little forced, like he was uneasy about the feel of the room.

So, an ass, but not an entirely stupid one.

Good. He enjoyed a bit of a challenge.

"Not at all. You'll just be dealing with me from now on."

"Oh, I get it. You're like his lawyer or something."

"Or something. Have a seat."

King eyed the lone empty chair in the middle of the three lined up in front of the glass-and-granite desk Richard sat behind. Sitting in it would mean being hemmed in between the silent men who already occupied the two end seats. Men who hadn't bothered to turn and look at him when he entered.

Grinning as though amused by the obvious intimidation ploy, he walked to the chair. But instead of sitting, he rocked back on the heels of his boots and shook his head. "Thanks, but I'm fine standing."

"Suit yourself."

"I usually do."

Oh, he was really going to love crushing this worm.

"So, Mr. King, I believe the amount you demanded was one hundred thousand dollars. Is that correct?" He slid a check out of the folder on his desk and centered it on the leather blotter in front of him. The other man's attention locked onto the piece of paper like he was a hound and it was a duck about to take flight.

Or a goose.

A big, fat, golden one.

He licked his lips and chuckled. "Demanded is a pretty strong word. It's more like me doing him a favor, and him doing me one in return."

"That favor being to not file a false police report against Amber Lovett?"

"Nothing false about the fact she's kept my son from me all these years."

"And why would she do something like that?"

"I dunno. Spite, probably. She never got over the fact I wouldn't marry her." His lips curled into a sneer. "Like I'd ever marry someone like her."

"Like her? You mean seventeen and pregnant with your child?" By the way King looked at him, he realized his tone had gotten a little too sharp. He grabbed hold of his slipping temper. "So, you knew about the child."

"No. Like I said, she hid him. Left my name off the birth certificate and everything."

"Then how did you come to find out about him?"

"I saw a picture of her and the kid, and I knew right away he had to be mine. I mean, he looks just like me."

Richard wanted to punch him for the way he preened over that statement. True, Derek might have some of King's outer features, but the kid had lucked out and was all Amber on the inside.

"So, you came to Boulder to confront her about it. To be sure."

"What does any of this have to do with the money, uh, favor?"

"Mr. Woodward wanted to be sure he had all the facts. I think a hundred grand is well worth satisfying his curiosity, don't you?"

You lying piece of shit.

Having his payday threatened, even vaguely, got King talking again, his words almost stumbling over themselves in his eagerness to comply.

"Right, I came here and talked to her, but she wouldn't let me see the kid. But she admitted he was mine."

"Why didn't you call the police when she wouldn't give you access to your son?"

"Like I told old Max, I thought about it, but I didn't want to traumatize the kid by having his momma hauled off in handcuffs and sent to jail. I mean, he's my boy. How could I do that to him?"

"How indeed."

If he hadn't known better, Richard might almost be inclined to believe him. But he knew the truth, and he was going to use it to take this smug son of a bitch down.

"So, aside from not having his mother charged with any crime, what are your plans?"

"What do you mean?"

"I mean, now that you've found out about having a son, one you obviously care about since you don't want to unnecessarily traumatize him, I have to wonder how involved you're going to want to be in the boy's life going forward."

The skin between King's eyebrows puckered. "I'm not sure I follow. I already said I didn't want to take him away from her. A boy should be with his ma."

How big of you.

"But shouldn't he also spend some time with his father? Surely, you'll want to get to know him. Maybe visit him here once a month, or have him come visit you back in Texas? Let him get to know the other side of his family."

He half expected to hear some kind of protest from the adjoining conference room, where Amber and a few other people were listening to everything over the open intercom on his desk. This had been the part of the plan she hated most, worried they'd be putting ideas in King's head.

Richard knew those ideas were already there, and not because of any nascent paternal love. He just needed to get King to box himself in with his own story.

"Much as I want to get to know my boy, I have to think about what's best for him." It was amazing how fine a performance King gave of a man torn but trying to do the right thing. There was even a catch in his voice as he spoke.

No wonder he'd been able to sweet-talk innocent young girls like Amber out of their virginity. He was a consummate con-artist.

One who looked forlorn as he shook his head. "After all these years, and with who-all knows what lies that woman has been feeding him about me, making him hate me, maybe even be afraid of me, trying to force myself into his life wouldn't just be hard, it would be downright cruel. Maybe later, when he's a little older and can think for himself some, he can decide if he wants to look me up. But for now, I think it's best I just let things lie."

Lie was a perfect word for it.

"That's good to hear." He reached into the folder again and withdrew a sheaf of legal documents. "Then you won't have any problem signing this."

King automatically reached out to accept the papers. "What is it?"

"A petition to sever parental rights."

Yanking his hand back as though snake bit, King scowled. "Why the hell would I want to do that?"

"Because you just said you wanted to do what's best for your son."

"Yeah, but…there's a difference between not seeing him and giving up my right to if I want."

"Even if it's the best thing for him? If, say, the man his mother might one day marry wanted to formally adopt him, make them a true family?" Richard's heart tripped at his own words.

He hadn't mentioned that possibility to Amber when they'd gone over the plan. He had no idea how she might be reacting right now. Hopefully she wasn't having a heart attack over it, because it sure felt like he might be.

King's reaction, on the other hand, was easy to predict. His eyes took on a calculating gleam. "Well, if good old Max really wants him, I guess I could be persuaded to sign those papers. For a price."

"You're already getting a hundred thousand." He tapped the check.

"That's a separate fee. I think something like giving up my boy is worth a whole lot more, don't you? Say, maybe another hundred?"

There were no words for the scum this man was.

Even though this was exactly what they'd expected, Richard still had to unlock his jaw to reply. "You want to sell the rights to your son?"

"I wouldn't put it like that. More like, it's another favor. You know, for peace of mind."

"Peace of mind that you won't be coming back six months or a year from now and change your mind about wanting to be a part of Derek's life?"

"You never know. If the door's left open, I just might be tempted one day to come see how he's doing." King shrugged, looking pleased with himself.

Prepare to crash and burn, asshole.

"We thought you might feel that way."

"Good."

"Which is why I can tell you in no uncertain terms there won't be any additional money coming your way. Not a single cent."

Rage quickly quenched the smug satisfaction on King's face. "What?"

"You heard me."

"Then you can forget about me signing any damn papers. In fact, I think I need to get myself a lawyer and see about some of those visiting rights you were talking about. Taking the boy back home to Texas for a few months might be just what he needs."

"What happened to all that talk about what's best for Derek? About not disrupting his life?"

"He's mine, and I'll take him if I want to."

"Does that mean you want to acknowledge Derek as your legal son, with all the rights and privileges attached to that status?"

"Damn straight."

The smile that made grown men's balls shrivel in the boardroom broke out on Richard's face. "In that case, you'll be wanting these." Shifting the first stack of papers aside, he withdrew the last two sets of documents from the folder.

"What's this?"

"The petition that's going to be filed first thing in the morning for retroactive child support. Ten years' worth, to be exact."

"Are you out of your fucking mind?"

"You said you wanted to be acknowledged as Derek's legal father. Being held financially responsible is a part of that."

"The hell it is!"

"In fact, this will just about cover everything you owe, so..." When he picked up the check and put it back on top of the folder, he thought King was going to launch himself over the desk. As it was, the man burned so red with rage he was practically purple.

"You can't do that! That's my money!"

"Not once the court assigns it to a trust for the benefit of your son."

"You're bluffing. No court will make me pay child support for a kid I didn't know about."

The angrier King got, the calmer Richard became, knowing it would infuriate the man even further. He steepled his hands on the desk.

"But I believe you did know. You and your parents simply chose to try and wipe away the fact Derek ever existed, bullying and harassing Amber until she had no choice but to leave town, taking your secret with her."

King shot his chin up. "Prove it."

"Oh, believe me, I will. And even if I can't, there's still this." He nudged the other set of papers forward. "As of this moment, you're fully aware of the existence of your son, and you've stated—in front of witnesses—that you want to claim your parental rights. So regardless of what you did or didn't know before, as of now you're legally obligated to pay child support until Derek turns eighteen."

"That's...that's..."

"Fatherhood."

"Bullshit! That's what it is!" Turning, King stalked away from the desk toward the door before stopping, fingers clenched in his hair as though trying to process what just happened. The money-making plan he'd walked into the office with had suddenly turned into a noose around his neck, and he was clearly feeling the pinch.

Richard waited. Cornered rats always turned and fought. The human kind were no different.

Sure enough, King spun back, his mouth tight with rage. "What if he isn't mine?"

"You already said he was."

"Just because he looks a little like me doesn't mean shit. That bitch spread her legs for anyone who'd buy her a milkshake down at the Dairy Queen. Who knows who the brat's father is? She probably doesn't even know. That's why she's tried to pin it on me from the get-go. Why not try to lay the blame on the guy with the most money?"

It wasn't until he saw Brennan Doyle start to rise from his chair with an alarmed expression that Richard realized he hadn't masked the powerful desire to rip King apart with his bare hands. It was difficult, but he stuffed the urge down, found his center, breathing through the tightness of muscles that were tensed to act. When he was sure he had himself back under control, he gave Doyle a quick nod. He had this.

Doyle didn't look so sure, but subsided.

"So, you're admitting you knew about the child all along."

"No. I didn't say that."

"Actually, you did." He let the bastard think about his words for a second, saw the moment he realized his slip. Then Richard went in for the kill. "In any case, a paternity test would clear the issue right up."

"I won't take one. It's an invasion of my privacy."

"The court can compel you."

"Then I'll sue for joint custody. Hell, maybe even full."

"Why? You clearly have no love for the boy. Why would you do that to him?"

King gave a smile filled with venomous triumph. "Because it would drive Amber Lee absolutely insane to know I have the kid and there's nothing she can do about it. If I can't win any other way, at least I'll have that."

Richard glanced at the second man sitting in front of his desk, who'd been listening with an expression of growing distaste.

With a nod, the older gentleman said, "I've heard enough."

"And who the hell are you?" King had been so intent on his back-and-forth with Richard, he looked startled to be reminded there were other people in the room besides them.

With the pleasure of watching a trap closing neatly on its prey, Richard made the introductions. "Judge James Walker."

"Retired," the judge added. "But that's not to say my word wouldn't still carry a lot of weight should I ever be called to testify at, say, a custody hearing."

For the first time, King looked worried. "You can't do that."

"I assure you, young man, I most definitely can."

"No." His gaze darted nervously to Richard. "You're a lawyer. What we talk about is supposed to be privileged."

"I never said I was a lawyer."

"Yeah, you did. Which means you lied. You can't use anything I said if you, what'cha call it? Misrepresented yourself." He looked to the judge. "Right?"

"I'm afraid not. He never claimed to be a lawyer. Nor can he be held responsible for your assumptions in that regard. Not to mention, privileged communication only exists between a lawyer and his client, not someone else's, so even if he were one, your argument would still be invalid."

"You...that's..." Impotent fury oozing from every pore, King glared at Richard. "You fucking *bastard*!"

Richard steepled his fingers again, going in for the kill. "There is one way out of this mess, you know."

"What?"

He picked up the first set of documents, took his time tidying the pages, then placed it front and center on the desk. "You can still sign the petition to sever your parental rights. Which will make all of this"—he waved a hand over the other documents—"go away."

He could see King was considering it, weighing his options, so he sweetened the pot by dropping the check on top of the papers.

"Plus, you get this, free and clear. The petition includes a clause where Amber waives her right to any past or future claims of child support."

King's fingers twitched, betraying his desire to take the money and run. That didn't keep him from trying to play it cool. He scrubbed a hand over his mouth. "I dunno. I need to think about this for a minute."

"Then think about this. Without that check, you have no way to pay back the money you drained from your parents' ranch to cover your gambling losses. What do you suppose will happen when they find out they're going to lose everything because you can't play poker worth a damn?"

King's face blanched. "How could you..." He clamped his mouth shut, but too late to prevent the damning confirmation of what Doyle's people at Praetorian Security had dug up in just a few hours.

With an almost audible snap, the trap closed the rest of the way, sealing King in tight.

Gotcha, fucko.

"The way I see it, you have two very different choices." Richard tapped one stack of papers. "You can sign the petition and leave your son in the loving care of his mother, while walking away with a cool hundred grand to solve all your problems. Or"—he touched the other pile—"you can try for custody, which is pretty doubtful given the eyewitness testimony the judge here can give to your true reasons for wanting it, and still be on the hook for child support payments when you lose."

"That's blackmail!"

"No, that's a choice," Judge Walker said. "What *you* were trying to do is blackmail. Which is worth about, oh, four to twelve years in prison, not to mention some hefty fines."

The muscle along King's jaw twitched as he digested the veiled threat.

Richard held out a pen. "Which is it going to be?"

With a foul curse, King snatched the pen and scrawled his signature on the petition ending his parental rights. Tossing down the pen, he snatched up the check, only to have Richard grab his wrist. A small twist and an application of pressure on the joint held him in place.

They stared at each other, their combined hatred almost thick enough to choke on.

"Gentlemen, if you could excuse us for a moment?"

As the judge and Doyle left the room, he reached over and switched off the intercom, leaving no one to hear what he had to say except the two of them.

"Let me make one thing perfectly clear. You're not to go anywhere near either Amber or Derek. Ever. You don't bother them, you don't harass them, you don't even talk about them. As of this second, they no longer exist in your world. And if I find out you've been causing them even the smallest amount of trouble, I'll come after you with all the considerable resources at my command, and I. Will. Crush. You." He tweaked his hold a little, earning a pained grunt. "Do I make myself clear?"

"Perfectly," King ground out between clenched teeth. When Richard released him, he shook out his wrist and flexed his fingers to ease the pain and numbness Richard knew would persist for a few more minutes.

Grabbing the check he'd dropped, he stuffed it into his pocket with a sneer. "You're a real tough guy when you've probably got a bunch of security goons waiting outside those doors to back you up. Why don't you come on down to Texas sometime, and we'll see how good you are when it's just you and me."

Richard slowly rose to his feet. He barely topped the other man by an inch or so, and King was broader and more solid across the chest from his years working on a ranch. But he had no doubts who would come out on top of such a matchup.

"You give me a reason, and I'll be there."

With his threat falling flat, King's expression turned nasty. "I guess that means you're fucking her, too. Figures."

Only knowing he might kill the man if he laid hands on him in that moment kept Richard on his side of the desk as King stalked to the door.

As he opened it, he gave a parting shot over his shoulder. "She must've turned into a much better lay than I remember to have all you rich bastards panting after her golden pussy this way." He gave a hard laugh. "Choke on this. No matter how many times you get your rocks off with her, you'll never know for sure if it's you or your wallet she wants most."

The door slammed behind him.

Rage swamped Richard's common sense. He found himself halfway across the office when the door to the connecting conference room popped open and Amber came rushing through. She threw herself into his arms.

"Oh, my God, I can't believe it worked!"

Concerned at how hard her entire body was shaking, he shook his head at Doyle, who nodded and closed the door, leaving them alone. He led Amber to the sofa against the wall and sat down, drawing her onto his lap. She went willingly.

"Everything's going to be fine." He stroked her back as the shudders slowly ebbed. "The judge and Doyle will sign as witnesses, and my lawyer will start the process of filing the petition first thing in the morning."

"But what if he changes his mind before everything's finalized? Hunter's not good about losing. What if he decides to cause trouble?"

"He won't. Not with the alternative hanging over his head."

And he didn't just mean the child support.

"I hope you're right." She looked at him with wide eyes. "Why did you give him the check? That wasn't part of the plan."

He shrugged. "It was the most efficient way to get the result we wanted."

"But, Rick, that much money—"

"Is money well spent if it gets the bastard out of our lives." Hell, he'd have given him the additional hundred grand if it had been the only way.

"But—"

"Let it go, sweetheart."

She looked like she was going to argue, then bit her lip and looked away. When she looked back, there was cautious hope in her eyes. "Is it really over, then?"

"It really is."

Her eyes closed, her body going soft as the tension drained out on a long sigh. After a few minutes of holding each other, she smiled up at him. "Thank you. For everything. This was...incredible. I can't believe you managed it all in such a short time."

"I was highly motivated."

"You were highly amazing." She hesitated. "Those things he said about me being with lots of boys...it's not true. He was the only one I ever slept with."

"I know not a thing that came out of his mouth wasn't twisted or tainted." But King's parting shot, which Amber hadn't heard, still lingered, poking at Richard's own worst insecurities no matter how hard he tried to brush it off the way he had the rest of his lies. He *knew*, without a doubt, Amber wasn't after his money.

And yet.

Damning both himself and Hunter King, he pushed all thoughts of money aside and kissed her softly. "What time do we have to pick up Derek?"

"Not for a couple of hours yet."

"Good. Just enough time to celebrate."

Amber smiled and leaned in for another kiss. "You read my mind."

Even as he sank into the kiss, all he could think was how glad he was she couldn't read his.

Chapter 21

"Well? How did everything go today?"

Amber dropped her purse and jacket on the floor of Rick's penthouse as she walked from the elevator straight into his arms. Burrowing herself into him, she let out a happy sound. Nothing had ever felt so good as being wrapped up in the safety of this man's arms.

Well, except when she was wrapped around the rest of his delicious body, but that was a totally different kind of good.

The hot, sweaty kind.

"It was awful. But it's finally over and settled, and that's all that matters." After three of the longest weeks of her life.

With Hunter so successfully routed, she'd felt the need to complete the purge of toxic people from her life. Which meant taking on Horny Hollingsworth and the good-old-boy network at the hospital. A terrifying prospect, but so was spending the next ten years going to work every day a massive bundle of nerves, feeling like she had a target on her back.

Or, more accurately, her ass and boobs.

She'd found an unlikely ally to her campaign in Ilsa. The icy blonde not only had first-hand knowledge of all the women her boss singled out for his "personal" attention during her tenure as Hollingsworth's PA, but she was also a victim of it herself. News which hadn't surprised Amber, although it did sadden her. As did the stories from the other women who'd been willing to talk.

It hadn't been hard to see the pattern.

Young. Pretty. Vulnerable. The ones most desperate to not lose their jobs, so least likely to report any sexual harassment, or pursue the issue further when HR told them there was no infraction in the rare instances when they did. Besides herself and Ilsa, she talked to over a dozen women who'd been subjected to Hollingsworth's harassment, but only four who were willing to come forward with them and take a stand.

One of whom was Belinda, which put her extreme reaction to Amber's supposed "services" in exchange for her promotion into better perspective.

After needing Rick to solve the Hunter problem—and sweet Jesus, she *still* felt her heart palpitate whenever she thought about the obscene amount of money he'd given away for her and Derek—she hadn't wanted to involve him in this issue, too. She didn't want him to think she was using him to make all her problems disappear.

She didn't want him to think she was using him, period.

And, of course, there was the not-so-insignificant fact she hadn't wanted to tell him all the awful things that had been going on since her promotion. The openly leering looks. The breaches of personal space. The increasingly suggestive innuendo. Things she'd purposefully kept from him despite their promise about no more omissions, because she'd been so damned ashamed.

It was that realization which finally prompted her to tell him everything. She'd done nothing to be ashamed about. But that was how abusers got away with their games for so long. They made sure the victims were the ones who felt at fault. A feeling Rick was swift to disabuse her of.

Then, like now, his comforting embrace had given her the strength to talk about things she would much rather forget.

"I could really use a drink," she sighed, snuggling against his hard chest. She'd been thinking about this all day. Coming home to him. It was a habit she was quickly coming to need in her life.

That kind of need for a man, any man, would have sent her running in the other direction a few months ago.

Now, with this man, it felt exactly right.

"I thought you might." He led her over to the sofa, where a bottle of wine and a glass waited on the coffee table. He poured her some as she sank into the soft cushions, kicking off her heels before curling her legs beneath her. "Don't keep me in suspense. What happened?"

She accepted the glass and took a long sip of the sweet, fruity riesling. "James had them quaking in their boots from the minute he opened his mouth."

Bored in his retirement, Judge Walker leapt at the opportunity to represent the women when they brought their grievance to the hospital board. Even insisting on doing it pro bono after he heard all of their stories.

"And?" he asked as he settled next to her with his tumbler of scotch.

"And they were appalled, concerned, surprised, and a bunch of other things, which all meant they were distancing themselves from knowing anything about the problems that have been going on, even though we had testimony from women going back over five years."

Besides getting the judge on the team, they'd also enlisted the aid of Praetorian Security, owned by the man who'd help dig up the dirt on Hunter's gambling debts. Brennan Doyle's experts tracked down dozens of former hospital employees who had either been fired when they threatened to cause trouble, or who'd simply quit when they couldn't take the harassment any longer.

"Closing ranks to save their own asses."

"Pretty much. They seemed very concerned about the possibility of a lawsuit. Which is why they were so quick to agree to the changes we suggested."

Like revamping the process for filing complaints, guaranteeing each one would be reviewed by a panel rather than a single person. There would be no more sweeping things into a closet and hiding them.

"What happened to your boss? Did they fire his ass?"

"Oh, yeah." She grinned, feeling the happy all the way down to her toes. That had been one of the best parts of the day. Knowing he wouldn't be there Monday morning took a weight the size of the Flat Irons off her shoulders.

"They're going to do an investigation into the HR department next, but I got the feeling it was just a formality before heads roll there, too."

"So, you accomplished everything you set out to do." He clinked his glass to hers. "Congratulations. You won."

"*We* won." It might have started out as her fight. But after hearing so many stories similar to—or worse than—her own, it had turned into a fight for every woman who wasn't able to stand up for herself. That made winning even more important. "Thanks to you."

Rick shook his head. "All I did was provide access to the resources. This was all you. I'm so damn proud of you."

Swallowing the lump in her throat at his words, she managed a wobbly smile. "Thank you."

An alarmed look crossed his face. "Why are you crying?"

"I...I'm not...oh damn, I am." Her vision blurred as the unexpected tears flowed. Rick plucked the glass from her hand before enveloping her in his embrace again. As his warm hand made soothing circles on her back, she sobbed out the last of the tears until she felt wrung dry.

He handed her a tissue. "Better?"

She nodded and blew her nose. "I don't know why that happened."

"Nerves. Your body needed to release all the tension you've been bottling up."

It made sense. She felt so much lighter inside now. And a whole lot messier on the outside.

After excusing herself to go repair her face in the bathroom, she came back to find both of their glasses topped off, the fireplace lit, and soft jazz coming from the integrated sound system. It would have seemed like a scene set for seduction if it weren't for Rick's alarmingly serious expression.

And the stack of papers now sitting on the coffee table.

Some of her earlier lightness fled under the weight of trepidation. Determined not to let it show, she retook her seat and waited, forcing her hands to still and not keep smoothing down nonexistent wrinkles in her skirt.

Rick cleared his throat, betraying his unease. "I didn't want to bring this up while you were dealing with everything at work. But now that it's all settled, I didn't want to let it go any longer."

"Okay, that sounds ominous."

"No! No, it's not. At least, I don't think it is."

She'd never seen him this nervous before. About anything.

"Rick, just spit it out."

"Okay. Well, you heard me say something to King in my office, and we haven't talked about it since, and I think it's time we did."

She'd heard him say a lot of things to Hunter that day. But she knew exactly which thing he was talking about. It had been the elephant heavy-breathing in the room with them for all these weeks, waiting for one of them to finally break the silence.

Thank God it was him.

"Okay. Go ahead."

"When I said the man you married someday might want to adopt Derek, I meant it. He's a great kid. Amazing. Any man would be lucky to have him for a son."

"Yes, they would." Her kid was the absolute best.

"I know it's been a crazy couple of months for us since we met, and we haven't really had a chance to talk about where all of this is going between us, but I'm kind of hoping we're on the same page here. I love you, and I want you in my life. And Derek, too." He took a breath. "But before that can happen, there's something I need to take care of, because I know Kitty mentioned this to you."

Richard's lawyers would never let him walk down the aisle without an iron-clad prenup in place.

Katherine's sneered warning was like an evil whisper in her ear, making her stomach twist. "The prenuptial agreement you gave her."

"*Showed* her."

"There's a difference?"

"Hell, yes! I never asked her to marry me, remember?"

She did. She also remembered Rick's words when he'd explained why he'd shown the prenup to that mercenary woman in the first place. *Because it's the only way I can ever know.* The misery in his expression still made her heart ache for him. A man whose money could buy everything.

Except trust in true love.

"Now, I know it might seem too soon to even be worrying about things like this, but this was something I knew I needed to handle now, before things go any further between us. Especially if we're going to have Derek as part of the equation. I don't want to risk either of you getting hurt." His expression softened. "You mean far too much to me to let that happen. I'll do whatever it takes to keep you both safe and happy. I swear it."

And he would. She knew it to the depths of her soul. This man would always be there for her and her son, protecting them, loving them, just like he'd been doing from the very start. She didn't need a piece of paper to know without reservation she was loved.

But he did.

Spurred on by the certainty it was the right thing to do, the only thing she could do to prove her unconditional love, she picked up the pen from the table, flipped to the last page of the prenup, and signed with a flourish.

She dropped the pen and smiled at his adorably shell-shocked expression. "There. Now you know."

<hr>

RICHARD COULD ONLY STARE at the confounding woman who'd just derailed his carefully planned out speech with one impulsive move that left him completely reeling.

"Know? Know what?"

"That I love you for you. Not for your money. Oh!"

Anxiety swamped him as she popped off the sofa and sprinted for the elevator. Was she seriously bailing on him *now*?

But rather than make a fast getaway, she merely grabbed her purse from where she'd dropped it on entering. Pulling out a sheet of folded paper, she brought it back and handed it to him as she retook her seat. "Here."

"What's this?" He opened it warily.

"A promissory note for the money you paid off Hunter with. James drew it up for me. It'll take a long, *long* time, but you can see we worked it out so I'll be able to pay you back every dime. Plus interest."

That's exactly what it was, all legally signed and notarized. Annoyance mixed with admiration bloomed. "I told you, I gave him the money because it was the most expedient way to get the result I wanted. I never expected you to pay me back."

"And yet, I am."

The stubborn set of her chin told him arguing wouldn't get him anywhere. Never let it be said he was a man who didn't know how to pick his battles.

"Okay, let's table this"—he rattled the paper before dropping it on the coffee table—"for now, and get back to the bigger issue at hand." He grabbed the prenup. "Why would you sign this without even looking at it? You have no idea what it says."

The sheer recklessness of the action made his blood run cold.

Even as it warmed his heart.

"It doesn't matter what it says. All I care about is making sure you never have to wonder why I'm with you. This was the most expedient way to get the result I wanted."

Hearing his own words echoed back at him in her smug tone made him want to laugh and cry at the same time. Had he really made her doubt his trust in her that much?

"I know why you're with me, sweetheart. I don't need any prenup to prove it."

Her smug expression faltered. "Then why give it to me?"

"Actually, I didn't. You took it."

"But...I don't understand."

"I was trying to make a point. Badly, it would seem," he added under his breath. "Kitty and the others...they all balked at the mere sight of a prenup."

"Because they didn't love you enough."

Her fierce certainty made him smile. Then it faded.

"To be fair, I didn't love them, either. Not in the right way. Which was why it was so easy for me to chalk them all up to being only after my money and move on. What I didn't figure out until very recently was that I kept setting myself up to fail. I kept choosing relationships with the same flaws, over and over again, and then wondered why they all ended up failing." He shook his head. "My brother tried to tell me, but, as usual, I didn't want to hear it."

"You were just being cautious."

"I was being an ass. But I think this time I'm finally going to get it right."

"What do you mean?"

"The only way I could think of to prove how different things are between us than with any of those other relationships was to show you the prenup, then *not* have you sign it."

Amber's hands flew to her mouth. "Oh, Rick."

"But now that you have, I guess there's only one other way to make my point." Prenup still in his hand, he got up, opened one of the glass doors on the fireplace, and tossed the papers in to the accompaniment of Amber's gasp.

She tried to grab the promissory note when he snatched that up as well, but he was quicker. With a deft flick, he tossed it into the flames, where it quickly blackened and curled before bursting into flames with the rest of the pages.

"Why would you do that?" She sounded horrified.

He watched the papers turn to ash with a sense of satisfaction he usually only got from choosing a stock that outperformed expectations. Then he turned to her. "I told you. I don't want any doubts between us. My surprisingly wise sister told me recently that you can't have love without trust. And I do. I love you. And I trust you. I don't need anything else."

"And I love and trust you." Jumping to her feet, she rushed to him, nearly knocking him back a step with her exuberance. Then she pulled back from the embrace to give him a stern look. "But you're out of your freaking mind if you think I'm not signing a prenup."

He had to laugh. "Are we really going to fight about this?"

"Of course not." She gave an impish grin. "I'll just have James write something up for me if the time ever comes."

"What do you mean, *if?*" Without giving her time to answer, he kissed her, putting every ounce of certainty he felt about their future together into it. "You're mine, sweetheart. Now. Always. I finally found you. No way I'm ever letting you go."

Pressing her forehead to his, Amber panted softly, trying to regain her breath. "Are you sure? I'm not exactly what you were looking for."

"No, but you're exactly what I needed."

"I'll probably embarrass you sometimes."

"I'm sure I'll do the same. I have been known to be an ass from time to time."

She laughed. "No kidding."

All humor fled as he hauled her in close, his eyes intent on hers. "Say you'll be mine."

"I already am. I just hope you don't come to regret it."

His heart soared at her words.

"Sweetheart, if there's one thing you've taught me since you first came into my life, breathing fire and ready to kick ass and take names, it's that a love like we have is worth any price. I'm more than willing to risk anything when the reward is waking up to you every morning for the rest of my life."

Tears shimmered in her blue, blue eyes. "And you said you weren't a romantic."

"Only with you." He kissed her again. "How about I prove it?"

She flashed him a saucy smile. "Give it your best shot."

That was all he needed to hear. Scooping her into his arms as she squealed with laughter, Richard headed for the bedroom and their future, leaving the ashes of their past behind.

A Note From the Author

I hope you've enjoyed Richard and Amber's story. But there are still two Beaumont men waiting to take the fall. Middle brother Theo is the next to meet his match in **Never Let Me Go**, releasing in spring 2024. Scan the QR code below to visit my website, nikarhone.com, and grab your copy, available from all major retailers. While there, you can also stay up-to-date on all future releases by signing up for my newsletter and following my author page.

And if you loved this book, please take a moment to leave a review at your favorite retailer. They're what feeds an author's creative soul. Thank you!

Also By Nika Rhone

<u>Boulder Bodyguards series</u>
What the Lady Wants
Finding Forever
Can't Help Loving You

<u>Boulder Beaumonts series</u>
Worth Any Price
Never Let Me Go (coming soon)
All I Need Is You (coming soon)

About the Author

Nika Rhone spent her childhood wearing out library cards as she read her way through the extraordinary worlds far beyond her small hometown on Long Island, NY. By her teens, her imagination was taking her places all on its own, forcing her to learn how to type (badly) so she could get all the stories down on paper. After a long love affair with science fiction and fantasy, she finally discovered romance, fell head-over-heels, and now spends her days crafting happily-ever-afters for the characters who still tell their stories faster (and better) than she can type them.

You can keep up with all the latest book news, events, and giveaways by visiting her website www.nikarhone.com and joining her newsletter.

www.ingramcontent.com/pod-product-compliance
Lightning Source LLC
Chambersburg PA
CBHW032015310726
48972CB00002B/414